RESURRECTION

BOOK FOUR IN THE DOMINION SERIES

S. E. LUND

ACADIAN PUBLISHING LIMITED

FOREWORD

"I, with a deeper instinct, choose a man who compels my strength, who makes enormous demands on me, who does not doubt my courage or my toughness, who does not believe me naive or innocent, who has the courage to treat me like a woman."

Anaïs Nin

CHAPTER 1

ON MY WEEKENDS alone at the cottage on the beach, I relish the quiet. While the world falls apart around me, I'm sheltered here for a while, listening to the sounds of the surf rising up over the dunes, the crash of the waves on the shore soothing in its regularity. At night, I sit on the beach and watch the Milky Way rise, remembering when I met Michel again and we spent time watching the stars. Or when Julien found me on the beach and fell to his knees in shock.

So much has happened in such a short time. I need the solitude of this place to help me come to terms with what it means now that I'm a vampire.

What would my dead mother think if she knew I'd become her sworn enemy?

And yet...

And yet she befriended both Michel and Julien. She changed her goals from killing off all vampires to curing them. Did the manuscript make the difference? Did she see them differently once she knew Michel and Julien and read their story? I know it affected me that way.

From my journal entries, I see that reading the manuscript affected me deeply. Instead of seeing all vampires as pure evil, I now see them with empathy, as victims of a cruel fate none of them chose, their actions as vampires largely determined by who they were as humans. They are predators of humans out of necessity, fellow victims doing what they must to survive in a time when humans armed with science have become far too adept at killing them off.

Once I recover and we defeat Blackstone—and we must—I plan on returning to Boston to continue my mother's mission to cure vampirism, and if not, at least end a vampire's need for blood. I'll try to discover the immortality genes, for that is like the Holy Grail of all our human dreams.

So while I should be in Boston at the makeshift command center set up to deal with the fallout of the plague, Michel and Julien both insisted that I stay uninvolved for a while. Dylan agreed.

I'll follow their advice, at least until I adjust and learn to control my blood craving.

On the Monday morning Michel is scheduled to arrive, I wait for him in bed, a hot water bottle beside me to keep me warm. After managing my time between the brothers for the past month, I feel as if my body no longer belongs to me. It belongs to them, and they've used me so well my brain is almost on a pleasure overload.

My weekends alone without their touch, psychic or physical, are time to orient myself to my new reality.

I never thought I could love two men equally. I wouldn't have believed it possible, but I do. When I'm with one of the twins, I'm happy, but part of me misses the other. Since the brothers agreed to this arrangement, I've done everything I can to keep our relationships separate and distinct. I've spoken to them both and warned them not to try to show affection towards me when the other is present. For my part, I don't show affection to either when we're all together to discuss the Council or our work as vampire hunters.

While they weren't jealous when they were both with Marguerite, they don't feel that way towards me. I can sense their jealousy at even the slightest hint of attention to the other brother.

I must manage them—and myself—carefully. I won't become Marguerite.

I won't.

A KEY SLIDES into the lock and my heart rate increases, for it's Michel. I sit up in bed and wait, smoothing my hair, which has become a tangled mess, the braid coming undone as I tossed and turned, waiting for him.

His footsteps mark his passage through the cottage, from the front door to the living room and then to the kitchen. With my enhanced vampire senses, I can hear every sound. He opens the ice box door and I hear the clink of glass against glass. He's getting some blood, probably thirsty and hungry after the trip from Boston. Then he cracks the bedroom door and peers inside, catching sight of me sitting on the bed, the blankets pulled up around me.

I can't help but smile when our eyes meet, for during the few days off between brothers, I started to miss him. It's been nine days since we were together and I feel a distinct sense of deprivation despite having spent a happy and very erotic week with Julien.

When I'm separated from him, I feel deprived of Michel.

"I thought you'd be sleeping," he says and enters the room, pulling his sweater over his head. He sits on the side of the bed, leaning over to take my face in his hands, smiling at me. His hair falls in his eyes but I can see desire in them. I can feel his need.

I close my eyes when he leans down, his lips hovering over mine for a moment before he kisses me, the kiss soft. When he pulls away, he brushes an errant strand of hair off my cheek. "I imagined sneaking into bed beside you, enjoying your warmth while you slept. I've missed you."

"I missed you. I haven't slept since dawn," I say and yawn. "I can't."

"Are you well?" A frown crosses his face, his brows furrowing. He takes my hand and feels my pulse. "Have you been drinking enough blood?"

I smile, his show of concern touching my heart. "I'm fine. I was just excited."

He nods and seems to relax. Then, he stands up and begins to remove his shirt, unbuttoning the cuffs and pulling it off his arms, discarding it on the bench at the base of the bed with his sweater.

"I brought some fresh fish," he says as he unbuttons his jeans, watching me intently as he does. "Even though you're a vampire, you still have to eat. You look far too thin for my liking."

"You here to fatten me up?" I say with mock affront.

He smiles, but looks at me from the corner of his eyes as he strips off his jeans, leaving him naked except for a pair of black boxer briefs.

"I like you on the curvier side, Eve. It's Julien who likes muscle."

I shrug. I have lost a few pounds since I became a vampire. The newness of the life and the effects of drinking blood tend to mute my hunger for real food. Plus, I haven't been training properly, so I've lost some muscle.

Finally undressed, Michel stands beside the bed and watches me. He's well-muscled, his skin smooth and pale, just like his brother. I smile like a child in a candy shop waiting for a treat, guilty that I have so much to choose from. I can't help but compare the brothers and how they approach me, how they touch me. Michel feels different from Julien. I can't help but compare them even at this moment when we've only reunited after being apart for nine days. Michel is so intense, serious, focused, and deliberate. Julien is playful, impulsive, and expressive.

Both twins make my heart race and my body and mind respond, but I shouldn't be thinking of Julien with Michel next to me.

Michel crawls on top of me, straddling my hips, and takes my hands in his. He raises them above my head, restraining me before leaning over me, his eyes intense.

His small show of power shocks me back into the moment and into our relationship, which is so very different from that with his brother.

"Look into my eyes, Eve," he commands. "Focus."

I do, and all thoughts of Julien vanish as I shut off my mind, shut off the tendency to compare, and turn myself over to him, gasping when his mouth moves down from my cheek to my jaw, down my neck to his bite mark, which he licks softly, slowly, sending a shiver through my body. He moves lower, his mouth claiming a nipple while he squeezes my breast. I writhe in exquisite pleasure beneath him. He possesses me completely, I forget Julien and lose myself in Michel, in his expert control of my body's responses.

I feel complete bliss in his arms and the world outside, with all its troubles and hardships, falls away into nothingness.

LATER, Michel lies beside me, watching me, one hand reaching out to stroke my cheek. "I love you, Eve. Never forget that."

I turn to face him. "I love you, too, Michel."

He leans in and kisses me softly. When he pulls back, his face is somber. "Things will happen that…" he says and hesitates. He closes his eyes for a moment, as if he doesn't want to admit it. "Things will happen," he says again and opens his eyes, his expression intense. Almost afraid. "Things will happen that make you hate me."

"I could never hate you," I reply. How could I hate the beautiful, soulful man beside me? How? I love him with all my heart despite what he's done in the past. I understand why he did everything and understanding has opened my heart for acceptance.

He's heroic in his willingness to deny his own happiness for the sake of humanity. A lesser man would run from what Michel has faced. He didn't. He remained loyal to his cause.

"You could hate me and you will, Eve. Please remember, when you do find yourself hating me, that no matter what, I love you. I always have and I always will."

His expression is so serious, so determined, that I know it's no good protesting.

"I'll remember," I say to appease him and make him happy.

"I'm serious, Eve," he says and his intensity makes me pause. Once more, he takes my hands and holds them in his to show how serious he really is. "You will hate me. Remember that everything I do is to protect you and fight Dominion."

We stare into each other's eyes for a moment until he's certain that I appreciate how important it is.

"When that moment comes, and it will," he says, his voice soft. "When you do hate me, remember this moment, here and now." He stops for a moment as if he's too full of emotion to speak. "Remember how we feel for each other."

He drops down the walls between us and this wave of love, need and devotion from him floods into me and it's so intense, it brings tears to my eyes.

"Oh, Michel," I whisper, my voice breaking. I pull my hands out of his and wrap my arms around his shoulders, kissing him to stop all this darkness.

Being a vampire, he responds immediately and I do my best to make him forget everything except our mutual passion.

ON THE FOLLOWING SUNDAY MORNING, I'm alone. Michel left early Saturday. I spent the day walking the beach and the evening watching the stars. I snuck under the covers as the sun rose.

I pull the quilt up now, almost covering my eyes, but I can still see thin sunbeams shining in through tiny slits between the drapes that I never seem able to close completely. A million motes of dust dance in the sliver of light, and for a moment, I miss the sun. I miss it so completely that a stab of regret chokes me up because it reminds me that I'm no longer human. I draw in a deep breath and tell myself that soon, Dylan will get me Blackstone's drug and I'll be able to return to the sunlight.

Until then, I'll spend my days trapped inside.

Despite being tired, I can't sleep, on edge because of the message Dylan sent me through the HAM operator in Davis Cove. A young messenger boy on an old bicycle delivered the hand-written message Saturday evening. It was cryptic, but I was able to figure out what he meant.

HERE's a bit of scary news. The boxes holding Schrodinger's thirteen cats were empty when scientists went to check on them this morning. Just empty boxes with no cats inside, and the security guards protecting the experiment from tampering were dead. Can't explain, but not a good sign for our theories of physics. Until we know if the cats are dead or alive, scientists will have to be extra careful when talking about causality.

P.S. I'll be by tonight to discuss.

TRUST DYLAN TO code his message using physics. Schrodinger's cat refers to a theory in physics about uncertainty and causality. What Dylan means by referencing it is that somehow, the tanks holding Soren and the Twelve were empty when the security shift changed that morning. He doesn't say what they think happened to the "cats," but I can guess. The bodies in stasis were either stolen by someone in Soren's coven in hopes of reviving them, or Soren and the Twelve found a way to fight off the infection and escape, killing the guards on their way out.

Either way, it doesn't bode well for those of us who took part in their (temporary) destruction.

Me in particular.

I toss and turn, trying to find a comfortable position, clearing my mind, but have no luck. Finally, a drowsy warmth overtakes me and I must slip into a dream because I'm in a dark room in bed, my vampire eyes adjusting to the low light.

I feel someone's breath in my ear. A brush of lips on my cheek makes me smile. I can't make out the words at first, and frown, wishing whichever twin it was would speak up.

"What?" I say, reaching behind me to feel for hair so I can know whom I'm with in bed this time. Is it Michel, returned because he forgot something? Or Julien arrived early? Instead of Michel's collar-length strands or Julien's short hair and scruff, I feel long silky hair—far too long to be Michel.

"Eve," the voice says, speaking barely above a whisper, "Eve... you've been a very naughty girl..."

"Who—" I turn and see pale skin, white-blond hair, and red eyes. And the most evil smile I have ever imagined.

I sit up in bed and pull my covers around me, gasping at the image of Soren's face in my dream. I glance around the room. No, he wasn't here. I'm still alone.

But I do know one thing with absolute certainty.

He's free.

WHEN I FINALLY GET UP FOR the night, once the sun has set fully, I've had only a fitful rest. I lay with my eyes open for hours, my mind racing as I tried to figure out what to do. As a result, I'm exhausted and in need of blood. I stagger out of my bedroom and find that Dylan is waiting for me, seated on the sofa looking out over the ocean, his arms thrown over the back. He looks as tired as I feel.

I sit beside him and he leans in and kisses me on the cheek.

"You look as though you've haven't slept at all."

"Tell me," I say, impatient to hear the latest news.

"What's there to tell?" he says and sighs. "Someone stole the bodies and we have no idea where they are or what they're planning to do with them. Put them on display for worshippers? Use their bodies to obtain more supporters?"

"He's alive," I say, my hand on Dylan's arm. "No longer in stasis."

He turns to me, his face immediately dark, his brow furrowed. "How do you know?"

"He entered my mind when I was trying to go to sleep." I shiver and pull my sweater around my shoulders more tightly. "He spoke to me using telepathy."

Dylan shakes his head as if in disbelief. "How? Any blood you shared should have left your system by now."

I shrug. "He spoke to me."

"What did he say?"

"He said I was a very naughty girl."

"That's it?"

I nod. "It was enough to let me know he's alive and remembers what happened…and knows I'm the one responsible."

Dylan sits for a moment in silence, staring at his hands, which are folded in his lap. I can almost see the wheels turning in his mind as he tries to figure it all out.

"If he's alive, we really are in the dark about what he is. He should have been killed by the nanovirus. He should have." His hands fist and for a moment, I see him grind his teeth. He turns to me once more, his warm brown eyes full of concern. "You're in danger, Eve. We must get you somewhere safe. I'm sure Michel and Julien will agree."

"I don't want to leave. I love it here," I say, knowing that I'm being foolish, but I can't help it. I don't want to face reality just yet. "Beef up my security at the cottage."

He shakes his head. "No. You're too vulnerable here. We can't police the ocean. We can't protect you from the sky here. You'll have to go to a safe house somewhere in Boston."

"I don't want to go to Boston. It's so…dismal there."

I think of what has become of my beloved city due to the plague and general unrest. Buildings destroyed by fires no one can extinguish, whole blocks gone as the fires burn until they're out of fuel. Stores looted. Roving bands of thugs stealing food, fuel, weapons—stealing women.

Vampires are attacking at night—the attacks sporadic for now, but still a threat. Other vampires are corralling humans and hauling them away in covered wagons to who knows what destiny—most likely to warehouses where their blood is harvested.

"This isn't about what you want," Dylan says, his voice low. "It's about the future of humanity."

"Don't put that on me." I shake my head, my body tensing at the thought. "It's too much."

"You know it's true. You're key to everything. We have no choice but to use you—Michel, Julien, and I—or Soren will. Blackstone will."

I sigh, for I do know what he says is true. "That doesn't mean I have to like it."

He smiles ruefully. "I know. Believe me, I wish the two of us could live quiet lives here, but we can't."

I wrap my arms around myself, suddenly cold. "Sometimes I wish I would have died instead of them saving me."

"Don't say that," Dylan says, leaning closer, his expression hurt. "You don't really mean that."

"Don't tell me how I feel." I move away from him, angry that my brother sees me as just a tool as well and is willing to use me. I know that it's true—that I am a tool—though I can't help but wish that at least one of the men in my life would see me first and foremost as a woman they love and not as a means to an end.

LATER THAT NIGHT, both Julien and Michel show up at the cottage.

"Eve." Julien enters first. As usual, he looks devastatingly handsome in his leather bomber jacket, white t-shirt, and a deep blue scarf highlighting his blue-blue eyes. His hair is military-short and there's a bit of scruff on his very square jaw. He has a sword in a scabbard on his hip and I know there's a stake hidden somewhere on his body. He's a warrior once more, a vampire killing vampires for the Council—whatever remains of it—staking them before beheading them with his incredible strength and exceptionally sharp blade.

He comes right over to me and for a moment, I want to embrace him, but I put my palms on his chest, stopping him, trying to be professional. Both Michel and Dylan are watching.

I can't help but steal a glance at Michel and even from across the room, see the jealousy in his eyes. He's dressed in a long black cassock coat, black jeans, and a black t-shirt. The black highlights his pale skin and piercing blue eyes. He's not wearing a sword, but I can see the leather strap of a holster crossing his chest. A gold cross dangles around his neck. Dressed all in black like that, he could be a priest.

"Michel," I say, and smile. Despite our recent week together, I feel a need to hold him as well, but instead, I deny myself. I promised to not show affection for one in front of the other and I intend to keep that promise.

"Eve, you have to come to Boston," Julien says from across the room, drawing my attention from Michel, which I'm sure was his intent.

I'm determined not to be like Marguerite. I can't show one brother affection and not the other.

How can I choose between them?

In this moment, I almost believe in God—a God who is punishing me for being greedy enough to want them both.

WE GO in the living room. For a moment, I don't know where to sit, for I don't want to show either brother any favoritism. I eye the chair across from the sofa and take it so I don't have to choose. Michel sits on the sofa across from me, Dylan takes the chair beside mine, and Julien leans against the wall, his arms crossed.

I tell them about Soren invading my mind and Dylan describes the latest information he has on the break-in and deaths of the guards, and the escape or capture of Soren and the Twelve. Julien quizzes him, asking about the security measures that were in place and if there were any changes in the staffing or procedures, but there was nothing out of the ordinary.

"Soren and the Twelve either all came out of stasis at the same time or Soren came out first and somehow found a way to take the others with him," Dylan explains. "With limited electricity, we don't have great surveillance. It's impossible to know exactly how the breakout happened. We only know it did. Regardless, we have to respond."

Julien turns to me. "You're going to come to Boston with us and live in our safe house."

Michel nods in agreement. "With Soren free, it's only a matter of time before he comes for you."

"Michel's right," Dylan says. "Soren will come for you. He won't be content to just torment you in your dreams. He'll want revenge."

I sigh, resigned. "Where will I stay?"

Michel speaks, his voice soft. "You'll live with both of us in a reinforced building with 24-hour security. We have to be ready."

"Why don't we go somewhere else?" I turn to Julien. "We could go to some small fishing village along the northern coast and hide out."

Julien shakes his head. "He'll know where you are as long as he can get in your mind. You shared blood with him and until the effects wear off, he can read you wherever you are."

"How long before it wears off?" I ask. "Can't we stop him from getting into my mind?" I frown and clench my fists. "Pain stops either of you from connecting with me. Maybe I should see if pain can block him as well."

"Maybe being in stasis prolonged the effect. Besides, you can't be in constant pain, Eve. No." Julien shakes his head and walks back and forth, pacing. "We need you to be in a safe house we control so we can protect you, keep him from taking you."

"Can you?" I ask, looking in Michel's eyes for a moment to see if I can detect deceit. "Can you really protect me from him? Or is this a done deal? Should I just give him what he wants?"

"We'll do whatever it takes," Michel says and leans forward to take my hand, squeezing it and rubbing his thumb over my palm. "We should know soon enough what he plans to do—kill you or capture you and use your powers. He's obviously weak from fighting off the virus, so it will take him some time to be strong enough to do anything himself. We have to be ready for anything."

"What do you see?" I say, my voice low.

He frowns for a moment. "You don't believe I can see the future."

I shrug and glance quickly at Julien and Dylan before leaning closer. "What do you think you see?"

He smiles briefly. "Too many futures to know which one comes true. In one, Julien and I die. In another, we both live. There are so many permutations, Eve. Choices we all make alter them. It's too much for one person to control. I know that now."

I look in his eyes to see if he's being truthful, but I can't read him. He's too good at deception.

"If he's going to kill me, he'll want to do it himself. Letting someone else do it wouldn't be good enough for Soren. If he wants to kill me, he'll want to do it with one hand around my throat so he can watch me die when he stakes me."

Julien frowns at Michel and finally, Michel releases my hand.

I sigh and lean back. The three of us working together is going to be tricky.

"I really don't have a choice here, do I?"

Julien shakes his head. I turn to Dylan. His arms are folded and he's frowning.

"Eve, we have to protect you. We have to prevent Soren from using you to gain power."

"All right, I'll go to Boston," I say. "But I need one more night here. I'm not budging on this," I say, my voice firm. The sky has been so clear the past few days and I want to enjoy it before I leave.

Michel shakes his head. "You should leave tonight. If you insist, you need to pack your things and prepare to leave by tomorrow night. No later, Eve. It's not safe here."

He's right, of course. There's no other option now that Soren's free.

WHEN IT COMES time for them to leave, Julien stays behind, lingering by the door. It's his week starting tomorrow and he won't let me forget it, but I hate to have Michel leave with Julien here. There's no need to foster more jealousy between the two of them.

I pull Julien aside. "Come back in the morning," I say. "Slip out when Michel's sleeping."

"It's my week," Julien says, his voice filled with muffled protest. "He knows that. He's got to be a man and accept it. He doesn't hesitate to speak of being with you when it's his week."

"Just do it, Julien," I say, and push him, my palms flat on his chest. "I want peace between the three of us. I won't become Marguerite and have you in front of each other. Those are my conditions for this to work."

He sighs and makes a face but relents. "I know. I'll be back before sunrise." He leans in and gives me a quick kiss but I see Michel waiting in the driveway.

He's seen us.

His frown says everything.

CHAPTER 2

"A flower cannot blossom without sunshine, and man cannot live without love."

Max Muller

I spend the rest of Sunday evening sitting on the patio watching the night sky. Down below on the beach, two guards take turns patrolling the perimeter of the property. On the street to the west, another set of guards monitor the road.

While I realize I have to move somewhere safer, I want to stay by the ocean and smell its scent tonight. I wanted to stay here until Dylan gets the daywalking drug from Blackstone. I'm still too new to this vampire lifestyle to be doing anything but adjusting. I need this peace and quiet for my sanity. At the cottage, the rest of the world, with all its tragedy and heartbreak, seems to vanish and it's just me and the sound of the surf, the seabirds, and, when they're with me, one of the twins.

∽

AS PROMISED, Julien arrives an hour before dawn, when the sky is still dark enough that I can sit outside with a blanket around me and breathe in the fresh air without being too cold. I hear the lock turn in the door and then the sliding door to the patio opens.

He stands behind my chair and his hands squeeze my shoulders as he leans down to kiss my cheek.

I take one of his hands and squeeze it back. "You were able to escape?"

"We're staying at the hotel. We sat up talking strategy and meeting with a few people about security in Boston. I think Michel was trying to stay awake as long as possible in case I left early, but when I didn't, he finally went to his own room. I waited at least twenty minutes before I left, so if he was listening to see if I left early, it's his own fault for being jealous." Julien takes my hand and pulls me up from the chair. "Come inside. It's cold out here."

I try to resist. "I like it out here. The sound of the water calms me."

"I don't want you calm, Eve. I want you all breathless and excited. If you're leaving tonight, I want you now."

He grins and I can't resist that de Cernay smile. I relent and let him pull me inside the house, my heart rate quickening at the thought of making love.

"You can't wait?"

"I can't wait any longer," he says and removes the blanket from around my shoulder. "It's been nine days," he says, his voice dropping lower in register. "That's more than long enough."

He sits on the bed and pulls me between his knees before pulling me against him. I cradle his head in my arms and we remain in that position for a few moments as our senses finally join and mingle, our flesh becoming an indistinguishable mass of desire.

He glances up at me, and our eyes meet. "I missed you," he whispers. "When we're apart, I feel like this huge part of me is empty. I only feel whole when we're together. Alone. This being apart for nine days at a time is hell, Eve. I don't like it. I want us to be together all the time."

I feel the same ache he describes when I'm separated from one or the other twin. Even when I'm with one, my heart aches for the other and I feel guilty for denying him.

"We can't be together all the time, Julien. You know that."

"The heart wants what it wants."

He kisses my neck where he first bit me, and the feel of his lips makes my breath catch in my throat. Then, he rolls over onto his back and pulls me on top of him. I straddle his hips and admire him beneath me for a moment. The expression of desire on his face as his eyes slide over me is incredibly arousing.

"Fuck me," he whispers as his hands grip my hips. I lean down and kiss him and before we connect senses, I can't help but think of how different he is from his twin.

Briefly, for a short time, I forget everything—all the stress of discovering that Soren is free. The worry about moving to Boston. Daywalking. Being a vampire. It disappears in a blur of flesh and mouths and tongues and fingers as our bodies press against each other, our limbs entwined, our breath joined.

WE SLEEP THE DAY THROUGH, wrapped in each other's arms, the sheets and blankets a tangle around our bodies. Before dusk, I send Julien back to the hotel where the twins are staying so that he can change clothes. They both stayed at the hotel in town. Neither one wants to be too far away in case Soren comes for me.

And come he does, all too soon, and the peace I have known at the cottage is forever shattered.

THAT EVENING, Dylan and the twins arrive to help me pack up and before we can even start, one of the guards enters the cottage wearing full SWAT gear, stake and sword on his hip in twin scabbards. He removes his helmet, his face vampire pale.

"We got traffic on the road."

"What?" Michel goes to the window and pulls back the drapes. "Damn…" He turns back to the room and his eyes find me where I stand. "Get Eve in the most central room."

Julien nods and takes my hand, dragging me to the bathroom, which is located in the center of the cottage. "Stay in here," he says. "Lock the door and don't come out unless one of us tells you. Do you understand?"

I stop and pull my hand out of his. "In case you forgot, I spent two weeks at the Abbey learning to fight…"

He shakes his head, his blue eyes dark under a frown. "You're too valuable to put in danger. Just stay here."

"Julien," I say, angry that he won't let me fight, "why did you go to all the trouble of training me if I don't use the skills I have?"

"Because," Julien says and grabs my chin, forcing me to look in his eyes. "Because if this is Soren, he has older and much stronger Adepts and ascended vampires helping him. You're no match for them, even with training. Leave this to us."

I try to pull away, but he stops me, his hands on either side of my face. He kisses me and his kiss is almost desperate.

"Please…" he whispers. "You know I love your independence, but for once in your life, just obey…"

I exhale, caught between a desire to protect myself and following orders. I don't want to obey if the brothers are just being overprotective, but maybe they're right. I don't have a chance against much stronger and older Adepts or ascended vampires.

"Okay," I say with reluctance, trying to be a good soldier.

He pushes me towards the bathroom and I enter, closing the door and locking it. I sit on the side of the tub and wait, my acute sense of hearing keeping me informed. Since I can't see anything, I focus on the sounds, attentive to the noises of the house and yard.

Michel shouts to Julien, ordering him to take up position in the back of the house. I hear the two of them moving through the halls, then I hear the slice of Julien's sword as he removes it from his scabbard. I hear Michel checking his pistol to make sure it's loaded, the click of the magazine as it slides into the gun. Dylan leaves the house with the guard, their footsteps crunching on the gravel as they run down the drive to the road that borders the coast.

I wait, my heart pounding. Is it Soren himself? I can't imagine it's anyone else. He's come to kill me in revenge for what I did to him and the Twelve.

It's only then I realize that I don't have my own swords. In the haste to get me to a safe place, the twins didn't think to arm me. I hesitate for a moment, not wanting to disobey orders. I don't want to be left alone to defend myself. Without a weapon of any kind, I'm a sitting duck.

The cottage is quiet. I listen at the bathroom door, but I hear nothing from the street or yard. The only sound is a low moaning of wind through the trees, a branch groaning as it moves back and forth, a hiss and crackle as the wind rustles the dry leaves. I turn the lock very slowly, for whoever, whatever is out there has hearing as good as or better than mine. The lock clicks open with a metallic sound that rings in my ears.

I turn the knob and slowly open the door, leaving the bathroom and hurrying on tiptoes to my bedroom, where my own sword and stake are located. I lift the cloth they're wrapped in and slowly unwind the package, taking the sword and wooden stake in my hands before creeping back to the bathroom. If Michel and Julien have heard my movements, they don't try to stop me. I'm surprised and a little unnerved. I thought one of them would hear me and come running, but perhaps they're so focused on the external threat, they don't notice.

Once back in the bathroom, I close the door, clicking the lock shut. I stand with my sword in one hand and stake in the other.

I won't be killed without a fight.

LONG MOMENTS PASS and my heart rate slows a bit in the silence. Nothing has happened and I begin to think that it was truly nothing of concern. I let my guard drop a bit, the sword heavy in my hand. I sit back down on the side of the tub, my sword resting across my thighs, and wait, placing the stake on the counter across from me. It's in easy reach if I need it.

A huge explosion rocks the cottage and the floor shakes below my feet. I hold on to the side of the tub and wait, my heart speeding. Dust falls from the ceiling, which seems to have been warped from the explosion. Shouts and the sounds of gunfire break the ensuing silence —single shots, one after the other. My nerves are all on edge, adrenaline pumping through me.

"The beach!" Dylan shouts and Michel responds that he'll check it out.

I stand and hold my weapons up, ready for whatever might come through that door. Another loud explosion pounds nearby and the house shakes once more, plaster dust falling from the ceiling. Are they trying to destroy the house?

I smell smoke, the scent unmistakable. Fire is one of the only things that can kill a vampire and immolation is not a pretty way to go. I remember the manuscript and the description of Marguerite screaming when she woke to find herself standing on a pyre, flames surrounding her.

Is Soren planning on burning me to death the way Marguerite died, to punish Michel?

I can't stay in the bathroom or I'll die, so I open the door and rush out, my weapons at the ready. I'd rather die with a stake through my heart than burn to a crisp. There's no sign of either Michel or Julien as I run through the cottage to check on the damage. Fire in the living room blocks the doors, so I run to the back of the house. There's a hole in the wall and fire there as well, orange flames licking up the drapes.

Where are they?

"Michel!" I shout, desperate for a way out of the cottage. I enter the office and put down my weapons so I can open the window, but the frame is jammed. I pick up a heavy lamp base and try to break the glass, but it's tempered and triple glazed. The lamp bounces instead of shattering the pane.

"Julien!" I gather my weapons once more and run to the hallway, desperate for a way out. Fire blocks the exits to both doors.

I'm trapped.

I run to the third bedroom and see that Julien is on his back on the floor. A soldier dressed in SWAT gear has a sword at his throat. Julien's unconscious, his eyes closed, his arms thrown over his head. I see something protruding from his chest and I scream.

"Julien!" I rush the figure and raise my sword and stake, yelling as loudly as I can manage, falling into fight mode, but the soldier meets my sword with his and he's far too strong. He's a vampire and must be old because my moves are pitiful in comparison to his. I try to see his face behind the mask, and catch a glimpse of pale hair and white skin —is it Soren himself?

He attacks me, pushing me back until I fall to the floor, and straddles me. He takes off his helmet and I see it isn't Soren. It's someone I haven't seen before.

He leans down, his sword across my throat, the stake pressed between my breasts. "Soren says hello." He smiles a completely evil smile and presses the stake against my breastbone until it hurts, cutting into my skin. "He has a message for you. You can't escape. Turn yourself in for your punishment or your beloved twins will die."

The sword bites into my skin, the pain slicing through me.

His eyes widen in shock, his expression a grimace, teeth gritted.

As I watch, a sword slices through his throat. Blood erupts from the wound and from his mouth. He tries to look down at the sword, his hands gripping it like he wants to stop it from moving. A stake protrudes from his chest and he stops completely, his expression freezing, his eyes staring blankly ahead. The sword retreats and the soldier slumps to the side.

Behind him stands Michel, Julien's bloody sword in his hand.

He kicks the body aside and kneels down to me, checking my throat and chest for wounds. "Are you okay? We told you to stay in the bathroom…"

"I smelled smoke. I didn't want to be burned to death. I'd rather die fighting."

He nods and leans down, pressing his forehead to mine for a moment, his eyes closed and his long hair brushing my cheeks.

"Julien," I say and Michel sits up, helping me up in the process. "He was staked."

I glance over to where Julien lies, but the stake has been removed and he's starting to awaken. A groan escapes his lips.

"Damn, that hurts," he says when Michel helps him up.

"Let's get out of here," Michel says, squeezing Julien's shoulder with affection. "There's no fire service. This place will burn to the ground."

I follow them to another room and this time, Michel's able to get the window open. It's a good thing because the air is thick with black smoke. I cough so much I have tears streaming down my cheeks.

After throwing our weapons out the window, we jump out to the lawn and run to the front, Michel in the lead and Julien behind me. I hold out my sword in case I have to fight.

When we arrive, there are several bodies on the lawn. Dylan runs up to me, checking me over. He gives me a hug.

"Thank God you're okay."

I hug him back. "I thought you didn't believe in God," I say and smile.

He squeezes me. "Not the way Michel does." He releases me and one of our guards runs up.

"We got them all, but the cottage is destroyed. It'll burn to the ground."

I turn to Michel. "Where will we go?"

"Your parents' cottage," Michel says to Dylan. "There's lots of room."

Dylan hesitates. "I don't want to put them at risk," he says, shaking his head. "There are a lot of abandoned cottages we can use."

"Your parents' cottage is strategically located. We could see anything coming for miles. It's our best hope."

With reluctance, Dylan nods, but his jaw is tense. His parents have suffered so much. They lost their daughter and their son is a vampire, so I completely understand his reluctance to involve them.

We take the cart, leaving a half-dozen dead behind, two of them our own but the rest Soren's men, including the one who gave me Soren's message. I take in a deep breath, trying to calm myself after the battle. My legs suddenly feel like jelly and tears spring to my eyes.

"The one you killed gave me a message," I say to Michel as the carriage drives down the street to Dylan's cottage.

"What did he say?"

"He said I had to turn myself in to Soren or both of you would die."

Julien leans over and brushes a tear off my cheek. "Don't worry. Michel and I are pretty much the most powerful ascended vampires in existence besides the Twelve. There are only a few who can beat us. Soren won't have an easy time of it."

"One of his men had you on the ground with a stake in you."

"He ambushed me." Julien reaches down and feels the place where he was staked, the fabric dark with his blood. "He couldn't kill me anyway. Only Soren can. This was just a threat to scare you." He grins in spite of it all.

"Julien's right," Michel says, his blue eyes dark. "A stake can't kill either of us. Not anymore. All it does is disable us temporarily. Only Soren or an ascended vampire who is older than us can kill us. There aren't many of those."

Julien turns to Michel. "I learned that the hard way." He grins again, referring to the Abbey when Julien tried to have Michel staked, but it didn't work and only temporarily disabled him.

How he can joke after what happened is beyond me, but he's a warrior. All his existence, he has fought battles like the one we just endured. He turns to me and, as if reading my mind, smiles softly.

"Joking makes it bearable."

When we arrive at the cottage, there are no guards and it's dark, the door open.

"This isn't good," Dylan says, his voice low. He takes out his sword and approaches the property.

The guards are on the ground. We find them just inside the gate. Julien kneels down to check each one, but they're both dead.

"How long have they been dead?"

Julien shakes his head. "They're both really cold, so this didn't just happen." He turns to Dylan. "When was the last time you were here?"

Dylan takes in a deep breath. "Days ago. Last week."

We move cautiously to the door, walking between two rows of cedars taller than we are and I feel threatened from all sides. Michel and Julien walk beside me as if to protect me, with Dylan leading the way.

Dylan steps over the threshold carefully. Michel follows and motions Julien to the back of the cottage and then follows Dylan through the doors, signaling to me to follow him.

"Stay close," Michel says and I do, my body tense.

Dylan and Michel clear each room and finally, Julien joins us from the sliding glass door that looks over the ocean.

"They're gone," Dylan says. "It looks like there was a struggle. It's possible they were taken, and I can guess who took them."

We stand together in the jumble of cushions and lamps that litter the floor.

"Soren's taken them," Michel says.

"Or Blackstone," Dylan replies.

"Aren't you on good terms with him?"

"I thought I was." Dylan sits on a wooden bench and covers his face with his hands for a moment. I sit beside him and slip my arm around him, squeezing. He rubs his face and turns to me, his expression a mix of fear and anger, his jaw set. "Whoever took them, I'll hear about it soon. Then, we'll know who I have to appease."

WHILE JULIEN, Michel, and Dylan talk in quiet voices in the dining room, I find the bathroom and wash myself quickly, wiping the soot and tears from my face. When I'm done, I stand in the doorway and watch the three of them. Besides my foster parents, these three have become my life. I haven't seen or heard from either of my foster parents in too long, come to think of it. That's where I want to go next.

"We have to go to see my parents," I say. "I can pick up some things there."

Julien glances at Michel and they both say nothing for a moment.

"What?" I say, moving closer. "Tell me! Did something happen to my parents?"

Dylan comes over to me and rests his hands on my shoulders. "I checked on my way over. They're gone."

I stare into his eyes. "And you were going to tell me this when, exactly?"

Dylan exhales loudly. "In case you didn't realize, we just fought a battle. We haven't had time to discuss things. Besides, I didn't want to alarm you."

I pull away from him and sit on the couch, resting my face in my hands. I feel nothing, the events of the evening far too overwhelming. I want to cry, but I can't. I just sit and close my eyes, breathing in deeply to try to keep calm.

I look up. "Soren has them," I say. "He must have taken them to use as bargaining chips."

"I think you're right." Dylan says.

"Why didn't he come and take me first?" I ask, glancing from Michel to Julien and back.

"Because one of us has been with you the entire time. We should have beefed up security for them. I was planning on it, but…" Julien closes his eyes and I can see pain on his face, in the tightness of his jaw and the lines in his brow.

"I'm going to kill him," I say, my voice low. "Can we go to their cottage so I can pick up some clothes? Some of my things are still there."

"If you want to."

"I want to." I close my eyes and a wave of fatigue flows through me. I have nothing left to draw on.

I think of the other people in my life whom Soren might take and use as bargaining chips. There are so few. My father, who is locked in some mental institute. Cecile, who I haven't seen since before the plague. I wonder if Soren has sent out a raiding party to capture either of them. Is my father even alive?

I sigh and adjust the sword in a scabbard on my hip. Julien comes over to me, making a point of touching my hand and letting it linger when he helps adjust the belt that holds the scabbard.

"I'm sorry," he says. "It's my fault they're gone."

I shake my head. "It's Soren, not you." I stare up into his eyes and when he takes my hand, I feel a surge of love from him. He's angry with himself, along with all the fear.

"When we go to Boston, it's still my week," he says, his voice low.

I stare up into his eyes and my body responds to the idea of being with him again, despite what we've just been through. Maybe because of it. The two of us are helpless against our desire for each other.

Michel turns his head towards us. Of course, he can hear every word with his acute vampire hearing.

I force a smile. "Maybe we should hold off on our arrangement for a while," I say, breaking our contact. "Re-establish a schedule once we know what's up." I tilt my head just a bit to remind him that Michel's in earshot.

Julien closes his eyes briefly and inhales. "Dammit," he says. "Fucking Soren…"

"You can wait," I say chidingly, but I'm unable to keep a smile off my lips.

He grins back at me, his eyes narrowing suggestively. My cheeks warm at the thought of his naked body.

"I hate waiting…" he says, his voice a whisper.

"You can wait." I hit him playfully on the shoulder, amazed that despite having just fought a battle, being staked, and killing enemies, he still wants me. I'd be happy to stay here with him all week the way the schedule has been planned, but that's not going to happen.

I turn away from him and catch sight of Michel's frown. He glances away, his fists clenched and his jaw tight.

These two...

CHAPTER 3

"We are all born for love. It is the principle of existence, and its only end."

Disraeli

My foster parents' house feels so strange without them here. I walk through the mess left by whoever took them, surveying the damage. Furniture has been overturned as if there was a struggle. Drawers are opened as if their abductors were searching for something.

Information about me?

I pick up an overturned chair in the kitchen and cover my mouth, imagining the fear my parents must have felt when Soren's men came for them. Michel stands next to me and touches me briefly, his gaze meeting mine. I see sympathy in his beautiful blue eyes.

"We'll find them," he says softly.

I nod, but inside I don't believe it. I turn away and catch sight of Julien watching us, a look of hurt on his face at seeing me with Michel. Even that small show of affection was too much for him.

I turn away, wondering if I can do this. Can I possibly live with them both? It's too much to deal with at the moment for my emotions are overwhelmed at the thought of my parents being captured and possibly tortured by Soren. I need to focus on the work at hand. I don't have much here any more. Most of the clothes are meant for summer, fit more for the beach than winter. When I sift through the boxes of old clothes, searching for something big enough to fit me, I find nothing but bikinis and cover-ups from my early teens. There's some memorabilia from my high school days, but very few items I can take with me.

We're scheduled to leave soon for Boston and I'm sad. I felt peace in Davis Cove for a short time during this period of transition and change. As I stand in my old bedroom, I don't know what the future has in store for me now that the three of us are to live together in the same household.

Keeping the brothers separate and allowing them to visit on alternating weeks with a weekend in between has made me feel less guilty for wanting them both. They don't see me with the other brother and I never have to hide my affection and desire for either man. I can be free to enjoy them openly when we're together and the other doesn't have to be jealous.

Living together will be very stressful.

Before we leave, Julien pulls me aside and whispers in my ear. "When we get to Boston, if we're going to have to wait, don't touch him when I'm around," he says, his brow furrowed. "I can't take it."

"Julien!" I stroke his cheek quickly when Michel has his back turned.

"Seriously. I can't stand to think of you with him, but seeing you touch him…" He shakes his head. "Please, just don't."

"That applies to you, too," I counter. "Don't touch me in front of Michel."

He grins for a moment and the old, playful Julien returns. "Now that I can't promise. Michel will just have to deal."

I hit him on the shoulder in mock anger and step away when Michel turns around and sees us standing together. He frowns but says nothing. Living with the two of them under the same roof won't be easy, but it's their choice, not mine.

I finish packing what few items I have and stand in the doorway, surveying the cottage. I wonder if we'll ever return here and a deep sadness fills me, the sense of foreboding so strong, I feel like I've had the air knocked out of me. I hold my hand to my chest and try to breathe in deeply to calm myself. Soon, my heart rate slows.

I don't know how I'll survive this, but I must be strong. I have to remember my mother and how she fought to the very end, defying Soren even though it cost her life.

I will as well.

THE TRIP into Boston takes hours despite using a vehicle with a hydrogen cell battery because we're taking back roads to avoid abandoned vehicles on the highway. It's the same road that we took when Julien and I went to Boston that first time. I have vivid memories of the vampires attacking and Michel rescuing us. When we pass the place where the battle occurred, I look at Michel and exhale.

"This is where it happened," I point out and take his hand briefly. "Thank you for being there when we needed you."

He turns to me, leaning close so that his face is just a few inches from mine. His eyes look haunted. "I'm so glad I was there." He leans in and kisses me softly, one hand tangling in my hair as he pulls me closer. That kiss could become intense so easily, but he pulls back before it does.

I steal a look at the front seat, but Julien hasn't noticed. Dylan, on the other hand, is looking at us from the rearview mirror, his brow furrowed.

I don't think he trusts Michel. There's been nothing concrete to point to, but I feel it even so. He and Julien seem more simpatico when it comes to personality.

WE STOP for a break and I hide in the bushes to pee. When I return, Julien is in the back seat and Michel is in the front.

Do they have to share everything? Even the drive to Boston?

I sit in the back beside Julien with a heavy sigh. "Was that the halfway mark or something?"

Julien grins but says nothing, then glances outside, his smile lingering as we drive on. After a few moments, he slides his hand over the seat to take mine and holds it, keeping his face turned away, his focus outside of the car. I feel like a teenage girl who can't choose between boys as I glance quickly at Michel. Luckily, he's busy looking out the front and doesn't notice, so I let Julien hold my hand—for a while. He obviously feels deprived because of the interruption in our usual routine.

Besides, I want a bit of human contact. This is all so upsetting. Just when I thought our battle with Soren was over, I realize it's just beginning.

I have quickly-fading scars on my throat and chest to prove it. I run my fingers over my wrists and the scars from Julien's knife when he saved my life. Those scars will never fade completely because they were administered before I was a vampire, and are a constant reminder of what happened that day I tried to kill Soren and the Twelve.

Julien fusses over them when we're together, kissing them and apologizing. Michel only sighs and touches them gently, regret in his eyes, as if he should have prevented it. These new scars from the battle we just fought will fade when I next get some blood, but for now, they itch and I'm uncomfortable as we drive down the road to Boston.

WE ARRIVE in the outskirts of the city, the streets dark, no lights on because there is no power. We pass abandoned houses and entire neighborhoods, the streets littered with newspapers that blow around in the wind. Trash is piled up and abandoned cars crumble on the roads. Overhead, the sky is littered with a million stars. Without the light pollution, the Milky Way is visible as a froth of bright dust in the blackness, the beauty of the heavens in stark contrast to earthly devastation.

"Where have the people gone?" I ask, staring into empty houses, the doors left wide open.

"They've escaped," Dylan says from the front. "Either to the borders to try to get out, or they're going where there's food. A lot of people are living by the ocean so they can at least fish."

When we get deeper into the outlying neighborhoods, I see bodies littered on the sidewalks and lawns, bloated and grey.

"They've been attacked by vampires," I say, noticing their ripped throats. A shock goes through me at the realization.

"Blackstone's vampires have been here, taken people, killed them," Michel says and nods slowly, his gaze moving over the bodies. "We knew that would happen eventually. With Soren out of the picture—temporarily—Blackstone wanted to execute his plan for Dominion."

"Have they killed everyone?"

Dylan shakes his head from the front. "No," he said, his voice low. "They're warehousing humans, using them as feedstock. They probably killed the men and any who fought them. They'll have taken the children and women. They're easier to manage."

"Feedstock," I say, the horror of the idea once again filling me with nausea. "How can they feel that way? Have they lost their humanity completely? I want blood. I need blood. I know what it feels like to desire humans, but I won't kill one."

"You're brand new," Julien says and squeezes my hand. "You have options, like blood donations. We never did. We were monsters, and that was that. We had pets whom we bled dry slowly or we outright killed. The most we could do was take those already dying, but we still killed."

I shudder, glad that I do have options. I know the pleasure of biting into flesh and drinking blood—Julien and I play that game all the time—but I won't kill a human.

I won't.

Not for blood.

I will, however, kill vampires. Those who refuse the Treaty? They've rejected the only thing that keeps them alive, ensuring their survival. If so, I feel no hesitance to kill them for their blood. I haven't done so yet, but I look forward to it.

A small bit of revenge for the death of my mother.

I look at the back of Michel's head and think about him. He's so tortured by his past and all the human lives he's taken. He's the priest who intended to save souls, only to find himself cursed to spend his existence taking them. He killed so many and all because of Soren's desire to have a stronghold in the Languedoc region of France. I used to hate Marguerite, but now I see that she was just as much a pawn as the rest of us.

Michel killed my mother under compulsion. He liked her and he admired my father. He would never have done it voluntarily. I've forgiven him enough that I can be his lover, but he still hasn't completely forgiven himself. I see it in his mind when we connect. His pain is still there despite my complete forgiveness.

It's Soren who is guilty, and I want more than anything to be the one to kill him. To suck him dry would give me the greatest pleasure. But to see him dead, through any means, will be good enough.

WE DRIVE to one of the most central buildings in Boston, near the cathedral, and stop on the street. I glance up at the building to a row of solar panels on the roof. A garage door to an underground parking area opens slowly to admit us. Security cameras are mounted on the wall all down the block, pointing at the driveway into the parking lot.

The street has been cleared as if this is a protected zone, only a single vehicle parked on each corner like sentinels, watching for any approaching cars or pedestrians. The streets downtown are deserted. There's no food left and since people can't live in cities without frequent shipments of food, they've fled south or to the rural areas in search of food.

We enter the underground, brightened by floodlights. The solar power system set up on the roof must provide electricity to the entire building. We park near an elevator and Michel gets out from the front and opens the door for me, taking my hand to help me out. I don't need help, of course, but he does it so he can touch me once more and reestablish contact with me. He doesn't let go and I stop and look up into his eyes.

I touch his cheek, brushing a strand of his black hair from his cheek. "Michel, I won't be with either of you until we can talk. It's going to be awkward living in the same building as you. You shouldn't be touching me in front of Julien."

He nods, but still he brings my hand to his lips. "I just wanted to say how sorry I am about all this," he says, and I can hear the regret in his voice. "I'm sorry that your life isn't your own."

"Maybe someday." I force a smile and he smiles back, but his is just as forced as my own. I'm starting to believe there will never be a day when I can have my life back. Finally, he drops my hand and it's a good thing, for Julien appears at my side. I glance at his face to check if he saw us, but his expression is neutral.

We take the elevator to the third floor. The building is wide with five floors, one apartment on each floor. The apartment itself is luxurious and large, obviously once owned by someone wealthy. I walk through and glance in every room. The floors are either hardwood, tile, or plush carpet. There are three bedrooms, all nice enough to be in a five-star hotel. There are two bathrooms and a formal dining table on which maps and papers are spread. Michel and Julien have been using this apartment as some kind of operations center. There's an ancient HAM radio set up on a desk in the corner and a map on the wall with pushpins marking off locations.

In the kitchen, a pot of coffee sits on an electric stove.

Julien puts my suitcase in the largest bedroom and I peek into the other two and see that there are clothes and other items belonging to Michel and Julien on each dresser. Perhaps this is where they've been living all along, just waiting for me to come to Boston.

I turn to Julien, who stands in the hallway leaning against the doorjamb watching me. "You've been living here together?"

He nods and crosses his arms. "We've been using this as a home base. We've set up security for the twenty-four blocks surrounding this one with guards and sentries on each corner. 24/7 coverage."

"I didn't see anyone."

"You weren't supposed to."

I sigh. "You expected I'd come here eventually?"

He nods again, a crooked grin on his lips. "We've both been dreading it. The walls are thin."

I close my eyes and sigh. These two...

"You've got it all planned out?"

"We do," he says, biting his bottom lip to keep from smiling even more widely.

I turn away, frustrated with them, although they were only following my own wishes.

"Eve..." Julien frowns. "You're the one who insisted on this sharing thing."

"You accepted it." I shake my head and hold up my hand. "I know, I know," I say and exhale. "You're right. I did insist on it. But not like this, with the other in the next room. Maybe...can we hold off for a week while I get settled in and we figure out what our plans are? You know—our plans to fight Soren? There are some things more important than a fuck schedule..."

"What?" Julien says, only half in jest. "How is that possible?"

I ignore his attempt at humor. "Maybe when it's your week, Michel can stay somewhere else. You know, so we can have some privacy."

Julien makes a face. "Can't do that. We need someone to protect you when one brother is otherwise occupied. We don't trust anyone but each other to do that."

I exhale heavily. "Suit yourself."

Julien returns to the makeshift office in the dining room and I stand in the hallway glancing between his room, Michel's room, and what I take is going to be the fuck room.

I clench my fists. I don't know if I can do this—not with both of them under the same roof. I will not become Marguerite.

I will not...

AFTER A MEAGER MEAL OF BREAD, cheese, and some beer, I yawn and head for the bath. I turn on the tap but no water comes out, so I return to the dining room.

"I want to have a bath. Can I heat up some water?"

"Sure," Michel says, "but it will take some time to heat."

"Where do you get clean water?"

"Springs outside the city," he replies and helps me fill several big pots with water from a large container. "We truck it in and are almost self-sufficient. Solar panels provide all the electricity we need for most things, but water has been a big problem. That's why the city is deserted. Without the water treatment plant operating and without city workers, all our services are out."

"What about the plastics in the solar panels?"

From the table in the dining room, Dylan replies. "Blackstone's been busy for a while developing new technology that doesn't use plastics in production."

"They knew what was coming and were prepared?"

Dylan nods and joins Michel and me in the kitchen.

"Won't Blackstone be out for you and Julien?" I ask Michel, watching as the burners heat up. "They should know you were helping Soren—or at least appearing to do so."

"Lord Blackstone trusts me," Dylan answers. "He knows we're related and has given me authority over this sector of the city. No one but our own loyalists know Michel or Julien are here. They're being hidden from Blackstone as much as you are from Soren."

I turn to Michel. "I have no clean clothes."

"Take something of mine," he says, moving to his room and opening a chest of drawers to remove a t-shirt.

"Thank you."

Michel smiles at me and nods. I return to my bathroom and then look at myself in the mirror. I look terrible, my hair a mess, my eyes tired. My skin is now vampire-pale.

The Damned, Michel calls us. A hint of blood hunger nudges me, reminding me that I need to feed. It hits me in a way it hasn't before. I've never felt this starved in all the time since I became the thing I've hated the most all my life.

I HAVE a bath and even the shallow water revives me a bit, the stress of the day and the trip vanishing down the drain to the sewers, which apparently still work. When I'm dry, I slip on one of Michel's clean shirts and wash my underwear and shirt in the remaining water, hanging them on the shower curtain rod. Then I go to the dining room where Michel, Julien, and Dylan sit, poring over some maps. They all look up when I enter, and their response makes me self-conscious. Dylan has a pleasant look on his face, as if he's glad to see me, but there is a palpable hunger in both Michel's and Julien's eyes. The t-shirt is too big, but it's thin and in the chill of the room, my nipples are hard. I cross my arms to cover them.

I know where their minds have gone—to my bedroom, wondering when I'll break down and ask one of them to join me.

"I'm tired, but I need some blood," I say.

Dylan comes to me. "Let me get you some. It's in the refrigerator."

I follow him to the kitchen and stop him once we're alone. "I'm so sorry about your parents," I say, squeezing his hand.

"And I yours," he says. "How easily our hearts become targets to our enemies. How are you holding up?"

I sigh. In truth, I feel nothing except the desire for blood. It overwhelms everything else.

"I'm numb," I finally answer. "How are you?"

He shrugs and takes in a deep breath. "I should have had more security on both our parents. I didn't think far enough ahead to see that they could be used as pawns to affect us."

"Maybe it wasn't Soren or Blackstone. Maybe they left quickly and didn't have time to leave a message and the cottages were looted after they left..." It's a plausible theory, but even I know it's just wishful thinking.

I try desperately to come up with something other than the four of them being held captive to force Dylan's and my compliance. I grew fond of Dylan's parents during the short time I knew them. I can't stand the thought our families are being tortured—or killed—so I shut it off.

Numb is better.

"Someone will contact us in the next few days if they're being held," he assures me. "Until then, there's not much we can do."

I hug him, my arms around his shoulders, and he hugs me back. We stand like that for a moment before he lets me go. He doesn't seem to want to speak about this anymore, so I drop it.

He retrieves a bottle of blood from the fridge and hands it to me. "Here," he says, watching as I remove the cover and drink. "Don't take it all at once. We're rationed, so that has to do for a few days. We have to be a little hungry at all times now."

I nod, wanting to drink the entire pint, but I stop halfway. I hand it back to Dylan and he puts it back in the fridge.

"Where do you get it?"

Dylan shrugs and leaves the kitchen. I follow him back to the dining room office.

"We have donors. Let's leave it at that."

"Tell me," I say, grabbing his arm. "Are they compelled or voluntary?"

"I can't know for sure," he says. "It's either this or hunting. As I said before, no one was killed getting this. That you can be assured."

I exhale, not wanting to think the blood was from one of Blackstone's factory farms where humans have become the new feedstock.

I lean into the room and catch Julien's and then Michel's eye. "I'm going to bed. To sleep," I say with emphasis. "Goodnight. I'll see you both in the evening."

Julien blinks rapidly, as if he's frustrated. He had planned on spending the week with me and now this happens. I must admit I'd like to have one of them with me, for a deep sadness permeates me. I don't want to be alone tonight. I could cry if I let myself because everything seems overwhelming. My cottage burning to the ground, my parents and Dylan's parents taken. Being here in Boston and seeing it so devastated.

The blood wasn't enough to send me into a euphoric state and so I go to bed tired, hungry, and depressed.

I DREAM, captured in a nightmare vision of someone stalking me, following me though a dark forest, the moonlight casting scary shadows on the forest floor. In my dream, bare branches scratch my cheeks as I run through the undergrowth. I can hear footsteps behind me, dry brush cracking under the stalker's feet. I see a flash of pale hair and I know it's him.

Soren.

He's laughing and pointing in the distance. A cross appears in front of me, and it's upside down. I go around it and see that Michel is crucified, a stake through his heart, his naked body pale in the moonlight.

"No..." I cry. "You bastard!" I run to the cross and touch Michel's cold skin, checking to see if he's still alive.

"He chose this," Soren says, his voice gloating. "He died to save you."

A scream begins to build inside of me, finally escaping my lips.

"Michel!" I cry out and my voice is so loud, I wake myself up. I sit up in bed, my heart pounding, my body tense, my cheeks wet with tears.

In an instant, Michel enters my room, closing the door carefully behind him. He's naked except for a pair of boxer briefs, his body pale in the sunbeam from between the drapes. His hair is a mess, dark strands falling into his eyes. He sits on the bed and wraps his arms around me, holding me, and I'm a mixture of tears and gasps as I try to recover from the nightmare.

"Michel, oh Michel…" I grab hold of him and run my hands over his naked shoulders to reassure myself he's real and alive.

"Shh," he says, stroking my hair, his breath warm on my cheek. "You're okay. It was just a nightmare."

I pull back. "I saw you," I say, wiping my cheeks. "You were crucified, upside down. Soren was there… He said you chose death to save me."

"It was just a dream."

I shake my head. "No, it wasn't just a dream. Tell me the truth—it's going to happen, isn't it?"

He looks in my eyes as if deciding whether to tell the truth. "It's one possible future. Not necessarily the one that will come to pass. Soren was trying to scare you into giving up. Torment you. Don't worry." He strokes my hair, smiling, but I can tell it's forced. "We can make a different future."

"Michel, I don't want you dying for me. Don't ever chose death to save me. I couldn't stand to live if you did."

Michel shakes his head, smiling softly. "Don't worry. We'll all survive this if we do what's right. Now, relax and go back to sleep. I'll lie with you for a while if it helps."

I want to lie with him, despite this being Julien's week by all rights. I don't want to let go of him because that was a vision of the future and not a nightmare. Soren showed it to me to scare me.

Michel lies down on top of the coverlet. He pulls me into his arms and I lie back down, my head on his chest.

"Don't choose death," I say again, squeezing him more tightly. "I know you want to die, but don't. Please." I lift my head from his chest and stare into his eyes. "Not because of me."

He smiles once more and runs his fingers over my cheek. "I don't want to die anymore. You're the only reason I want to live, Eve. I love you."

Tears spring once more to my eyes at his words. "I love you," I whisper and pull him down to me, our lips meeting in a kiss.

It starts out chaste, just mutual love being expressed, but soon it turns to desperate need and before I'm aware of it, his mouth is moving down my chin to my neck, to the sensitive skin beneath my ear where he—and Julien—marked me, claiming me. He sucks on the skin there briefly, pulling my t-shirt and then his briefs off before lying on top of me.

I welcome the feel of him against me. It's comforting, his body reassuring in its solidity. The sensation of his skin against mine is arousing and then our limbs entwine, our mouths joining in a kiss that sends jolts of desire through my body.

No words are spoken between us. The only sounds are when we touch and caress each other as we make love. Our senses join, the boundaries between us disappearing so there's only a blur.

~

AFTERWARDS, we lie together recovering, the sheets tangled between us.

"This was Julien's week," Michel says, his voice soft. "He'll be upset if he knows we've been together."

"I know," I say and sigh. "But I needed you after that vision. He has to understand…"

"He'll understand, but he won't like it. I wouldn't. You were supposed to be his this week. Tonight."

"I'm not his or yours." I sit up and look at him as he lies beneath me. "You can't treat me as a possession. I'm my own person."

"We've been over this before. You're ours," Michel says, running his fingers through my hair. "You're either with us or Soren. He won't let you be with anyone else."

"Soren doesn't want me that way. He's almost like my genetic father. I have his genes…"

"He's an angel. The body he took form in is merely a vessel. He doesn't see it the way humans do. He'd have you if we don't. You must understand that. You were made for us, to keep us in line. You were made to serve him."

"I have my own will."

"You do," he says and smiles, pulling me back down on top of him so that my face is above his. "Don't I know all about your will, Eve…" He chuckles. "Controlling you has been pretty near impossible, despite all my military, masculine and vampire wiles."

There's a crooked de Cernay grin on his lips; I'm surprised by his rare show of humor. He's been so somber lately.

"You want me tamed?" I say with mock affront. "You really want me as your pet?"

He strokes my cheek and is serious once more. "It's not that I want you that way. It's required. There's a hierarchy even among vampires. Age gives power and rank. You must obey or be compelled to obey if you won't of your own free will. Except you—immune to compulsion. You resist me every step of the way."

"I'm sorry if I've been difficult. It's just the way I am."

"I know. I love the way you are, even when it's not in my or your best interest."

We kiss once more and it's tender and sweet.

"I better leave," he says quietly. "I don't want Julien to wake up and find us together."

He leaves the bed and I let him go with reluctance, watching as he pulls on his boxer briefs, appreciating his very buff body.

He turns when he's dressed and leans down to kiss me once more, his hair in his eyes. He kisses me as if he can't get enough. Finally, he's gone. After I wash myself in cold water from a pitcher in the bathroom, I lie back down, but I don't think I can sleep. Despite the endorphin rush I got from the sex, I'm hungry and still slightly unnerved by the events of the previous night and by my vision of Michel crucified on an inverted cross.

Like St. Peter.

I lie on my back, staring at the ceiling as a sliver of afternoon sun coming in between the drapes crawls across the room.

CHAPTER 4

"I'M NOT upset that you lied to me. I'm upset that from now on I can't believe you."

Friedrich Nietzsche

WHEN THE SUN SETS, I wake, surprised that I did finally sleep. The sheets are wrapped around me and my body's cold because I haven't had enough blood. I yawn and stretch, wondering what the night will bring.

I splash cold water over my face, staring at my bleary eyes and pale skin in the bathroom mirror. After I dress, I go to the kitchen where a pot of coffee is brewing, the scent wafting through the apartment. Julien is up, dressed in his usual faded jeans, thick black belt, and white t-shirt. His very square jaw is covered in a few day's growth of whiskers, making him look like a male model from the pages of GQ rather than a vampire-hunting vampire.

His eyes meet mine, and I know in an instant that he must have heard us.

"Julien," I say and go to him, but he keeps his back to me while he watches the coffee maker.

I rest a hand on his shoulder; he pulls away from my touch. Unwilling to give up, I slip my arms around his waist and pull myself against him from behind. He smells so good, clean and masculine.

"Eve..." he says, his voice low as if he's trying to be polite, but it's forced. It's hurt.

"You have to understand—" I begin, wanting to assuage his jealousy.

"I understand," he says a bit too quickly. "In case you forgot, we vampires have really good ears." He pauses for a moment and a sense of regret and embarrassment fills me. "I heard everything."

"I'm sorry." I lay my cheek against his back, my arms squeezing around his waist from behind. His washboard abs are firm beneath my hands. "I broke my own rule the very first night. Don't hate me."

He shrugs, but doesn't move away. Finally, he takes my hands in his and we stand like that for a moment while the coffee finishes brewing. As usual, I'm filled with desire for him and guilt that I want him so soon after having made love with Michel. I had them both within one day of each other, hours of each other, and I feel incredibly bad and greedy.

I hear Michel emerging from his bedroom, the door closing softly behind him. I try to pull away from Julien so that Michel doesn't see us together like this, but Julien won't let go. I realize he wants Michel to see me giving him affection.

Michel stops abruptly when he sees us. Our eyes meet and I smile, but I know seeing me like this with Julien will upset him. I should protest, but I realize that Julien wants to score some kind of point with Michel after last night, to prove he means as much to me as Michel does. Julien finally lets go of my arms when he feels my resistance.

I step away from Julien and turn to Michel. "What's on the agenda for today?"

Michel moves past us to the fridge, his jaw tightly clenched. He opens the door and stands staring into it. Then he bends down and removes a small cardboard box. I noticed it when I looked in the fridge before but never thought to ask what it was.

"This," he says and holds it up. "This is on the agenda for today."

"What is it?" I move closer and take it from his hand. It's about three inches by three inches square, wrapped in butcher paper and tied up with a string like a package from another century.

"Your freedom."

I glance up at Michel. "What is it?" I say. "Blackstone's daywalking drug?"

Michel shakes his head. "It's the waters of life. We want you to take it."

I hand it back to him quickly, as if it's poison. "I don't want it. You already know that."

"Julien and I agree and Dylan concurs. You should take it. If you go to Blackstone for his serum, he'll demand your loyalty. He'll expect you to obey his orders, whatever they are."

"This will make me a..." I was going to say monster, but stop. "Into something I don't want to be."

"This will solve almost everything, Eve," Julien says. "It will make you invulnerable to other vampires. Only Soren and the Twelve, as well as other ascended vampires, will be able to kill you. Soren won't so long as you're useful."

I shake my head, for it will make me an abomination. I feel bad enough that I've become a vampire. I won't become an ascended one.

"Come on," Julien says playfully. "No one will be able to push you around anymore. You can daywalk, you can join senses with others more easily, and keep others out. You'll be free."

"Free?" I shake my head. "I don't call what you are 'free.'"

"Dylan did this," Michel says as if it's the last resort to refer to my brother's willingness to ascend. "If you did, the four of us would be almost invincible."

I push Michel's hand away. "I'll take Blackstone's serum before I take that."

He exhales loudly. "You are so damn stubborn…"

"You love me because I'm stubborn."

"In spite of your stubbornness..." he says and finally gives in, returning the box to the ice box.

I pour myself a cup of coffee, my back to the brothers. I don't want to talk about this any longer. What they've become frightens me. They're otherworldly in a way that challenges all my views on science and religion.

It unnerves me.

~

I'M SITTING in the living room at the baby grand piano, half-heartedly playing some Chopin, when Dylan arrives.

His face is haggard. He's probably spent the entire day trying to discover what happened to our parents. His dark eyes go directly to me when he enters the room. He pulls off his jacket and comes over to the piano.

"Did you take it yet?" He looks a bit flustered, as if he's rushed over and is out of breath. "Have I missed the ceremony?"

"She didn't take it," Julien says, his voice tired.

Dylan sits on the bench beside me, shoving me with his shoulder. "Why didn't you take it?" he says, sounding frustrated. "I did."

I look at Michel and then at Julien. "I don't want to become whatever it is you are. But forget that," I say, impatient to hear about his parents. "What have you learned? What happened?"

Dylan shrugs and then leans back, rubbing his eyes with his hands. He exhales heavily and then turns to me and takes my hand.

"I've learned nothing. No one has contacted me and there are no demands. I spent the day looking through their cottages to see if there's anything that will lead me to who did it, but nothing. Some of their things were missing, their suitcases are gone from the closet, and some of their clothes as well. But the place is trashed. All the food is gone as well as a lot of useful items—tools, household goods. That kind of thing."

"Maybe they left for somewhere safe, unable to tell you at the time. Maybe," I say, hoping beyond hope, "maybe the place was looted when people found it empty. They could be safe on some farm somewhere." I say it but I really don't believe it. They would have let both of us know.

Dylan shakes his head. "They would have left something so we wouldn't worry. No, someone took them, and it looks like they were planning to keep them for the long haul. It has to be Soren." He closes his eyes for a moment, struggling with his emotions. "I guess we'll find out soon enough."

He looks at me, his eyes hard, his expression disapproving. "Why won't you take the waters? It's not what you think," Dylan says. "It's just activation of some special genes that protect you from being staked and from daylight. It enhances your telepathy. It makes you stronger. It's nothing mystical."

"Michel thinks it is."

"He's rather biased," Dylan says, smiling softly. "Everything is screened through his religious beliefs. I'm telling you, as one scientist to another, that it's merely gene activation using a special retrovirus that turns on certain gene sequences. Nothing religious."

"How do you explain the disappearing and reappearing wings?"

Across the room, Michel moves on the couch where he's sitting, as if interested in Dylan's explanation.

"Mental projection and telepathy," Dylan says. "When you're especially emotional, in specific states of consciousness, you project this image to those around you. I can't explain it exactly—why wings, I mean. Wings must be archetypal, deeply ingrained in human consciousness. But I know I don't have wings," he says and laughs as if it's the most ridiculous thing he's ever heard. "We're not angels."

"What are angels?" Michel asks from across the room. "Beings of power. The power to manipulate matter, to control human minds. Where did they get that power? That's the question science can't answer. Only religion can."

Dylan turns to Michel. "Genetic mutations. Random events that were so rare they became recessive, only showing up in a geographically distinct population. Northern European. Nordic. Hence, the white skin and fair hair associated with angels. Soren is a prime example."

Michel says nothing. Instead, he shakes his head in dismay.

Dylan turns to me. "If you won't take the waters, then you must take the serum. You can't go on like this, living as a simple vampire, even one who is an Adept. You're far too vulnerable."

I exhale, resigned to taking Blackstone's serum. "How do we get it? Do you have contacts in Blackstone so you can get some for me?"

He nods. "Lord Blackstone himself. We've become close," Dylan says and raises his eyebrows as if in surprise. "He's taken me under his wing, seeing me as his protégé."

"How can you even consider working for him?"

"I'm not really working for him, Eve. I'm trying to understand his capabilities and goals. For the Council."

"You're a good secret agent," I say, giving him a grin. "But it must be hard. Doesn't he know about Sarah? How can he think you'd side with him after her death?"

"He apologized to me. Said if he had known about Sarah, he would have warned me. We could have turned her before—she could have been healed. I blame myself for not pushing more, but I was trying to stay under the radar."

I nod and take his hand. Dylan looks at it and then smiles at me briefly before becoming serious once more. He pulls his hand away.

"Look, Eve, if you're not going to ascend, the first thing we have to do is get you Blackstone's serum so you can daywalk. I've convinced him that you did all this willingly, thinking it might kill Michel and Julien along with Soren, and that you wanted to become a vampire. You're going to have to meet him, though. Now that you're a vampire, he'll consider you one of his and you'll be welcomed into the fold. You're going to have to pretend you now share the goals of Dominion so that we can get you ready for battle. You can't fight effectively if you can't daywalk. If you won't ascend, you have to take the serum."

"I don't want to meet Blackstone. He's the bastard responsible for Sarah's death. For the fall." I turn to Dylan and frown.

I'm unsettled about having to meet Blackstone, but if it's necessary,

I'll do it. When I finally received my mother's research files—after years of fighting with the University to get them—I knew my life would be in danger if I chose to follow in my mother's footsteps as a vampire hunter. I can't back away now that I really am one.

"If you get me as close to Lord Blackstone as possible," I say, "I'll jam a wooden pencil into his cold black heart."

Dylan shakes his head. "Believe me, I felt that way after Sarah died. But if either of us did that, someone would replace Blackstone. He's important, yes, but he has a son and lieutenants who would be only too happy to replace him if we killed him. We must get to the heart of the organization and destroy it from within. All of it."

"How?"

"The Council is working on a plan."

"Tell me," I say, frustrated that none of them will tell me everything, as if to protect me. "I'm not going to tell anyone."

"Eve, you know why we can't tell you." He shakes his head. "You can't know the details now, because even I don't know them. We'll both find out once the mission is ready."

"Do you know?" I say, turning to Julien.

He smiles but says nothing and shrugs as if it's out of his control.

I sigh heavily. "Don't you trust me?"

"It's not that," Julien says. He comes over and leans against the table across from the piano, his arms crossed. "If I told you and you were captured, they'd torture you to get the information since you won't ascend. This is a need to know mission. Only those at the top know all the details. Those in operational mode only know what we need to know. We act when we receive the signal to proceed. Once the plans are complete, you'll be informed. Like before, you'll be given a drug to make you forget. Only when you're given the code word will you know."

That's the plan. Like the plan to destroy Soren, we'll strike from within. I'll know the plan, but it won't be available to my conscious mind until I hear the code word. That way, I can't be tortured to get the information. Organized madness.

"When will we go to Blackstone?"

Dylan stands up. "No better time than now."

I turn to him, dreading this meeting. "Where?"

"At his compound in Cambridge. I'll arrange a meeting with him later tonight. If you pass muster, and I know you will, you can take the serum. This will mean you can move more freely during the day."

As much as I'm reluctant to meet with Blackstone, there's no fighting it. I have to take the serum so I can daywalk. Not taking it is preventing me from moving around in the day. Even though I won't be ascended, being able to daywalk will give me an advantage over regular vampires. Besides, I want to feel the sun on my pale face once more.

"All right," I say, resigned to my fate. "Let's go."

Dylan nods and goes to put on his jacket. "Come with me to the compound. I'll introduce you around and talk to Blackstone's lieutenant to arrange a meeting. People from Blackstone will be very pleased to meet you. You're the legendary Adept who worked for the Council but who changed sides. The vampire who almost succeeded in killing Soren Lindgren and his Twelve. The woman who chose to become a vampire."

"I didn't choose it," I say a little too petulantly.

"No, you didn't, but they don't have to know that. Believe me, it will be a plus in their eyes. You're revered. Blackstone will be very pleased to offer you the serum so he'll have you in his debt."

Michel comes to me as I put on my jacket. "This is really important, Eve. Please cooperate. I know you despise him and with good reason, but your ability to daywalk is critical. Don't resist."

I nod and dread fills me. I realize now that this serum of Blackstone's will change me as well.

"How will the serum make me feel?"

"You'll feel like hell," Julien says, the only one of them who has taken it. "You'll sweat, you'll feel nauseated, you'll shake. You'll probably pass out for a while and sleep like the dead. When you wake up, you'll be transformed. It's like the waters, but not as complete. And it's temporary. If you don't keep taking it, you'll revert back."

"Is there any risk?"

Julien shakes his head. "They've almost perfected it. You feel like total crap for a while as the nanovirus infects you. It's really fast, but it's pretty safe."

"Pretty safe?" I say, hesitating. "Has anyone died because of it?"

Julien shrugs. "A few, but it's really rare. Don't worry. You'll be fine."

I take in a deep breath and look at them. I want to kiss and hug them both, but which one would I kiss and hug first? No matter which I approached first, the other would be hurt. Instead, I go to where they're standing side by side and stand between them, my hand on each of their shoulders.

"Kiss my cheek," I say. It's the only compromise I can think of that won't hurt either of them. They both hesitate and then lean down, each one pressing their mouths on a cheek. I pull them momentarily against me, both at the same time. I want to kiss them both but can't. Having them kiss my cheek will have to do. I let go of them with deep reluctance and turn to Dylan.

"Let's go."

CHAPTER 5

"To be trusted is a bigger compliment than being loved."

George MacDonald

We walk on foot for some miles through the city center to a garage that has been converted into a stable. Dylan lives in this neighborhood in North Boston, deserted now except for a few of Lord Blackstone's forces, which are scattered throughout the city, most in Cambridge.

The trip to the stable drives home how far civilization inside the protected zone has fallen. In the cold of early winter, the trees are all leafless and trash has rotted on the corners. Stores have been looted of everything salvageable and everything plastic or made from petroleum products has disintegrated into crumbly powder or sticky dark sludge.

We cross a bridge into Cambridge, skirting the dilapidated trucks and cars sitting abandoned on the overpass.

"What kind of surveillance does Blackstone have in place?" I ask, conscious of all the places where we could be watched. "Will they see us coming?"

Dylan shakes his head. "Don't worry. There's too much city and too few forces to monitor the entire place. Besides, Lord Blackstone will welcome you. You're his heroine."

"Why does he think that?"

"He thinks you wanted to kill Michel out of revenge for your mother, and Soren as well."

I frown, surprised, but I guess in Lord Blackstone's mind, it's impossible to imagine a vampire not sharing his goals for Dominion. I try to relax.

"But they lived," I whisper to Dylan. "Michel and Julien should have died as well. How did you explain that to Blackstone?"

"An error in formulating the nanovirus which allowed Soren and the Twelve to survive as well," Dylan says, leaning down so that his lips are by my ear. "It wasn't viewed as sabotage, but incompetence. The scientists involved in engineering the nanovirus are all dead so there's no one to tell the truth."

I nod, filled with guilt that scientists died because of me.

We're able to drive the carriage undetected until we get closer to Blackstone's camp in Cambridge. The lights we finally see in the distance signal that we're getting close. We arrive at a set of jerry-rigged gates made with police barricades and barbed wire, cordoning off one city block. One of Blackstone's guards greets Dylan and asks for his papers. I listen as Dylan describes our trip from the coast to the city, and the reason. The guard looks at me with real curiosity and then takes off his hat and nods, smiling. Maybe what Dylan said is true. Maybe Blackstone's forces do think I tried to kill Soren because I support Blackstone's goals.

The guard motions us through the makeshift gates and down the street, which is more residential than commercial, the buildings grand mansions set on large lawns. It reminds me of Michel's mansion and I wonder if we'll ever be able to return there.

We drive up to a gated and protected mansion of red brick with Georgian architecture. It's huge with three wings, a semi-circular driveway, and torches lighting the way to the massive set of double doors. Guards greet us at the driveway and speak with Dylan. They recognize him and pass us through, nodding to me once more, as if they're expecting me.

We dismount at the entry. Another guard takes the horse and leads it away from the front.

"Come," Dylan says, his hand at my arm. "Don't be afraid. Lord Blackstone is only too happy to meet you. You're his poster child for Dominion."

We walk up the steps to the doors and a servant opens them for us, admitting us into a wide foyer. As we cross the threshold, I look up to see a huge chandelier and a double staircase leading to the second floor. Our footsteps echo in the cavernous entry. In a room to the left, people are gathered in small groups and from their pallor, they're all vampires. They turn expectantly when Dylan enters the room. One of them, a young-looking vampire with short dark hair and a very muscular frame, stands and comes right over to us.

"Dylan," he says, nodding. Then he turns his eyes to me and I feel his gaze like a laser boring into me. "This must be Eve." He reaches out to take my hand and then kisses my knuckles. "Welcome. We've been waiting to meet you. I take it your trip from the coast was uneventful?"

I force a smile.

"Eve, this is Lord Blackstone's eldest son, William. He runs security for the compound and spent some time in Afghanistan during the wars."

I smile again and he finally releases my hand.

"My father's in a business meeting and won't be able to join us for a while," William says, so very polite. "But please, do come and sit with us. We're pleased to have you with us." He puts his hand on the small of my back and leads me over to the group of other vampires. "Have something to drink. You look famished."

He motions to a circle of plush chairs surrounding a central coffee table. On the table is a large carafe filled with what appears to be blood. Immediately, my bloodlust revives and my mouth actually waters.

"We're rationed," Dylan says. "Both of us are hungry." Dylan raises his eyebrows at me as if to warn me not to ask about the blood's provenance.

I don't want to drink the blood of slaves, but what choice do I have? My purpose is to get Blackstone's daywalking drug so I can be an effective fighter for the Council. I can't be effective at anything if I'm starving. I must compromise my morals for the greater good, but it chokes me to do so.

William pours some blood and hands us the delicate crystal glasses. They're beautiful, with an intricately etched floral pattern. I hold the glass up and nod to William.

"To Lord Blackstone," I say, hoping to get myself even more deeply into their good books.

Beside me, Dylan holds up his glass. "Here, here. And to Dominion."

I'm so hungry by that I drink the glass down without stopping, gasping a bit when I finish. It tastes so good. When I look up from my glass, I see that William has his hand over Dylan's glass, preventing him from drinking. It's then I realize things are not what Dylan has led me to believe…

I turn to Dylan. "Why aren't you drinking?"

Dylan doesn't answer. Instead he puts his glass down and turns to me. "Don't panic," he says softly. "The drug should start to work right away. You might feel a bit dizzy."

I frown and sit down heavily. "The daywalking drug?" I say, licking my lips. It's then that the room starts to feel far too hot. I glance around as the room seems to melt around me. "What's happening?"

"Truth serum," William says. He stands in front of me, his hands on his hips. "Do you really think Lord Blackstone wouldn't want to interrogate you before he accepts you into the fold?"

I try to look at Dylan but my muscles seem weak and it takes forever to turn my head.

"Dylan," I whisper, fear starting to fill me. "What's happening?"

He turns to me, his expression sad, his mouth downturned. "Sorry, sister, but they have my parents. You must cooperate now, for real. They know you can't be compelled, so they're using a truth serum to force you to tell the truth."

He shrugs as if it's all beyond his control. It's then I realize that he's betrayed me.

"You knew all along…about your parents…" I manage to whisper.

He nods. "I didn't expect that we'd have any reason to go to their cottage. I'm sorry I lied to you, but you can understand, Eve. They have my mother and father."

Adrenaline courses though me and what I'd like to do is get up and run as fast and as far as I can, but I can barely move the muscles of my face, let alone my legs.

"Lord Blackstone," comes a voice from the doorway.

I slowly crane my head and when I finally have the entry in focus, I see him.

Lord Blackstone himself.

He's younger than I imagined—not much older than his son—perhaps early thirties. He must have become a vampire and then turned his own son when he got to a certain age. That's the only way they could be so close in age, for they look more like brothers.

He has dark curling hair to his shoulders and green eyes, thick black lashes and a generous mouth. His square jaw is covered in dark whiskers. He's also well-built, wearing a black zip-up mock turtleneck and leather trench coat over black jeans. He's very handsome in a slightly fearsome way. Like I'd imagine a thug in the Irish Republican Army.

Not someone you want as your enemy.

"Ahh, Eve. The woman of the year."

He walks over to me and I follow him with my eyes, my body slumped back into the sofa, my muscles useless. He motions to Dylan, who moves aside, and then Blackstone sits beside me. He takes my hand and kisses it the way his son did. On his face is a warm smile, but his calculating green eyes betray his otherwise-friendly demeanor.

"I am so glad to finally meet you, Eve. Your brother here has told us so much about you. You have the de Cernay twins on their knees before you, you almost killed Soren and the Twelve… Everyone wants to ask you about the whole thing. But me?" he says and turns my hand over, examining my fingers. "I want to hear you play Chopin. Dylan tells us you were a child prodigy and performed in Budapest and Prague. How sad that things went so badly for your family."

He clicks his tongue, smiling at me while I sit helpless.

"So," he says and leans in closer. "I know you can't be compelled and I apologize for drugging you, but how can I trust someone I can't compel?" He shrugs as if this is out of his control. "Now that you've had the truth serum, I hope to get some answers out of you. Tell me, how much do you hate Soren?"

"I want to suck him dry," I manage to whisper. "Then I want to drive a stake through his heart."

Blackstone smiles at that. "Sadly, that would accomplish nothing. He would merely incarnate into another body. To kill him, and I completely understand your desire for his death, Eve, we must prevent him from leaving his body. We must destroy him and the body together. Our first attempt didn't work, due to incompetence on the part of my scientists, but I assure you that won't happen again."

I say nothing, barely able to keep my eyes open. In fact, I can feel them partially shutting so that all I can see is the bottom of his face, his very square jaw covered by dark stubble and his full, smiling mouth, his chin and neck with a prominent Adam's apple. It's only very slowly that his words finally hit me.

Our first attempt…

What does he mean? It was the Council who tried to kill Soren.

Blackstone shifts on the seat. "And what do you feel for Michel and Julien?" he asks.

I can't help but respond, for whatever drug he's given me is making me lose all control over what I say.

"I love them both more than anything."

He smiles at me and nods his head. "Yet you were willing to let them die so you could kill Soren?"

"I thought they might live." It's the truth, even if not the complete truth. I find I can tell a half-truth as long as part of what I say is true.

"You were willing to sacrifice yourself to kill him."

"Yes," I say. That is the truth. Of course I wanted to live, and I wanted both Julien and Michel to live as well, but apparently I wanted Soren to die even more. "Soren is a monster."

"That he is," Lord Blackstone says, his eyes narrowing. "And what do you think of Dominion?"

"It's wrong."

He nods again, as if he expected me to say that. "You support the Treaty?"

"Yes. Vampires shouldn't rule. We should share power."

"Sharing power," he says and shakes his head. "A nice dream, but only possible between equals." He crosses his legs and leans back. "Vampires and humans are not equals." He studies me for a moment, and then inhales as if he's decided. "In the end, Eve, it really doesn't matter if you agree with our goals or not. You still love your parents as well. You're an exceptionally new vampire and still have all those old loyalties. You'll do what I want to keep your father alive."

My father?

He has my father? Despite the drug, my heart thumps in my chest.

"You have my father?"

"Yes," he says. "If you want him to stay alive, you'll cooperate." With that he stands and goes to Dylan, who glowers at him, not hiding his contempt.

Dylan assured me that my father was well-guarded. Of course, at the time, I had no idea Dylan was under Blackstone's control.

"Quit looking at me like that," he says to Dylan and pats Dylan's cheek. "This is the far more humane thing to do, don't you think?" He turns to me and catches my eye once more. I don't see gloating in them—just a calm sense of competence. "Aren't you glad I took him to protect him from harm, Eve? I'm sure you'll comply with my wishes to ensure he remains alive. If I didn't take him, Soren surely would have."

With that, Lord Blackstone struts out of the room, his two guards following in his self-confident wake. I hate him.

Almost as much as I hate Soren.

I'm LEFT ALONE in a small, dark cell of a room in the mansion, the lights low, waiting as the drug slowly loses potency. I've lost track of time, but judging by how hungry I am, I'd say it's been several hours. Finally, Dylan comes to me, sitting on the bed beside me and taking my hand. Part of me wants to be angry with him, while the other part understands completely. With my father now under Lord Blackstone's control, I'll do what he asks. But I will also look for every opportunity to stop him.

"Don't hate me too much, sister," Dylan says with a strange detachment, his voice monotone, as if he feels nothing. "I screwed up and didn't protect our parents well enough. We didn't get your father to safety soon enough."

"I thought he was somewhere in upstate New York," I manage once my control recovers and I no longer want to scream.

"Blackstone found your father and brought him here. He has all angles covered, Eve. He's a master strategist."

"You say that as if you admire him." I drag myself up to a semi-reclining position, my back against the cement wall.

He shrugs listlessly. "I can admire someone's skill and still hate them."

"Can I see my father?" I ask. "If he's here in the compound, I want to see him. Tell Lord Blackstone that I'll comply with him, but only if I have proof that my father's alive. Otherwise..." I say to the ceiling, where a video camera is poised, watching and listening. "Otherwise, he can go ahead and kill me. What do I care?"

"Lord Blackstone assumes you'll cooperate to save your father's life."

"He's right," I say, but my heart is almost thumping out of my chest at the thought that my father is here. My foster parents deliberately hid his location from me because, in his brief moments of sanity in between those of complete insanity, he didn't want me to see him the way he was, and they agreed.

All I knew was that he was somewhere in an asylum, drugged and insane. I was always told he wouldn't recognize me anymore because he'd lost complete touch with reality and had become catatonic.

I make a terrible decision. If he truly is that way, if he is completely shut off from reality and I can do nothing to bring him back, I'll kill him myself so his torture and death can't be used against me. If he truly is catatonic and it isn't the result of drugs or compulsion, I figure he'd rather be dead than used to blackmail me and destroy human civilization.

"Please ask Lord Blackstone to let me see my father. Tell him that once I see he's truly alive, I'll do whatever he wants of me."

Dylan rises and straightens his jacket as if he's gathering his courage. "All right, sister. I will."

He goes to the door and knocks. A guard opens it, but before Dylan leaves, he turns to me once more, his face pained despite the smile he pastes on his lips. "Don't get your hopes up that your father will recognize you. From what I hear, he's practically a vegetable."

I nod and lie back down, my muscles too fatigued from the effort to sit up. I don't know what to do. How can I get myself out of this situation? Once I know whether my father is a vegetable, at least I can remove Blackstone's leverage over me. What will he do then? Kill me?

I'm totally at his mercy.

A WHILE LATER, a guard opens the door and motions to me with his head. "Come on. Lord Blackstone wants to see you."

I rise without protest and stand while he fastens my hands together with rough iron manacles from some bygone era, the iron rusted and rough on my skin. We trudge down a long, dim corridor to stairs leading up to the main floor of the massive house. Upstairs, the guard leads me through a half-dozen hallways with wood paneling and stone floors until we enter a large study with cathedral ceilings, the walls lined with bookshelves. There must be thousands of books in the library. Lord Blackstone sits at a wooden desk before the arched stained-glass window, a map spread out before him on the tabletop.

He looks up when we enter.

"Lord Blackstone, you asked to see her." The guard pulls me forward and I stand before him, my bound hands in front of me.

"Take off her cuffs, for God's sake, man." Lord Blackstone waves his hand at the guard, his brow furrowed. "She's not a prisoner. She's a guest."

The guard unlocks the manacles and removes them from my wrists, which I rub. The scrapes are slow to heal because I've had so little blood in the last few days and I wince a bit from the pain. I glance around, searching the room for potential weapons. There are few, but nothing traditional. A table or chair leg could be broken off and used as a makeshift stake if I had to...

"Guests are free to leave when they choose," I say, hoping to distract him while I survey his study for weapons. There's a coat of arms on a wall with two long blades—I could try to remove one and stick it through his heart if the opportunity arose.

Blackstone smiles, his eyes narrow. "Unfortunately, I've declared martial law over this sector of Boston and so no one is free to travel without permit. You have no permit, so..."

"And I suppose you're in charge of issuing permits?" I say, sarcasm heavy in my tone.

"Of course. It's a safeguard to ensure that there's no unnecessary traffic to interfere with keeping the order. And we must have an orderly society, mustn't we, Eve? Don't you think that order is preferable to mayhem and murder in times of chaos?"

"A free society is more important," I say, eyeing the chair's narrow wooden legs. One of them could be used as a makeshift stake in a pinch. "How inconvenient for me that you're the one to issue permits," I continue, unable to bite my tongue. "Does keeping the order include attacking humans, killing them, taking them prisoners, and farming them like cattle?"

"That's what humans are to us," he says, smoothing his hands over the map and turning his attention back to it. "Feedstock. Amusement. Toys for our pleasure."

"Not all vampires feel that way."

He nods and examines part of the map more closely. "That's entirely true. I intend to make sure that they all share my view of things. Those who don't will go the way of the dodo."

"You intend to kill off all dissenters?"

He glances up at me. "Whatever it takes to keep the peace."

"Your peace. Isn't killing another vampire one of the cardinal sins?"

He smiles but says nothing for a moment, examining me like I'm a disobedient child. Finally, he heaves a heavy, impatient sounding sigh.

"Dylan said you had a mind of your own." He looks back at the map and motions to me. "Killing vampires is something mortals have become very adept at doing. Too adept, your mother included. I had to do something to stop our extermination. Come and see what we've accomplished in such a short time."

I frown and refuse for a moment, but then realize that knowing his plans and what's happened could be useful. I walk over and stand in front of the desk. A map of the world is spread out on its surface. I recognize the continents and the oceans, but on the entire eastern seaboard of America, there's a wide swath of red extending from Newfoundland to Florida. It reaches all the way west to Chicago and down to New Orleans.

"Is that the extent of the plague?"

"Plague?" he says, and makes a face of mock offense. "You mean, the liberation of my brethren from the threat of humanity? I prefer to call it Dominion, and it will allow you to live the way you should as top predator. The highest on the food chain. An Immortal with powers unrivaled since the time of the old gods."

"Old gods?" I say and frown, wondering where he's going with this and what his religious beliefs are.

"Yes, old gods," he says and runs a fingertip over England, which is almost completely covered in red from the coast of my beloved Wales to the eastern coast. London is completely surrounded by red. He glances up at me. "Don't tell me you're an atheist like Dylan."

"I'm a scientist," I say. "A skeptic who needs evidence before I can accept something. I believe as much in the Flying Spaghetti Monster as I do in God or the gods of religion."

"How sad for you. To be such an empiricist is to deny spiritual experiences that go beyond the senses. The old gods!" he says and waves me around the desk to his side. "The old gods were like vampires are to humans now—powerful beings who had dominion over them until they gave us their powers and we vampires took over. That's all."

I go around the table as he indicated and stand at his side. He points to the western coast of the USA.

"That's our next release target. At the same time," he says and points to the eastern coast of Russia, near Vladivostok, "we will release the nanovirus here and here so that eventually, the entire world will be red." He smiles up at me. "What do you think? A blood red plague that covers the earth. Symbolic, don't you agree?"

I shake my head, my heart pounding at the thought. "You've already caused the deaths of millions of humans."

"Hundreds of millions, I'd think by now," he says matter-of-factly, as if he's proud.

I can barely breathe for a moment, let alone speak, my anger is so great.

"And you think we—that I—won't try to stop you? I'd be a monster if I went along with this, by any credo of religion or ethics."

"Pishaw," he says. "I have your father. If you don't comply, I'll kill him. And Dylan. And everyone you care about. You're necessary to my plans now that our first attempt to destroy Soren failed. If you really want to get rid of Soren, you'll comply. He's the only fly in my ointment at the moment, but even he will be useful for a while. Then I'll get rid of him as well."

It's then I remember what he said when I was first drugged.

"You said that before. What do you mean, your first attempt to destroy Soren?" I ask, a sense of dread creeping through my body. I understood that my attempt on Soren was a Council plan, not one of Blackstone's.

He looks up at me, a look close to gloating on his face. "Oh, that's right. You thought Dylan was working for the Council." He turns back to the map and straightens it, righting the corners once more. "That outmoded waste of time." Blackstone cricks his neck and moves the map a bit, repositioning it in front of him. "I'm the Council, now, Eve, and have been for decades. You've been working for me all this time. You never questioned how Dylan was able to get the nanovirus and use it against Soren?"

"He infiltrated your organization…"

"Or maybe I let him join?"

I stand in silence for a moment, taking this new piece of information in. He's the Council?

I'm at a loss for words, snarky or serious. All I can think is that we're screwed if there truly is no Council independent of Blackstone. If he's telling me the truth, then we'll have to start a new Council free of his influence.

"If you expect me to cooperate with you, you'll have to let me see my father."

He shrugs and smiles up at me then turns back to his map. "I'll let you see your father later. We're moving him to the compound so you two can be together. He was kept in terrible conditions. And now, if you don't mind, please leave. You're free to enjoy the compound, but don't for a moment think you can escape." He snaps his fingers to summon the guard and then I'm forgotten. He opens a file of papers and busies himself reading some document as if I'm now invisible.

The guard shows me to the door and closes it behind me, leaving me alone in the hallway.

I know he meant what he said—I'm free to wander around the compound undisturbed. So that's what I do, determined to find a way to escape.

CHAPTER 6

"IT IS MORE shameful to distrust our friends than to be deceived by them."

Confucius

I WANDER around the compound and note that while no one stops me from exploring each room, they seem to keep an eye on me. I've spotted plenty of surveillance cameras overhead, watching every corridor and room from all angles. After I've checked in each room, I try the rear door and find that it opens. I walk out as calmly as I can and stand for a moment to glance up at the stars, breathing in the cool night air. I wonder where Michel and Julien are and if they're worried about me.

Can they imagine what's happened—that Dylan has betrayed us—that Blackstone is the Council and we're working for him all along? Do Michel and Julien both know this and once again, I'm the only one in the dark? I can barely believe it myself, but that's what appears to have happened.

I take a moment to examine the security arrangements. A ten-foot tall fence surrounds the grounds with barbed wire and floodlights. Several guards walk along the inside of the fence. Even if I could reach the fence and climb it, I'm sure one of them could get to me in time to either shoot me or stop me. My only hope would be to overpower one of them and then climb the fence unnoticed, escaping over it and running back to the city.

I sit on a low retaining wall that circles the patio and watch the guards patrol for a while. They move along the fence in a defined pattern, guns in their hands. Once they reach a predetermined point, they stop and then return to their initial position.

Beside me is a pile of wood that must be used for heat in the old mansion and a shed that looks as if it's used by a gardener. Of course, my mind goes to the implements inside—hedge clippers, hoes, lawn sprinklers, pots and trowels. The clippers could be used as a weapon, and the smaller branches meant for the fireplaces could be stakes.

There's no use. Even if I armed myself with a sharp weapon and found a piece of wood to use as a stake and even if I managed to take down one of the guards, the others would be there in seconds. Besides, my father may be on his way to the compound and I want to see him, to make sure he's still alive.

If it's still him inside.

So instead of trying to run, I sit on the retaining wall and watch the stars, waiting for someone to come and get me. Nothing happens for hours, it seems, as I watch the guards walk back and forth along their respective paths. Finally, the door opens, emitting a swathe of light from the mansion, and Dylan joins me.

"Here you are," he says and sits beside me, close enough so that our shoulders touch. I pull away, not yet ready to be on friendly terms with him. In truth, I want to scream at him, shake him, demand he tell me everything here and now, but I take in a deep breath. I'll hear him out.

"You have every right to hate me," he says. His eyes are bloodshot and his face is haggard.

"I don't hate you," I say and sigh heavily.

"Don't bother trying to escape. Blackstone has fantastic security."

"How long have you known that Blackstone was in control of the Council?" I say, my voice barely under control. I'm still not certain how to treat Dylan or how truthful he'll be.

"I didn't know for certain. When Vasquez took over, I wondered what happened. He seemed far too interested in Soren. In fact, he sent you right to Soren, as if he was giving you to him, when he should have been trying to keep you away from him."

I frown. "He was giving me to Soren." Vasquez's behavior makes sense now. He was under Blackstone's control. Blackstone wanted me in with Soren so he could use me to kill him.

"We were working for Blackstone all along and didn't know it," I say, almost to myself. "Maybe we were wrong to try to keep the existence of vampires secret. Maybe if we had compromised, if we had worked together, we could have prevented Blackstone from releasing the plague to gain power."

Dylan shakes his head. "It's too late for maybe, Eve. The Treaty may have been wrong, but there's no way of knowing if we could have prevented what's happened. Even if vampires had been able to walk among humans, they'd never accept doing so as equals. The only reason we have a treaty at all is because vampires became afraid humans would find a way to destroy them. Some believe that they are the superior predator and as such, they can take what they want."

"So what now?" I say and turn to Dylan, watching his face in the moonlight.

"You meet with your father. You take the daywalking drug. Then, you become part of the plan."

"Which plan? Blackstone's? I don't want to be part of his plan."

"Our plan."

"The plan to stop Dominion?"

Dylan nods but says nothing.

"Tell me. I need to know that there's a Council outside of Blackstone."

"You'll know in time," he says, his voice sounding tired. "That's all I can say. Take comfort that there are a few who still hold to Council values. They're working on it even if we can't."

"Not good enough," I mutter and turn away. Damn these men and their protective instincts. Why can't they treat me as an equal?

Of course, it's because I'm physically not an equal. Blackstone's drug will let me walk during the day, but it won't make me practically invulnerable the way the waters of life would. I shudder at the thought of taking it and becoming like them, but there's a small part of me that fears it will come to that one day, no matter how much I fight it.

The door opens and a guard approaches us. He stops in front of us and nods to Dylan. Then he turns to me.

"Lord Blackstone wants to inform you that your father has arrived. You're to come with me."

My heart leaps in my chest and I stand up, eager to see him but afraid at the same time.

Dylan stands as well and puts an arm around my shoulder. "Prepare yourself."

THE GUARD TAKES us to the recesses of the building and down a staircase at the back to a basement that is more like a dungeon than a living space. The walls are cement, the rooms are tiny, and the only light comes from lanterns hanging on the walls. In one of the cells is a man I don't recognize. He's small and wizened, crouched in the corner, his hair long and matted, a thick beard shot through with grey reaching down to his chest.

This can't be my father...

My father was a handsome man with dark hair and sharp brown eyes. He was meticulous about his appearance and always looked professional with his bow tie and blazer. I barely remember the last time I saw him. I do remember him at my mother's funeral; there was no indication that he would lose his mind. In my memories, he appeared as a man who could not be broken, but from what my foster parents told me, during the weeks following her death, he fell apart. Soon, he couldn't even care for me.

This man looks like someone who spent years in the Tower of London instead of a psychiatric hospital. The smell emanating from the cell is overpowering, as if he's been living on the street for months.

"That's not my father," I say, shaking my head. I hear movement behind me and turn to see Blackstone, his eyes narrowed.

"Rest assured that he is the one and only," he says, his voice hard.

I step away from the door. "My father was in a hospital. The insurance from my mother's death paid for the finest care. My foster parents—"

"Your foster parents told you what they were supposed to. They are compellable, unlike you. He was kept in solitary confinement and treated as a violent patient with dementia."

I glance back inside the cell at the man who is supposedly my father and swallow hard. There's a lump in my throat that feels very much like a scream.

I turn to Blackstone and tears well up in my eyes. "How long have you had him?"

"I only found him a few weeks ago. Apparently he was moved from time to time, but kept in solitary for the duration of his stay."

I shake my head slowly, my fists clenching. "Why are you keeping him like this? He needs medical care. A bath. Clean clothes."

"His comfort is the least of my concerns, Eve."

"You bastard."

"Assuredly not a bastard," Blackstone says, a grin on his face. "An actual lord, believe it or not. My title stretches back to the eighth century."

I frown. Eighth century England? He's older than the twins.

"Are you…" I say, not wanting to imagine it's possible.

"Am I what?" he says, a look of supreme satisfaction on his face as he realizes what I mean. "Ascended? How else could I outsmart Soren for so long?"

"They never told me. No one told me."

I look back inside the cell and try my best to figure it all out. Blackstone said he was the Council but the Council has, for decades, been fighting Dominion—fighting Soren. I'm so confused and upset, I can't think.

"So…" I begin, my mind working, trying to piece it all together, "the Council has never been fighting against Dominion. It's always been which version of Dominion, yours or Soren's, would be in place —not whether it would."

"There have been a few who have fought for a third way," he points out.

"Michel and Julien. And my mother."

"Smart girl. Not smart enough. Michel has never been under my sway. He's always been more allegiant to Soren. For a while, I thought I might have convinced Julien to my way of thinking. Certainly, I have Dylan."

"Only because you have his parents."

"Think what you will."

"So no one ever told me the truth. Not even my mother."

"The truth shall drive you mad," Blackstone says and exhales heavily.

I stand in silence for a moment, my heart racing in my chest, biting my lip to stop the tears. My father, my brilliant, talented father, is muttering to himself in the cell, his words indistinguishable.

"What do you want from me?" I ask, my voice breaking.

"Your compliance."

"You expect me to stand idly by while you destroy humanity?"

"Not destroy. Just bring to heel. The way it should be."

I'm filled with revulsion at what he says and how cavalier he is about the subjugation of humans. "I can't cooperate. I can't. I'd rather die."

"Oh, you won't ever die, Eve. Not by my hand nor by Soren's, so don't think he'll kill you either. No," Blackstone says, his voice weary. "If anyone dies, it will be your beloved twins. And your father. We knew you'd sacrifice yourself to protect them and get rid of Soren. We used that to our advantage. Love—it's such a powerfully illogical emotion."

"And if I cooperate?" I say, hoping he'll explain his plans to me. "What is it that you want me to do?"

"Help me destroy Soren when the time comes."

"I thought you said you wanted to share the world with him."

Blackstone shakes his head. "Do I seem like the kind of man who wants to share anything?" Then he smiles a wicked smile. "If you want your father to live upstairs, get his medicine, and come back to life, you'll cooperate and soon. Like this afternoon. Agree to help me destroy Soren once and for all. This cooperation bullshit makes me ill." He turns to the guard, who snaps to attention. "Let her stay for a few moments, then bring her upstairs."

He leaves me standing in the narrow hallway, staring into the dank cell that holds my father. For a moment, I'm unable to speak, my anger is so great, but then I try to calm myself with a few deep breaths.

"Father?" I say, my voice wavering with emotion.

The man in the cell, who appears more like a wild animal than a human being, doesn't respond.

"Father," I say again, this time with more force. "It's me. Eve."

He scrunches down even more tightly in the corner as if he's afraid of me, turning his head aside.

"Father, don't you remember me?"

He doesn't respond, one hand covering his eyes as if the light from the hallway hurts them.

"Please say something," I whisper, tears in my eyes blurring my vision. "Anything."

He remains where he is and doesn't respond. If anything, he makes himself even smaller, like he's trying to disappear, and I can only imagine what hell he's been through—ill and mistreated, kept in solitary confinement in a dungeon in the dark.

I hate Blackstone. I hate whoever did this to my father.

But I will cooperate long enough so I can get my father upstairs and see if I can restore him to some kind of normalcy. If he is insane, I'll decide what to do at that point. I know I must cooperate at least until I can find a way to free my father and remove Blackstone's hold over me.

The guard stands at attention, waiting for me. Finally, I turn from the window that looks into the cell.

"Let's go," I say with a sigh.

The guard escorts me back to the library on the main floor where Blackstone is seated. His son stands behind him and together they examine the map spread out on his tabletop.

They look up when I walk in and I'm struck once more at how close in age they appear. They could be brothers instead of father and son.

"So, Eve," Lord Blackstone says and folds his hands on the table, "have a seat." He gestures to the armchair across from his desk, but I stubbornly stand.

"I'd rather stand," I say but realize it's a silly response.

"Suit yourself. I wanted to go over our plans for you."

I say nothing, staring straight ahead because I don't want to look at his face. After everything that's happened, I feel like I could break into tears. I bite my cheek so hard to stay in control that I taste blood and that brings me some satisfaction. It calms me.

Blackstone stands as if he can't tolerate me remaining where I am. He walks over and faces me, his arms crossed. I feel his gaze move over me, but I refuse to meet his eyes except briefly.

"Such a rebellious girl," he says. "Michel and Julien have a handful with you."

I still refuse to respond, taking in a deep breath to try to slow my heart rate.

"Very well. Let me describe our plan for you. You're going to go back to Soren and you're going to agree to help him gain power. At the appropriate time, you'll help destroy him. This time, we won't fail."

I frown and glance at him, unable to resist, to see if he's serious. He wants me to help Soren gain power?

"I thought you wanted him dead?" I asked, confused. "I thought you didn't want to share. If he gains power…"

"If he gains power, he'll bring a lot of humans under his wing, so to speak," Blackstone says, a grin on his face. "They'll be more docile. Easier to manage if they have the fear of the Lord in them. Then, when the time comes and things are under control, you'll help Michel and Julien kill him. Once he's gone, I'll put my own people in place. Soren is a wildcard. He can't be controlled. He's even older than me."

"How old are you?" I say, unable to resist.

"Old enough," Blackstone says. "Old enough to have seen things only written about in myth and legend, but not quite as old as Soren, and our kind has this thing with age and rank."

"Why won't you tell me when you were born?"

"Some things are best left a mystery, Eve. But it was before either Michel or Julien were born, so that puts me above them both."

"You've ascended?"

"You don't believe in it," he says, smiling.

"I don't believe it's anything to do with God or gods," I say, unable to keep a hint of ridicule out of my tone. "It's some kind of genetic engineering."

"You're right, of course," he says, tilting his head to one side. "A natural form of it, discovered long ago and kept secret for thousands of years. Only those connected to others of our kind know of it. You should take it yourself, but I hear you're stubborn."

"Why did the virus fail to destroy Soren?"

Blackstone walks away from me and returns to the desk, taking a seat. "He must have a genetic mutation that makes him immune. He was able to keep it from completely taking over in his body and the Twelve. Don't you hate the Twelve, Eve?" he says, a look of disgust on his face. "Twelve? I mean, how manipulative can he be, replicating Christ and the Apostles!" Blackstone shivers dramatically and shakes his head.

"You're not religious?"

"I'm not a monotheist, if that's what you mean."

"So you believe in the gods?"

"Belief isn't the appropriate word, Eve. Knowledge of is more accurate."

"They're not gods," I say and shake my head, my back stiffening. He stares at me as if to check my response, his eyes narrowing.

"Call them what you will," he says. "They were gods to humans just as vampires will be now."

"You think he's like you—a vampire who has ascended—but he's different. That's why the nanovirus didn't work."

"Obviously. But the difference is one of degree, not kind."

"He claims to be an angel."

Blackstone shrugs. "He can claim anything he wants. I know better. He's like me, but has some strange genetic variant that makes him just a bit harder to kill. That's all. Now, please," he says and takes in a deep breath, "I'm growing tired of this question and answer session. You're going back to him and you'll help him do his little magic tricks and calm the masses. Then, when the time is right, you'll kill him."

"Won't he know your plans? He can force me to tell just as easily as you can. The drug you used he can use, too."

"We'll block your memory the way we did before. You won't remember until you hear the magic word." He grins at that, as if this is all a fun game.

I have to keep telling myself that everything I thought about the Council was wrong. That the plan I was involved in before wasn't from the Council. It was his plan. I was working for him, not for humanity.

I'm so sick of being used by everyone, manipulated, lied to, drugged, my memory wiped, that I feel like screaming. I know that would accomplish nothing but make me look like a weak child, so I bite my lip hard to regain control over my emotions.

He points to the guard standing behind me. "Take her back to her room. We'll speak later."

The guard takes my arm and leads me out of the library. When I reach the door, I glance back to see Blackstone's son bending over the map while Lord Blackstone points to it. I'm forgotten, just a pawn in their game of power.

Julien said I was the queen, but at that moment, I certainly don't feel like one.

CHAPTER 7

"LOVE CANNOT LIVE where there is no trust."

Edith Hamilton

I SLEEP for several hours in my cell and wake up with a hunger for blood and regret for everything that's happened since I found that online journal of mine. How would my life have been different if I'd never found it?

I don't tend to prefer ignorance over knowledge, but at that moment, I'm so tired of all the revelations and anxiety about the future that for a moment, ignorance seems preferable. Living an ignorant but idyllic life with Michel at the beach cottage before I found the journal seems preferable to what I now face, but there's no going back.

Right now, I want more than anything to go back to that day when I opened the file box from the University and found the manuscript. I wish I hadn't been so damn curious and instead of trying to get it translated, simply filed it away as something to deal with later and then forgotten it. I wish Michel had been able to compel me to forget him and the Council and everything connected to it.

Then I think of the brothers, and my heart can't imagine life without them in it. For all the bad in my life since I met them, there has been some good. I saw my abuser die, I learned the truth about my mother's death, and I've felt intense and deep love for Michel and Julien despite everything. Plus, I met Dylan and learned I had a brother. Could I blame him for betraying me? He thought he was doing the right thing. He thought he was infiltrating Blackstone in order to use their technology against them and was then betrayed when Blackstone took his parents.

I sit up, barely refreshed and in need of some blood. I know I'm free to roam around the compound, but I feel more like crying than exploring more. My father won't respond to me, and it's fruitless to stand outside his cell and speak through the bars when he's crouching in the corner.

I'm so sick of feeling helpless. I'm sick of being told half-truths and full-on lies. I'm sick of people drugging me and wiping my memory and hiding the truth to protect me. I want to take a sword and stake and shove them both through Blackstone's and Soren's hearts.

It's while I'm fantasizing about murder that my door opens and Dylan enters. I glare at him, caught up in a fantasy of bloodshed, and he visibly winces, as if my very expression hurt him. I still don't feel entirely comfortable around him, knowing what I now know, but I still think he's more friend than foe.

I pat the bed and motion to it with my head. "Blackstone's told me his plans, or at least the part he wants me to know. I take it I'm supposed to go back to Soren and help him gain power so he can calm the masses using religion? Then we kill him once things are under control?"

Dylan sits on the bed and leans forward, his elbows resting on his thighs, regarding me. "That's what I understand," he says. "One more try with the nanovirus to destroy him and the Twelve."

"Does he really believe Soren will accept me back? Does he really think Soren won't suspect some kind of plot against him?"

Dylan shrugs. "Soren will expect it, of course. He's no fool. But he's as caught up in this as Blackstone. They both need you. They both want to use you to destroy the other. They'll use you and they'll each hope to be the one who gains the temporary advantage that will let them prevail."

"I'm so tired," I say and lean back against the wall.

"I know," Dylan says and takes my hand, squeezing it. "When this is all over, we'll go away somewhere. Live in peace."

"Do you really think that will ever be possible?"

Dylan raises his eyebrows, but he exhales heavily, as if exhausted. "I have to keep believing it's possible or else I can't go on. I have to believe that there will come a time when Blackstone is vulnerable and I'll be the one to shove the stake through his heart."

I stare at Dylan, seeing the anger in his jaw, the tightness to his lips pressed together. "Revenge for Sarah's death?"

He nods. "And for everything else."

"I'll do the same to Soren," I say, and smile softly. "We'll both get revenge."

"Your mother. My sister. They think they can do these things with impunity. The only thing that keeps me going is the possibility that one day, they'll both pay."

We sit in my tiny dark room and discuss our childhoods, waiting for Blackstone to call for us. Dylan speaks of his parents with such fondness, and of Sarah; I feel my heart squeeze for his loss. I hear his fear for his parents in his voice.

For my part, I try to remember my own childhood, but my memories from before my mother's death are so fragmented. I can remember snatches of the past with both my parents—our cottage on the Pembrokeshire Coast, the salon in Vienna, various apartments where we lived. I was happy, that much I know. I loved my father and mother deeply and tried to please them both by playing really well.

After about an hour, a guard knocks at my door and orders us to follow him. He takes us to a large dining room where there's a feast set out. Outside, the sun is setting and servants are busy lighting candles. Places are set and we're led to two seats near the end of the table.

We sit and wait, and in a few moments, others enter the room— more of Blackstone's officers. Then William enters and nods to us.

Dylan and I speak to each other in quiet voices while the others sit and the servants pour a dark liquid into our cups. I take a sip after I see others drinking and I discover that it's not wine but blood. I can't help myself and drink down hungrily. The waiter fills my cup once more and I drink that down as well.

I feel satisfied for the first time in days.

Finally, Lord Blackstone himself enters with one of his lieutenants. They're deep in discussion when they come through the huge double doors and barely acknowledge the rest of us when we stand.

"Gentlemen," he says to the others. Then he turns to me. "Lady."

He nods at me and I nod back and sit down once more, determined to go along with him at least on the surface. I'll lie in wait the way Dylan said we should, for our moment. It might not come for a while, but we're both determined it will.

"Please," he says and motions to the plates of food and decanters of wine. "Help yourselves. Let us enjoy the bounty we have before us."

While my thirst for blood is slaked, at least temporarily, my stomach still grumbles and so I take some meat off a plate. It looks and smells like venison, the meat bloody. It tastes amazing and I wolf it down as if I haven't eaten in a week. Dylan is silent beside me, busy eating as well. Together, we fill our plates and eat the roasted vegetables, bread, and meat that is set out on platters in front of us. The setting is rather rustic, with tapestries depicting pastoral scenes hanging on the walls. The servants stand against the walls watching, but there's little for them to do but refill our glasses.

When I'm full, I wipe my mouth with my napkin and sit back, my eyes on my plate, listening to the conversation. Dylan does as well, but he turns slightly towards me, his arm over the back of my chair.

Neither one of us speaks, simply listening to the discussions around us while we wait for Blackstone to say or do something. Several officers report to Blackstone on the problems they're having maintaining order in Cambridge. Someone talks about the quotas of prisoners and whether they're being met. Someone else talks about how far the plague has travelled in the last twenty-four hours.

I realize that this is no longer merely a war, but a conqueror establishing his empire. As the plague progresses and civilization falls even further, Blackstone and Soren are prepared to step in and establish control.

Finally, Blackstone puts his own napkin down and pushes his chair back from the table, crossing his legs and settling his arms on the armrests. I've been watching him out of the corner of my eye and when I feel his gaze on me, I meet his eyes.

He smiles. "So, Eve. Tell me—have you decided to cooperate? Once you do, we can get your father cleaned up and fed and I'll bring him up to see you."

"Of course," I say, keeping my voice calm despite my desire to scream at him. "I have no choice."

"Good," Blackstone says and waves to the guard who stands directly behind him. The guard bends down and listens as Blackstone whispers something in his ear. The guard leaves, and I wonder if he isn't going to bring my father up.

"Is he getting my father from the dungeon?"

"Patience," Blackstone says. "Now, because you can't be compelled, I'm going to have to insist on absolute obedience and a proper attitude from here on in. I don't want any resistance. I don't want hesitation. I'm not used to it and I don't tolerate it. If you want your father back, you must comply. Any sign of disobedience, and he's back to the dungeon. Do you understand?"

My instinct is to fight him but I resist. I nod. "Yes." I say it as respectfully as I can manage given the circumstances.

"You promise? Say it out loud."

"I promise to follow your orders without hesitation." It makes me sick to say, but I do.

"Good girl. I'm having your father washed and dressed and his hair cut. He'll be brought to my study when he's presentable. In the meantime, I have a little test of your loyalty and willingness to follow my orders."

Blackstone waves his hand and a guard goes to the door and opens it. Other guards shove three men into the room. They stumble inside, their hands shackled to chains attached to their manacled ankles. They look like they're drugged or compelled—I can't tell which. They're zombie-like as they stand before the table where Blackstone sits, their eyes on the floor before them.

Blackstone turns to me and points at the men. "Kill one."

I know what he means, but I feign confusion, frowning, my heart going into high gear and blood pumping in my veins. When I do nothing, Blackstone clicks his tongue.

"Tsk tsk, Eve. Not off to a very promising start."

"What do you want?" I say, my voice wavering, my hands gripping the armrests. "Do you want me to kill one outright or drink his blood?"

He makes a face as if I'm stupid. "What do you think, Eve? You're a vampire now. Own it. Vampires drink blood. Why waste a perfectly good human by killing him outright? Drain one. Any one of them."

I stand, but my knees are weak. "Who are they?" I ask, stalling for time.

"What does it matter? Under Dominion, vampires need no license to kill for blood. Only hunger. But if it makes you feel any better, these three were caught looting and pillaging among their own kind in the city. They're going to be put to death for their crimes, and so I thought," he taps his temple, "what a great opportunity for Eve to show her loyalty to me. Her willingness to follow my orders. Without hesitation. Without question." He emphasizes the last phrase.

"I've never killed before."

"A virgin vampire? Gods above, that I could be so lucky. My favorite thing of all. A vampire's first kill."

He smiles a feral smile and comes to my side. My heart pumps fast, the blood rushing in my ears. He grabs one of the three men by the scruff of his collar. The man has dark hair shaved almost to his scalp, a grizzled chin, and filthy clothes. He visibly recoils when Blackstone pulls him close.

"Why not this one?" Blackstone says, glancing over at me. "He's as good as the next."

I frown. "If all he did was loot, death isn't an appropriate sentence."

"It is under my rule."

I say nothing, a feeling of panic filling me. I grind my fingernails into my palms to try to regain control over myself and turn to Blackstone, my eyes stinging with tears. "I can't."

He shakes his head, a world-weary expression on his face. "This one, then. He raped a mother in front of her child. Surely that deserves death. I mean, after all, Franklin got the knife, didn't he?"

I stare at Blackstone. He knows about Franklin?

"Am I not right?" he says, an amused expression on his face. "If Franklin deserved death, why not this man? Who knows how many women he's raped? Even killed? These are not nice men, Eve. Surely a vampire can take their blood without guilt."

I hesitate. Is Blackstone telling me the truth?

"Ask him if you don't believe me," Blackstone says. "Use your powers to compel him to tell you the truth."

Blackstone motions to the man, who stands sullenly in front of me, his eyes on the floor.

I stand in front of the man, who continues to stare at the floor despite my presence. "Look at me," I say, my voice breaking.

Finally, he drags his eyes up to meet mine.

"Look in my eyes."

He does, and when our eyes meet, when they really meet, I speak to him. I don't know if I'm doing it right for I've never tried to compel anyone before.

"You're going to tell me all the crimes you've committed in your life."

He clears his throat. "When I was sixteen, I drove a truck while I was drunk and got in an accident. My license was taken away. I drove without a license anyway. When I was eighteen, I helped steal a shipment of clothes from a warehouse and sold them to a fence."

I shake my head. "More recent. Since the plague."

"Since the plague, I have stolen food and supplies from several grocery stores. I broke into a home and took it over when the owners left. I—"

"This is taking too long." Blackstone grabs the man by the neck with one hand, the man's chin in his other hand. "Tell her why you've been arrested."

When Blackstone releases him the man coughs and clears his throat.

"We broke into a shelter and took their food. We—"

"What did you do?" Blackstone demands, his voice a growl. "Forget what the others did. What did you do personally?"

"I," he says, his voice low as if he's embarrassed to admit it. "I had sex with a woman…"

"Not sex," Blackstone says, his voice firm, a hard edge of anger in it. "Tell the truth."

The man squeezes his eyes shut. "I forced her."

"In front of her child?"

The man nods.

"Say it out loud for all of us to hear."

The man swallows, his fear visible. "I forced her in front of her child."

"And then what?"

The man hesitates, licks his lips. "I held her down while the others had her as well."

"And what shape was she in when you left?" Blackstone walks around the man, his hands clasped behind his back like some medieval inquisitor.

"I don't know—"

"Don't lie to me. What shape was she in?"

The man shakes his head. "Unconscious."

"And the child?"

"I don't know," he says. "He was screaming and I hit him…"

"Stop," I say and hold up my hand. "I don't want to hear any more."

I wipe tears off my cheeks. The man's story can't help but arouse hatred in me. Maybe enough hatred that I can kill him and drink him dry. I pause, thinking this has all been orchestrated so very carefully to accomplish just that.

I go to the man, who looks terrified. He's a foot taller than me and much heavier. I honestly don't know how to do it. I turn to Dylan and find him looking at me with a horrified expression. He mouths some words and I can hear them despite how quietly he speaks.

"I'm so sorry…"

But I've already forgiven him.

"How do I do it?" I ask, turning towards Blackstone.

Our eyes meet and he nods as if he understands. He picks up a chair from the table and brings it over to where I stand. He places it beside me and motions to the rapist "Sit."

The man obeys, but I can tell he's terrified. He can't help but comply with Blackstone's orders, but he's fully aware of what's happening.

The mother was aware of what was happening to her as well. But is my killing him really just punishment?

I stand in front of him and hesitate. "Have you ever killed anyone?"

The man nods. "A pharmacist. When we stole their oxycodone. I didn't mean to, but he resisted…"

"There," Blackstone says, as if he's won some kind of bet. "See, Eve? He doesn't deserve to live. Taking advantage of a woman, killing someone for drugs. This should be easy for you, even if you weren't a vampire and needed blood to survive."

"It still isn't easy," I say, and it isn't. Even knowing the man is a murderer and rapist.

"Yes, your human morals are still fresh in your soul. Give yourself a few centuries and they'll fade. Now, go behind him and drink him dry. Don't lie to me and tell me you haven't desired to sink your teeth into human flesh and feel blood run in your mouth. Every vampire has. It's our curse, to have all this power and the gift of immortality but to desire human blood more than anything else."

I can't lie. I have desired it. Every single day since I became a vampire, I've desired human blood, craving the feel of my teeth breaking warm skin, the blood gushing into my mouth, almost choking me with its rush. Biting Julien and Michel have been substitutes, but there's something about the thought of biting a human that makes me weak and breathless the way I am when filled with sexual desire.

I tilt the man's head to the side, baring the flesh beneath his ear. I can almost see the blood rushing in the vein, smell the blood through his skin. This close to a human, I feel the pull of bloodlust despite having enjoyed two glasses of blood at the dinner table.

I bite down hard and am immediately lost to it, my desire for blood overwhelming my human morality. I barely hear the man's gasp of pain when my teeth rip into his flesh, his heartbeat so loud in my ears I can't focus on anything else.

While I drink, we connect and I sense his fear, his horror, for he didn't really believe that monsters roamed the earth. He thought it was all a story to keep people in line. He never imagined that a beautiful young vampire, a woman, would be the one to take his life, always thinking he would die in a shootout with police.

I drink, unaware of how much or how fast, until my stomach is full and I feel gorged. I pull back, my mouth covered in blood, and gasp for breath. The man slumps in the chair, his head thrown back, his eyes still open, but only slits. I can hear his heart even now, beating fast, thready and weak, for he has far too little blood. He's close to death, but not quite.

"Finish him off," Blackstone says, his hands on his hips. There's a gleam in his eyes, almost lustful, as if he gets off seeing a new vampire with their first kill.

"I can't," I say, barely able to speak, wiping my mouth with my sleeve. "I feel like I've had too much."

I go to my chair and sit, leaning my head on the table as I feel something similar to post-coital bliss overwhelm my other senses.

"You can never have too much, Eve."

I raise my head and watch as Blackstone finishes the job, taking the man's head in his hands and biting down on the other side of his neck. It takes him barely a minute to kill the man. He would have died even if Blackstone hadn't bitten him, but it would have taken a while, and his blood would be wasted, spilled on the floor.

Blackstone pushes the man's dead body over so that it falls with a heavy thump on the floor. He takes out a kerchief and wipes his own mouth, but there's barely any blood on it.

"Are you satisfied now?" I say, unable to keep my revulsion for what I've done out of my tone. "I killed on your command. Bring my father up."

Blackstone sits in his chair and leans back, a satisfied expression on his face. "You enjoyed it," he observes. "I can tell. But you hated it all the same. I'll only be truly satisfied when you kill on my orders and without guilt, but that will come with time."

He watches me for a moment, and I meet his gaze, our eyes locked together. I don't pull away even when I feel his amusement at my forwardness.

He smiles. "As to your father, he'll be brought up later this evening. I'll call you back when he's ready."

He waves his hand in dismissal so I stand up to leave. My legs are still a bit wobbly so Dylan helps me, one arm around my waist.

I glance back when we're at the door and see Blackstone holding out his glass for more blood while the guards pull the dead body away from the table. The other two captive humans stand mute, their eyes still focused on the floor. I wonder how long before they're both dead.

A servant bends closer and pours the thick red liquid into the crystal glass in Blackstone's hand. Blackstone catches my eye before I'm able to leave and in his expression is gloating triumph.

I can't wait to see Dylan wipe that look from his face when his dagger thrusts deep into Blackstone's chest.

CHAPTER 8

"Keep love in your heart. A life without it is like a sunless garden when the flowers are dead."

Oscar Wilde

"Where should we go?" Dylan asks as we walk down the hall.

I shake my head, tears of anger and remorse for killing the man wet on my cheeks. "I need air."

Dylan helps me outside and together we sit on the retaining wall that surrounds the patio. I take in a deep breath, the chill of the night air refreshing me. Dylan removes his jacket and places it around my shoulders, but I'm so full of fresh blood that I feel too warm and I push it away.

"I'm fine."

Dylan nods in understanding and puts his jacket back on. "I remember my first kill," he says, his voice soft. "She wasn't a criminal, Eve. Just an unlucky human. Don't hate yourself."

"I don't," I say. "I hate him. I hate Soren."

"Good. Keep that anger fresh in your mind. Use it to help you comply while we wait. We will kill them both, Eve," Dylan says and I can hear the edge of anger in his voice. "We will."

I sigh and stare up at the black sky. The moon is rising in the distance, its orb almost full.

All of a sudden, I miss the twins so much I ache. I want to go back to them both and forget everything else. I want to live on the beach with them, one after the other. Nothing but us and the sand and surf and night sky. But I can't forget everything. My father is being cleaned and dressed so I can see him. Blackstone is no doubt making plans to send me on a mission to help Soren resurrect the Twelve and calm the masses so they're more compliant with Dominion. When he has an effective nanovirus—one that they're assured will destroy Soren and the Twelve—we'll make our move.

Blackstone must know that, for Michel, it will be real. Michel will do what he can to save as many souls as he thinks possible while formulating a plan to fight Blackstone, restore the Council, and enforce the Treaty.

I know that will be his only goal. Michel doesn't want Dominion. Everything he does is calculated to see its end, of that I can be sure. It's the only thing I can hold on to, besides the twins' love for me. The only hope I have left besides my father recognizing me and my parents—and Dylan's parents—being freed.

AN HOUR PASSES. We speak in soft voices about what has come to pass since we met. It's when we're discussing Soren that a guard opens the door, casting a wide shaft of light from the interior onto the patio where we sit in the darkness.

"My Lord Blackstone will see you now."

I turn to Dylan and he takes my hand and squeezes.

"Give your father time to remember you," Dylan says. "It's been ten years and you're a grown woman now. Remember that you were only a little girl when he last saw you."

I nod and together we follow the guard inside. We take now-familiar hallways to the study where I met with Blackstone earlier. I scan the occupants for my father and finally recognize him. He is far thinner than I remember, and smaller, but perhaps that's the result of me growing up and him shrinking from his disease. His hair is shorn now, almost to his scalp, and shot through with gray. His face is sallow, his skin marked by age spots and wrinkles even though he's only in his forties.

He doesn't look up when I enter the room. Instead, he remains cowering in a chair beside Blackstone's, his body curved in on itself like before, as if he's trying to disappear.

He looks mad.

"Father?" I say, my voice barely above a whisper. "It's me. Eve."

I step closer and bend down, trying to meet his eyes, but he turns his head this way and that to avoid me. I kneel in front of his chair, trying to catch his eye that way, but he closes his eyes. Is he afraid to make eye contact with anyone?

"Daddy," I say, my voice pleading. "Daddy, don't you remember me? It's Eve. Your daughter."

He whines as if he feels pain and squirms in his chair, twisting like he wants to escape me. I touch his knee and he jerks it away from my hand as if my touch burns.

It's no use. He's clearly not there. This man isn't the father I knew and loved. He doesn't recognize me and shrinks farther and farther away from me the closer I get. I give up, covering my mouth with a hand to hold back my tears. I catch Dylan's eyes and he shakes his head, then he pulls me into his arms.

"I'm sorry," he says softly. He pulls me over to a sofa and we sit together.

My father twists and turns in his chair. He obviously can't get comfortable, and he's squinting like the room is too bright for his eyes.

"Now that you're here, Eve," Blackstone says, as if my attempt to communicate with my father isn't important, "play the piano for us.

I've heard Dylan rave about your talent. Play something by Chopin. Dylan says he's your favorite composer."

A grand piano sits in the corner of the room by the huge window, but I don't want to play. Yet I have sworn to obey Blackstone without hesitation or question. I want my father to be cared for properly until I can determine if he can ever come back to me, so I stand reluctantly and make my way to the piano.

I play an arpeggio to get my hands warmed up, followed by some scales. Finally, I pause with my hands poised over the keys, uncertain what to play, not wanting to play anything.

"Play Chopin. Ballade No. 1," Dylan says. "It's my favorite."

I sigh and start to play. The introduction is slow and dark, the melody somber. I watch my father, and if he recognizes the piece, he doesn't show it. He sits still, his arms wrapped around his body, his head down. He looks like a frightened animal held captive and completely focused inward. But when I get to the end of the first section, as the tempo increases and the sound reaches a crescendo, he frowns and I can tell he's listening.

Does he finally remember, at least the music? This was his favorite piece and I play it with as much passion as I can muster, pouring all my emotions into the performance. When I come to the first change in tempo, the music soft, light, dreamy, he lifts up his head.

He's listening. He still doesn't look at me, but I know he's finally present in the moment.

The piece is so beautiful, especially the middle section, the meno mosso. It's my favorite part of the piece, the touch so light, so soft. Then it's back to the main theme and I see him sit up straight. He's truly listening now.

My heart is in my throat. I'm torn between playing and rushing over to him to try to make him recognize me again, but for now I play, my hands flying over the keys as I move through the complex chords and progressions.

I come to the part that I find most difficult—the part that Julien forced me to learn all those months back when I was in his loft in Boston. I'm glad now that I did practice for it was here where I stopped when I was a child, when my mother died and I was torn from my father as he sank into madness.

Tears fall from my eyes and I don't care. Maybe the music will remind him who he is and break through the walls he's built around himself to keep the world out.

I finish and wipe my eyes. If he knows who I am, he doesn't show it. But he's no longer coiled up with his arms twisted around himself. He's sitting like a normal person, his eyes fully open, alert at least to the music. I rise from the piano and run to him, kneeling down once more, trying to catch his eye, but he frowns and looks away.

"Daddy!" I cry, my heart breaking from dashed hope. "It's me, Eve. Your daughter!"

Nothing.

He starts to close up again, the moment gone. I rest my head on his knee and he tries to pull away, apparently horrified to be touched.

He doesn't know me. Some part of his brain remembered the music, but that's all. I cry, covering my face with my hands, until Dylan finally comes over and pulls me up, wrapping his arms around me and rocking me while I weep.

I push Dylan away and rush at Blackstone, not thinking, only feeling so much pain and sheer hatred that I don't care anymore. I reach him before he can respond and try to strike him, my fists searching for his face. He grabs my hands before I can even touch him, holding them firm while I struggle, my eyes blurred with tears.

He does nothing but hold me still while I twist and turn, trying to free myself. Soon, I give in and stop fighting as he holds me there, imprisoned in his steel-like grip, and I cry without caring that he's watching me, his face only inches away from mine.

I weep, my sobs loud, but in his face I see no anger. I see patience and even understanding. He finally releases my hands and I stand there with my palms covering my face. I'm no match for him and I know it. I could never kill him using my own measly powers as an Adept vampire.

I can't even daywalk.

"I didn't do this to him, Eve," Blackstone says.

"Then who did?" I ask between sobs. "Who did this to him?"

"Ask your beloved Michel." With that, Blackstone leaves, a guard trailing behind him.

"What do you mean?!" I shout after him.

He stops and glares at me. "You think so highly of your precious Michel. You love him. But perhaps he's the one who has told you more lies than anyone. Certainly I've only ever told you the truth."

Before he goes through the door, he turns to the guard standing over my father. "Take him to his room. She can see him if she wants."

Then Blackstone leaves.

I turn to Dylan, wiping my eyes on the backs of my hands. "What does he mean by that?"

Dylan shrugs. "He's playing with your mind, Eve. I doubt he's telling you the truth. Michel loves you. I don't like him much, but I know he loves you."

The guard puts his arm under my father's and lifts him up.

"I'll help," I insist, taking my father's other arm.

My father acknowledges neither of us. He merely stares straight ahead and lets us lead him down the hallway to a set of stairs and then to the upper floor. We practically carry him down the hallway, Dylan trailing behind us, and into a room on the left with a huge canopy bed and a window facing the grounds.

I point to the wing chair by a fireplace and the guard and I lead him there. He sits without protest, his face blank, eyes staring straight ahead. I take a blanket from the bed and cover his legs with it, tucking it in around him, for the massive room is cold.

"I'll look after him," I say and the guard nods and goes to the door.

"I'll be outside," Dylan says, leaving me alone with my father.

I kneel down in front of the chair and adjust the blanket. My father slowly turns his head towards the door as if searching for the guard.

He turns back to me and our eyes finally meet. "Eve," he whispers and my heart almost stops.

"Yes!" I say, my voice breaking with emotion. "Yes. I'm Eve, Daddy! You recognize me?"

"Shh," he says, a finger to his lips, his eyes wide, "or they'll take you away again. Pretend you don't know."

"No," I say. "It's okay if you remember me."

He shakes his head vigorously, his eyes wide. Too wide. So wide I can see the whites above his irises. "They'll take you like they took your mother. Pretend I don't recognize you."

Frustration fills me. Is this his paranoia—his mental illness—speaking or is he right?

"Please, Eve," my father pleads. "Trust me."

"Okay, Daddy," I say and force a smile. "We can talk when we're alone, but when someone else is around, we'll pretend you can't talk."

He nods and visibly relaxes, his muscles going limp. He exhales heavily, as if he's been holding his breath, and rubs his eyes with a bony hand before running it over his nearly-shaved head.

He looks like a Holocaust survivor.

"Are you hungry?" I ask, noting the bones of his shoulders through his sweater and his pronounced collarbone. "I can get you something to eat."

He shakes his head. "Already did. Just some hot tea, please."

I go to the door. Dylan is waiting outside, leaning against the wall. "Can you ask to have some tea brought up?"

Dylan nods and I close the door and return to my father. I pull up a chair beside him and he reaches out and takes my hand.

"He said you love Michel—does he mean de Cernay?"

I nod. "Yes." I look at his hand in mine, so bony and weathered, the nails too long and in need of a trim. I look up in his eyes. "I'm in love with him."

He shakes his head slowly. "He's very bad, Eve. Don't trust him. Stay away from him."

I frown and adrenaline courses through me. "Why do you say that?"

"He betrayed your mother. He killed her."

"It was Soren Lindgren who forced Michel to kill her. He cared for Mom and tried to help her. He felt so bad—"

"Don't believe him, Eve. He's a liar just like the man said." My father's face is pale, his eyes wide, as if he's truly afraid for me.

"Why do you say he's a liar?"

"He lied to your mother. He doesn't support the Council. He is Soren's servant."

I squeeze my father's hand. "He was cooperating with Soren only to learn his plans so he could stop him. He supports the Council—at least, before Blackstone took it over. I know this, Daddy. Michel and I worked together for the Council. The Special Cases Unit."

My father shakes his head, his eyes closed tightly under a frown. "He promised to keep you out of it and look what he did. He recruited you into the very organization he promised you'd never join. You were supposed to go to school. Study music. He promised…"

"I studied science so I could become a doctor and be like Mom. It was me who found him. He stayed away from me until I contacted him…"

Of course, that's not really the way it happened. He actually contacted me when I went searching for a translator. After I received my mother's files. He found me and contacted me because he was looking for the manuscript. He had no idea that it was given to my mother…

Or did he?

And just like that, a seed of doubt is planted in my heart and mind. Michel found me so quickly, within hours of me placing the ad. He claimed that he had a service that scanned the web for requests for translators of thirteenth century manuscripts…

"How did you meet him?" my father demands. "He was supposed to have hidden you from the Council."

"It was by accident," I respond, although now I doubt the very foundation of my trust in Michel. His story of how he found me, his tale of how he'd hidden me away when I was taken away from my father and had no idea where I was, and that it was purely because he was looking for the manuscript that we met…

I hate Lord Blackstone for planting this seed of doubt in me. I hate him for calling Michel a liar.

Yes. He did lie to me. He hid things from me, including his role in my mother's death, but I truly do believe that he didn't want this fate for me. He tried to compel me into forgetting him, forgetting everything, but he failed.

I'm confused and upset about everything. The revelations about Dylan, our foster parents being held hostage, my father's return and mental state. Now Michel. I can't think straight.

"Don't trust him," my father repeats. "He wants his own kind of Dominion."

I force a smile for my father's benefit because he seems so agitated. He needs to rest and recover from his years of captivity, not argue with me.

"We'll talk more about this later, Daddy. I want you to rest now."

The door opens and a servant brings in a tray with cups and saucers, a teapot, cream and sugar, and a small tray of sandwiches and biscuits. He places it on the coffee table in front of the sofa and then leaves us alone.

"Here's some tea for you. And some food, if you get hungry." I check the tea and then pour a cup for him. He always had a sweet tooth, so I put two cubes of sugar in his cup and stir. When I hand it to him, he takes it with obvious relish.

"When was the last time you had a proper cup of tea?"

My father shakes his head and brings the tea to his lips, blowing before taking a small sip. He swallows and closes his eyes as if in ecstasy.

"Far too long. Years."

I spend the next hour sharing a cup of tea with my father, listening to him recount his years in a facility somewhere up north, surrounded by truly mentally ill people.

"No matter how I protested, the guards and staff had all been compelled to believe I was insane. I was drugged and kept starved. I was barely able to walk a few feet without help, so I couldn't escape."

"But why?"

My father shakes his head. "To keep me quiet. To keep me from finding you and stealing you away, raising you the way your mother and I wanted you to be raised. As a musician."

I wanted to say that Michel tried to have me raised that way, but that my case got lost by the Council. Instead, I was placed in an abusive foster home, but my father doesn't need to know that. It would only upset him that he wasn't there to protect me. When I was rescued, I was placed with my current foster parents, who allowed me to study what I wanted. I wanted to be a vampire hunter like my mother. It was all that really kept me going.

That was my choice. I loved music, but my life was dedicated to finding my mother's killer and bringing him to justice.

Of course, I found her killer, and while Michel did the deed, it was on Soren's command. Michel was helpless to refuse.

Still, I feel a creeping doubt about Michel. I try to shove that doubt down deep in my mind so it doesn't make me too upset. I have other things to think about at the moment. My father's well-being is number one. I have to keep him safe at all costs. He's paid for my life with years of his and I'm going to do whatever I can, short of helping Blackstone achieve Dominion, to keep him safe and healthy. One day I will free my father and we'll be together for whatever years of life he has left.

I found my father. I'm not going to let him go anytime soon.

Something nags at me, though, biting away at my resolve to push the doubt about Michel down deep.

"Did Michel know you weren't insane?" I ask, trying to keep my voice light.

"You'll have to ask him," my father says, shaking his head. "I can't see how he didn't know. He was the one who was supposed to arrange my transfer to the asylum."

My muscles all tense at that. Michel always said that my father went insane and was placed in an asylum to keep him from harming himself. That's what my foster parents told me, and they discouraged me from ever trying to find him, telling me he was a shadow of his former self and wouldn't recognize me.

Now, I find that to be a lie. He was always well. He was a prisoner.

Of whom? Blackstone? Or Soren?

After my father finishes his tea, he's so exhausted that he falls asleep in his chair by the fire. I go to the door and invite Dylan inside. We take chairs by the fire and I tell him about my father and what he suggested about Michel.

"I don't know what to say." Dylan shrugs. "He's lied to you before. You forgave him for those lies. What's one more?"

I shake my head. "I don't think I can forgive him this one."

Dylan tells me what he knows about his parents and where they're being kept. He's seen them and they're being kept quite comfortably in a set of rooms somewhere in the mansion, but Dylan's father was roughed up as a warning that worse could happen if Dylan doesn't comply with Blackstone's demands.

Finally, we help my father to his bed and cover him up, fully dressed, for he waves me away when I ask if he wants to change. I leave him in the cavernous room, a guard at the door to protect him. The only real danger is from Soren or Blackstone. I realize now that there's no real protection for any of us until both of them are gone.

CHAPTER 9

"THE WAY TO love anything is to realize that it may be lost."

G. K. Chesterton

WE'RE CALLED to an audience with Blackstone once more before the night is over. As guards escort us to his study after midnight, I find myself curious and anxious to get the daywalking serum so I can sleep when I want and move around when I want.

Blackstone, his son, and several other people I don't recognize are standing around Blackstone's desk. They glance up when we enter and Blackstone sits back in his chair, an expectant expression on his face.

"Well, there you are," he says, his voice amused. "How did your visit with your father go, Eve? Not quite what you expected, I trust."

"It went fine, thank you," I say, trying to keep my voice even. "He's not insane after all. Just exhausted and stressed due to solitary confinement for a decade."

"All thanks to your beloved Michel."

I shrug, not yet willing to concede anything about Michel's guilt, and especially not to Blackstone, whom I despise with every ounce of my being.

"I expect you want the serum now," he says. When I nod without speaking, he motions to one of the men standing by his side. "Very well. Doctor? If you please."

A tall man, whom I assume to be the doctor, reaches into his pocket and removes a small ampoule with yellowish liquid in it. Seeing it makes this all real and for a brief moment, my heart races as I imagine what it will do to me.

"That's it?"

The doctor nods. "Yes, and you'd better be sitting when you take it. It has immediate neurological effects and you might be a bit dizzy for a while. In fact, you'll probably want to sleep for a long time."

He motions to an armchair in front of Blackstone's desk and I take a seat, holding on to the armrests, my knuckles white. I take in a deep breath and try to relax, blowing out the air through my pursed lips as I've been taught to manage anxiety. It works after a few breaths and then the man is standing in front of me, the ampoule in his hand.

"Break the tip and drink it down," he says. "It's vile tasting but it won't make you nauseated."

I take the ampoule and break off the tip as instructed. I hold it up and nod to Blackstone and then meet eyes with Dylan for a moment before pouring the liquid down my throat. I swallow as fast as I can because the doctor is right—it's extremely bitter—like vinegar. I hand him the empty ampoule and the broken tip and hold on to the armrests once more, waiting for the dizziness he described.

Sure enough, in mere moments, I feel the room spin, my bearings mixing up, my vision blurring. I bend my head down and close my eyes, gasping as vertigo strikes harder than it ever has in my life. But then, almost as soon as it struck, the vertigo passes and my eyes are merely blurry, as if clouded with tears.

I lift my head and feel a warm drowsiness take hold, like I've had too much wine to drink, my limbs heavy and my tongue thick. I feel drunk but not happy-drunk. Just a bit lethargic, and not at all anxious any longer.

I try to speak but find my mouth won't work. No words come out, so I sit in silence. I can hear people speaking around me, but their words are muffled, as if I'm hearing them from underwater or with earplugs in.

No one tries to speak to me and I give up trying to speak to them.

"Should I take her back to her room?" Dylan says, his voice sounding distant.

"No, leave her here. Let her sleep it off."

Then, darkness.

When I next awaken, I'm lying on the sofa in Blackstone's study, a blanket thrown over me. Dylan is sitting beside me, watching me. He smiles when my eyes open fully, and I try to smile back, but I have a bitch of a headache. It strikes like lightning behind each eye. The light is far too bright; I have to shade my eyes.

"Oh, God," I moan, squeezing my eyes shut. "Is there a remedy for this headache? It's like a migraine but on both sides."

Dylan holds out a glass of reddish-brown liquid, like cold tea. "Here's a bit of willow bark tea. Nature's aspirin. There's salicin in the bark, and it's converted into salicylic acid in your body."

I take the glass and drink down the tea, but it's nasty as well. "Could you have added some honey at least?"

He laughs softly. "Believe me, it doesn't make it much better. Best to just down it quickly."

I drink it all down as fast as possible to get the worst over with and then lie back. In the corner of the room, Blackstone and his men are speaking together in quiet voices. I can't quite make out their words.

I regard Dylan for a moment. "Now what?"

He shrugs. "He wants you to appear to help Soren get power so the people have the church as a calming influence. Then Soren dies."

"Why can't they share power?"

"I'd wager that neither Blackstone nor Soren are good at sharing."

I sigh, wondering what will happen next. "So I'm supposed to present myself to Soren and make him think I'm going to help him do his miracles?"

"I guess. Blackstone seems to think that he'll help establish some kind of law and order. If people believe God or the gods will protect them, they'll be more likely to follow orders. Once order is restored, Soren is gone." Dylan shrugs as if he can't believe it. "Blackstone will let the plague circle the globe and he'll take power, installing his own people in the Church and in the military."

"Do Michel and Julien know this?"

"Michel thinks that Soren will stop the plague before it destroys everything. That's why he's temporarily on Soren's side. But he wants Soren to die as well, and for the Council to be restored. I believe him when he says he doesn't want Dominion, either by Soren or Blackstone."

I nod. I hope that's Michel's plan. If not, everything I ever thought and believed about Michel and his motives is all a huge lie.

Blackstone sees me speaking with Dylan and gets up from his desk, striding over to the sofa.

"So, Eve. How are you feeling now? You slept straight through the night. The headache lasts for a day or so, and your eyes will be very sensitive to light for a bit, even at night, but you should be otherwise physically well. I'd say wear sunglasses, but alas, they're all mostly plastic and like all fake things from the old world, they disintegrated with the rest of it."

"I happened to like plastic," I say, sitting up straighter.

He chuckles. "That's what I like about you. Irreverent and stubborn to the end. But for our purposes, Eve, try to cooperate and appear to be somewhat chastened by my power. Even if only for the sake of appearances."

"I never cared much for appearances."

"So I gather." Blackstone looks at me closely for a moment, his eyes narrowed. "Are you well enough to travel?"

I feel a bit tired, but I could manage a trip to Boston if needed. "I think so."

"Good. I want you to go to Soren as soon as possible. You can say a temporary goodbye to your father, but then I want you on the road back to Boston. I've reached out to Soren, offering him a truce, and access to you, in return for my control of the streets. He's agreed."

"He won't kill me in retaliation?"

"He needs you to complete his little performance piece. Fireworks, miracles, acts of wonder. You know what I mean."

I nod. I know exactly what he means. "And you want me to help him? I thought you'd want to stop him."

"I wanted him dead," Blackstone says, his expression thoughtful. "At least at the start. But humans have proven unexpectedly rebellious since the plague started. Soren will have to go eventually, but he'll be useful for a while. The mortals need something to control them now that their precious civilization has fallen. Firepower is good for keeping the streets under control, but mortals need to believe some higher power is looking out for them or they'll lose heart. Soren does the avenging angel shtick so well."

"You two are going to play the 'good cop, bad cop' routine?"

"Exactly."

"How will you destroy him?" I ask pointedly. "The serum you made before didn't work."

"Don't trouble your pretty little head about it. We have a plan in place. Just play your part and things will work out well for us all. You're my bargaining chip to enforce a short détente before I deliver the deathblow. Once we succeed in getting rid of Soren, you'll be reunited with your dear father and your beloved twins, and I'll have what I want." He eyes me from under a furrowed brow for a moment as if appraising my value. "Now, you might be a bit weak for a few days, but I want you to take the vehicle and go to Boston before dawn."

"I can go out in the sun right away?"

He nods. "It acts very fast. By dawn, you should be ready to go." He glances at the men still standing around his desk by the window.

"Now, if you'll excuse me, I have some logistics to go over with my officers." He bows low to me and turns on his heel, leaving Dylan and me behind.

"I don't believe he's actually letting me leave."

Dylan takes my hand and helps me up from the sofa. "He has what he wants—your father. He's certain you'll do anything to keep him alive. As I will for my family."

I look at Dylan and force a smile. "Our families and those we love are our weakness. Speaking of which, I want to say goodbye to my father."

I wake my father up when I return to his room. There's only an hour or so before dawn, and I want to say goodbye in case I don't come back for a long time. Or ever. There's always that possibility.

"We're going," I say when we have him seated by the fire. "We have to obey Blackstone's orders and go to Soren."

My father shakes his head. "This is what your mother and I tried so hard to prevent. You serving any of these monsters."

"I know," I say, taking his hand and squeezing it. "But that's our fate. Or at least," I continue, correcting myself since I don't believe in fate, "that's the only real choice we have. I have to trust that Julien and Michel have other plans and that one day, both Blackstone and Soren will be defeated."

"I can only pray for that."

I sigh. "Better to act than pray," I say, belligerent to the end. My father isn't truly religious, but he was raised in a Catholic home and can't escape its legacy.

"Come back," he says and takes my hand, holding it between both of his. "I've only just found you. I don't want to lose you again."

"Me either," I say and lean over to kiss his cheek. He's so frail compared to what I remember of him from my childhood. He was always my teacher and my protector. He seemed tall and strong. Now, he's a shadow of what he used to be, thin, pale, and greying.

It breaks my heart to see him like this. It's something every child must face—that moment when their parents no longer seem invincible and all-powerful. I thought it would be years and years before that happened to me, when my father was much older, in his seventies perhaps. Instead, he's in his forties, thin and frail, his eyes wide and his cheeks gaunt. I should be staying with him for a week or more just to ensure he eats properly and starts to recover from his ordeal, but I know Blackstone will never tolerate it. I wish I could take my father with me, but then Blackstone would have less leverage over me.

I think of my foster parents. In the shock of learning my father wasn't mentally ill at all, I realize I've neglected to think of them at all and a sense of guilt fills me.

"My foster parents!" I blurt out. "I want to ask Blackstone about them. He never mentioned holding them."

Dylan closes his eyes as if he too only now thought of it. "I would've thought he'd throw that in your face as a way to pressure you into cooperation. Maybe he doesn't have them after all."

"But then who? Soren?" I try to imagine what Soren would do to them, how he'd treat them, but can't.

"Has to be Soren," Dylan says, frowning, "unless they picked up and left and were unable to send a message to you. But that doesn't sound like them."

"I want to speak with Blackstone before I leave," I say. I hug my father once more. "I'll be back," I assure him, although I can't really promise anything. "One day, we'll move to the Pembrokeshire Coast and live in a cottage by the ocean."

He smiles. "Like the one near St. David's?"

"Yes," I say and kiss his cheek once more, tears biting at the corners of my eyes. "With a garden filled with wildflowers."

"Your mother loved them. Especially lavender."

I force a smile and leave him, pushing out of the door and down the hall, then down the stairs to Blackstone's study. I stand at the doorway and see him deep in conversation with some of his men. He glances up and waves me in.

"Eve," he says as if we're old friends and not sworn enemies. "How is your father? Rest assured I'll keep him safe, comfortable, and well-fed while you're off slaying dragons for me."

I smile to be polite, but of course, I hate him. "I appreciate that. Do you have my parents as well? My foster parents? We went to their cottage the other day and it was empty. It looked as if it had been looted. All their possessions were gone."

He shrugs. "I don't have them. Perhaps Soren took them as bargaining chips. He's not the sort to leave things to chance, but if he has them, he said nothing to me when I sent my offer of sharing the spoils of war. He gets the pews and I get the streets, as I said before. For a while, at least."

"You can't really believe he'll cooperate with you," I scoff. "Don't you think he's planning on getting rid of you as well?"

Blackstone shrugs. "If he wasn't planning on it, I'd think far less of him. Soren's a worthy adversary. I imagine he has plans for every eventuality. I do."

He turns his back on me to speak with his lieutenants. I take that as my cue to leave. Dylan takes my arm and leads me out of the study. One of the guards escorts us to our cart and horse and we ride off as if nothing's happened.

I can't believe what I've just lived through. Meeting Blackstone and his son. Finding my father alive and sane. Learning of Michel's possible deceit about my father's well-being. The mystery of the disappearance of my parents. Taking the daywalking serum and my newfound freedom to live in the sunlight.

It's almost too much to take in for one week.

We drive through the deserted streets of Cambridge to Boston and the sector of town Michel and Julien have under their control. The sun is rising steadily, and for the first time since I became a vampire, I'm able to watch the dawn and feel the sun's warmth as it rises over the ocean. After we stop in to speak with Michel and Julien, we'll make the trip to Soren's stronghold in Davis Cove and see what he wants of me. I imagine I'll play his little Adept and funnel power to him from his worshippers the way I did before my transformation.

Dylan wanted to bypass a stop in Boston, afraid perhaps that I'll become too upset by Michel's lies, but I must see him—and Julien—once more before I go to Soren, perhaps to my death.

On the trip, Dylan and I speak of the Council and what it means that Blackstone has control over it. We can't go to those we once trusted. A new Council has to be formed by people we know for certain share our goals.

"I know you have no reason to trust me, Eve," Dylan says, his voice filled with pain, "but you have to know I'm going to do everything in my power to fight Blackstone and Soren. To free my parents. If you and Michel are going to Soren, Julien and I need to find a way to fight Blackstone. I have to keep up the front that I support Blackstone's goals while working to stop him."

I nod. "Julien can help. He has more reason than most to want Blackstone dead."

We have to sit down as a group and figure out how to respond. We need a plan.

As I think about going to Soren with Michel, I remember what Blackstone said, casting doubt about Michel's role in my father's imprisonment. I'll confront him about my father and see what he says. I want to watch his face and hear his voice when he denies it—or confirms my worst fears. Did he know all along my father was sane and keep him out of my life so I would study science and take up my mother's place as an Adept for the Council?

I shudder as the sun finally rises above the horizon. The morning sky is blood red. I can't help but think of the symbolism.

"Red sky at night, sailor's delight," I say.

Dylan smiles ruefully. "Red sky at morning, sailors take warning," he replies, completing the old adage. "Looks like there's a storm on the horizon."

"I'm afraid you're right," I say and pull my scarf more closely around my neck.

CHAPTER 10

Anaïs Nin

WE PASS through one guard post after another until we finally arrive back at the safe house. Michel and Julien rush to me once I walk through the door to the apartment, both of them reaching out to me. I glance from one to the other, not knowing how to handle this. Of course, they're both concerned about me, considering I was at Blackstone's residence and took the daywalking drug, but who do I acknowledge first?

"How are you?" Julien says, taking hold of my shoulders before Michel can. "How do you feel after taking the serum?"

Michel steps back, reluctance clear in the frown that creases his brow.

"Like crap," I admit, removing Julien's arms. I glance at Michel. "But I'm glad to be able to go outside during the day. I missed the sun." I smile at him and he smiles back, his frown diminishing. I step back and exhale, my gaze moving from one brother to the other. "We have to talk."

~

JULIEN IS FURIOUS.

"No," he says, chopping his hand down on the palm of his other hand. "I won't let you go without me."

"It's not up to you," I say and cross my arms in defiance. "Blackstone has my father. He's working with Soren for now, but he plans on destroying him once the Church has established some kind of order. He expects me to help Soren gain temporary power, do his miracles. Then, when they have the virus perfected, we'll take Soren down permanently. Once we do, we can deal with Blackstone separately."

"It sounds so easy," Michel says and I hear the doubt in his voice. "You and I go and help Soren gain power, and then when Blackstone decides it's time, you administer the virus. Sounds far too good to be true, Eve. I don't like it."

I turn to Michel. "You said that Soren plans on using you as well, Michel. As his high priest. You're part of this. Have you changed your mind? I thought this was a scenario you had to see through."

Michel shrugs but says nothing.

"What about me?" Julien says. He turns to me, his expression dark. "If you think you and Michel are going to go to Soren and leave me behind…"

"Julien," I say, frustration filling me. "We need you and Dylan to get a plan in place to take Blackstone out. You two are all that's left of the real Council of Clairveaux. Blackstone's infiltrated it for the past few decades and has been in control, manipulating those on the Council without your knowledge." I take his hand and squeeze it. "You need to develop your own plan to take down Blackstone."

Julien shakes his head and opens his mouth to speak but stops. I already know what he was going to say. He knows all this, but he doesn't care about the rest of the world any longer. He doesn't care about Soren or Blackstone or Dominion. I feel it when we connect. He's tired of fighting. He wants some happiness for a change.

"You have to stop thinking about us, about me," I say, my voice soft. "We have to make sacrifices. Our relationship is nothing compared to what's going on."

He doesn't feel that way any longer. He's almost at the point of not caring and if he could, he'd take me away from everything so we could live together in peace, somewhere far away from Michel and Soren and Blackstone. It's pure selfish desire on his part, and he knows it.

Michel still cares. The fight always comes first for Michel. He's always been one to sacrifice himself for the greater good, giving up his personal happiness if need be. He wants to end this battle over humans. He wants to reestablish the Council and find a cure for vampirism. Then, if possible, he wants to live with me for as long as we're happy.

Everything Michel's done, he's done for the greater good. I have to keep telling myself that when I think that he may have been involved in my father's imprisonment. In the lie that my father was insane. In the attempt to keep me away from him so that I'd follow my mother into the life of an Adept.

Even though that's what I wanted, and I'm glad that I did choose this path, the thought that Michel has kept the truth from me all this time… It hurts me. My chest constricts, and when I look at Michel, there's a part of me that sees him as the grand manipulator that Lord Blackstone called him.

Is everything an act with Michel, right down to our relationship? Is it all to get my cooperation with his overarching plans?

I shiver for a moment at the thought.

I have to speak with him alone.

THAT NIGHT, after we've had a meal and sat around talking about the safeguards we'll put in place, I say goodnight and go to my room. Julien frowns when I leave, for I know he wants to stay with me, given that this is his week, but I don't invite him. I want to speak with Michel alone. I want to get Michel relaxed and calm and then I'm going to reach into his mind and find out the truth about my father.

Of course things don't always go as I plan...

I tiptoe into the hallway after everything is quiet in the apartment, and just when I get to the door outside Michel's room, Julien shows up from the living room.

"Going somewhere?"

I startle, surprised that I didn't hear that he was still up. I glance into the living room and see that he had been at the table, reading some papers. Was he specifically waiting to see what I'd do? I don't like to be suspicious, but I can't help but think he was.

"Julien, I need to speak with Michel."

"Why didn't you speak with him earlier? Or are you planning on getting some practice in as his concubine?"

I exhale loudly and in frustration. "Julien..."

Julien steps closer and brushes an errant strand of hair from my cheek. His gaze moves over my body, across the thin t-shirt, and down my bare legs. I have nothing on underneath since I was planning on seducing Michel into a compromising position.

"You don't look like you were going in there to talk."

I step away. "You have to stop being possessive. You know this is going to happen. There's no other choice."

"Yes, but you should be with me tonight, since you're going away. You could at least wait until you're at Soren's to fuck him!"

Julien turns away from me, his fists clenched. He stomps away and just then, Michel's door opens and I see his bleary eyes through the crack in the door.

"What's the matter?" he says and rubs his eyes.

"Nothing," I say and leave Julien to himself. "Michel, we need to..." I say and hesitate. "Talk."

Michel opens the door to admit me and I push past him to go deeper into the room. He's in his boxer briefs and his skin looks luminous in the light from outside. Of course, my body responds to his male beauty and I hate myself for being so manipulative. I go right over to him and cup his cheek, pulling his head down to kiss me.

He's surprised. I hear his sharp intake of breath, but he pulls me against his body and kisses me back without question. Luckily, I've developed an ability to block him from my thoughts, so all that he gets when we join senses is a wave of desire from me. I sense his mind trying to figure out what I'm doing—why I would want to make love with him instead of Julien, especially since we're leaving tomorrow—but the feel of my mouth on his, my hands stroking up his back erase all those thoughts.

Of course, being the alpha male that he is, he has to take over, so he pushes me over to the bed and strips off my t-shirt before covering me with his body. I wrap my legs around his hips and sigh as he begins to kiss my throat.

He's completely immersed in the sensations and so I state it point blank.

"You knew all along that my father was sane."

He's shocked back into the present. I can tell by the way the walls go up between us that he's trying to hide the full truth from me, but at least I got the momentary sense from him that he did know my father was sane.

There's more to the story, but the rest of it will have to wait. At least I now know the truth.

Michel rolls off me and sits on the side of the bed, his head in his hands for a moment as he rubs his eyes. He sighs and runs his fingers through his hair. "Eve…"

"Don't say anything else except the truth or I won't go with you to Soren's. I'll run away with Julien."

"No you won't," Michel says, his voice tired. "You want Soren dead as much as I do."

I sit up beside him. "You knew my father was sane. Admit it to me. I want to hear it from your own lips."

"Yes," he says. "I knew he was sane. It was for the best that he went away, Eve. You have to believe that. If he hadn't, he would have died when Soren's men came for you. He was sent away for his own protection."

That makes me mad. "Did you know the conditions he was kept in? Like a medieval dungeon!"

Michel turns to me and despite the darkness, I can see pain in his eyes. "It had to be that way. He had to appear to be insane to keep him safe. This wasn't my choice, Eve."

"It wasn't his choice."

Michel shakes his head. "This is bigger than us all. Some sacrifices have to be made."

"I think my father has made more than enough. He lost his wife, he lost his daughter, and he lost his freedom. He almost lost his mind after being in that asylum for a decade."

"But he's still alive, Eve," Michel says and takes my shoulders, shaking me a bit. "You're still alive."

"Hardly," I say and pull away from him.

"You know what I mean." He shakes his head. "Would you rather that he was dead? Would you rather that Soren had found you and taken you when you were eleven? You think you had a hard time with Franklin? You have no idea…"

"I'll never know what might have been different, will I?"

Michel exhales loudly. "No, but I know what would have been different. You wouldn't prefer what you would have become had Soren found you when you were eleven."

I touch his shoulder deliberately, trying to join with him. "Show me."

He pulls away, frowning. "No," he says, his voice low. "I don't even want to see what might have been had you not been taken away, had your father not been put in the asylum…" He finally turns to face me once more. His expression is earnest when he speaks, his voice breaking. "There was no choice for me, Eve. No choice."

"Show me, or I won't believe you. I want to know." I move closer and weasel my way onto his lap so that I face him, our eyes almost on the same level. When he looks in my eyes, I feel how my body affects him, how his heart races, how his limbs all become heavy, how desire for me infuses him.

"Eve…"

"Just a brief glimpse," I say, my voice soft. "Think of it as evidence for why you did what you did. Show me what I would have become."

"You would have become like Marguerite, happily being with all of us at once," he says. "Why do you think she tried to make Julien and me jealous of each other? All she knew was sex. She used sex to manipulate us and it was Soren who taught her, beginning at a young age. He took her in the fourth century, Eve, from her family. Wealthy women and women of noble birth were married when they were twelve. Soren wouldn't have hesitated to take you as his own when you were eleven."

I don't really want to see what I would have been, but I need to in order to believe Michel. "Just a brief image, then," I encourage. "Nothing too explicit."

He sighs, closing his eyes as if he can't bear to face it with them open.

We connect, our minds joining, and I see what he sees. In his mind's eye, I'm sitting on Soren's lap in a grand house, the surroundings not familiar. I'm wearing a gown of diaphanous material and jewels that are far beyond anything I have ever seen except on television or in movies. I look maybe sixteen. My arm is around Soren's shoulder and I have a pouty, petulant expression on my face as he feeds me fresh cherries. He's reveling in feeding me, and then he leans in to kiss me, like he wants to taste the cherry juice on my lips.

I pull my mind away from Michel's before he does, disgusted by the scene, not wanting to see any more. "Enough!" I say and break our connection. It makes me ill. I don't care if those were the norms for the medieval period. They were barbaric. That he would be willing to follow the old ways in modern times disgusts me.

"How young was I when he first—" I started to ask, not able to finish.

"In that version? Fourteen. The minimum age of marriage with parental consent is fourteen in Massachusetts."

I shudder at the thought. "I thought he made me for you and Julien."

"He did, but that doesn't mean he wouldn't have preferred to marry you so that you'd be his possession, to give to us when he chose."

"You would have taken me if he gave me to you?"

Michel sighs. "No," he says. "We agreed that we wouldn't have you —neither of us—but we knew that's what he'd want. We'd fight Soren instead. Soren created you as bait, but Julien and I agreed not to accept his bait. We were, despite our differences, united on that."

I nod, knowing deep down that while both would have wanted me, trapped by their seemingly timeless love for Danielle, they wouldn't have used me the way Soren wanted to. The fact I was kept out of Soren's life, that I escaped that fate, meant I was free to choose between them.

Part of me forgives Michel for his deception, but there's a part of me that holds back complete forgiveness. Why couldn't he have told me the truth? Did he think I'd run off to the asylum and try to rescue my father?

When I think of it, that's exactly what I would have wanted to do. It would have tortured me to know he was sane but being kept locked up. I would have fought both Julien and Michel, insisting that we try to rescue my father.

Michel reaches out and takes my hand. "I'm so sorry, Eve. There's nothing I can do to make this up to you. I know that. Please believe me when I say I was faced with two impossible choices. I chose the best I could at the time."

"What else are you hiding from me?" I ask, not yet ready to forgive him enough to continue what we started. I slip my hand out of his, maintaining the distance between us.

Michel doesn't say anything in reply. That tells me one thing: he is keeping other secrets.

"Tell me that whatever other secrets you're keeping are to protect me at least," I implore.

He turns to me, his eyes haunted. "If I could tell you everything, with no harm to come to you, I would." He moves closer and there's nowhere for me to go. "Don't you understand that if I could, I'd take you somewhere far away so that it was just the two of us?" He reaches up and runs the backs of his fingers against my cheek. "I love you, Eve."

When he leans in and kisses me, I don't stop him. I kiss him back, but when his lips part to deepen the kiss, I pull away.

His expression is hurt but he doesn't protest. He knows that it's too soon. There have been too many revelations in too short a period of time for me to simply fall into his arms the way he might want me to and the way I might have only a week ago.

"I better go back to my room," I say and rise from the bed. I pull the t-shirt over my head and leave Michel. When I reach the door, I turn to him. "Soren will expect us to be together at his residence the way we used to be, but you have to know I can never go back to that."

"You don't love me anymore?" His voice is low and choked with emotion.

"I'll always love you," I assure him, "but I'm not sleeping with you again. Not until this is all settled and I have my father back."

"And Julien?"

I sigh. "He hasn't lied to me again and again."

Michel exhales, and turns his head away. "Don't be too certain of that."

I stop, the door partly open. "What do you mean? If you know something he hasn't told me, tell me now."

Michel turns back to me, his eyes finally meeting mine. "Ask him yourself. They're his secrets to tell, not mine."

I frown, angry at Michel for laying the groundwork for doubt about Julien in my mind. I leave his room, closing the door behind me.

I TIPTOE through the hallways back to my bedroom, but Julien is standing in the hallway just outside my door.

I come to a stop, my breath catching in my throat.

"Julien…" I hold my hand against my throat. "I didn't see you. Have you been waiting outside my door for long?"

"Long enough to hear you speaking with Michel."

I push past him, opening the door to my room. He follows me inside. I don't face him because right now, I'm too upset. "Then you know I went in there to find out the truth about my father, not for sex, so stop being jealous."

I hear the door to my bedroom close and then a low chuckling from Julien.

"Not ever going to stop that, Eve. Give up on that hope now."

I turn and see the hint of a grin on his lips. It makes me relax just a bit and I close my eyes in relief that he's able to joke. That means he's not too hurt.

I take him in with one long glance. He's standing just inside my bedroom, dressed only in a pair of black boxer briefs, the rest of his very buff body illuminated by the moonlight flooding in from the window. He's breathtakingly beautiful with his short dark hair and several days' growth of whiskers on his very square jaw. A tattoo marks his forearm and his neck below his ear. He is perhaps the most desirable man I've ever met—besides Michel. His blue eyes regard me possessively and that sense of possession sends a jolt of desire through my body.

"If you're going with Michel tomorrow, I want you tonight."

As much as my body thrills to those words and the way he's looking at me—like a predator surveying its prey—I think it's a mistake to make love with him. I'm still upset over learning the truth directly from Michel's lips. I'm upset from seeing my father. I'm upset at having to go to Soren's and pretending all is well with Michel.

Most of all, I'm upset that it's come to this. My becoming a vampire was for nothing. Soren is still alive and now is cooperating—at least temporarily—with Blackstone in instituting Dominion. I have become my worst enemy and have gained nothing except my imprisoned father. Now I'm strapped with a hunger like no other.

"Go away," I say and throw myself down on my bed. I grab on to a pillow and can't stop from sobbing into it. I feel like a petulant child in doing so, but I can't help it. Everything is just too overwhelming all of a sudden.

Julien comes to the side of the bed and sits down. He lays his hand on my shoulder. His touch does something to me and I cry even harder, unable to control myself. Soon, without knowing how it happens, I'm in his arms. He doesn't try to kiss me. He rocks me, his arms wrapped around me, his face in the crook of my neck.

"I'm so sorry, Eve," he whispers, squeezing me more tightly in his embrace. "So sorry..."

Then the walls between us fall and we connect, not consciously doing so, but out of sheer habit, I feel his love for me, feel his regret and sympathy, feel his overwhelming need for me—not only for sex, but for love. He needs my love so deeply it chokes him and chokes me. I didn't plan on it, but with no barriers between us, it's impossible to resist each other. Desire wells up inside of me, whether from him or my own body, I don't know.

Our mouths find each other and we kiss deeply, our tongues searching each other out, our lips pulling at each other. He pushes me down on the bed and continues to kiss me as if his very life depends on it, biting my bottom lip gently before kissing my cheek, my chin, and then my throat.

I'm unable to resist him, his touch overwhelming any lingering resistance.

I'm lost to him. The rest of the world fades into nothingness.

CHAPTER 11

"Looking back, I have this to regret, that too often when I loved, I did not say so."

R. S. Baker

I sleep all that day and wake up in the early morning hours of Saturday, still not back in sync with the normal daytime / nighttime cycle. Julien's body is next to me on the bed, sheets tangled between his legs. I didn't ask him to go back to his room because I have no idea if or when we will be together again. All I know is that I needed him to be with me when I awoke off and on, contemplating our next move with Soren.

Julien stirs, rolling over so that he's on his back, a pillow over his face. "Did you sleep?" he asks, his voice soft.

"Like the dead," I reply, snuggling closer to him, throwing one of my legs over his. "I feel as if I could sleep for a week."

"It's the daywalking drug. You need more sleep for a few days."

"I'll sleep on the trip and when we get to Soren's."

"You'll have to sneak off and spend some time with me or I won't be able to go through with this," he says as he slips his arm around my shoulder, pulling me closer. "I can't stand the thought of you being with him not with me. I hate this, Eve."

I run my hand over his pectoral muscles, the skin smooth and warm beneath my fingers. "I'll try. Won't Soren want you there too? He likes the fact that the three of us are together."

"Soren really has a blind spot when it comes to Michel. Hates and loves him. He sees me as being too tainted by my relationship with Blackstone. He's suspicious about my involvement."

"You didn't know about the plan either," I say in protest. "Dylan pulled one over on all of us. I didn't know about the plan until the last minute. I mean, I knew about it and approved it, but I didn't even really know about it on a day-to-day basis."

"I truly didn't know about the final details," Julien says, "but I knew the Council had some plan. I thought I'd be involved in it in a completely different way than I was. Soren knows I saved you and that Michel didn't want to. He still wants Michel to be by his side. I'm persona non grata."

"I don't like being separated from you," I admit, "but we have to do this. There's no choice."

"I know." He rolls over on top of me, making me breathless.

Then, someone—Michel, of course—knocks at the door to the bedroom.

"Eve?"

It's Dylan, returned from whatever errand took him away earlier

"Yes?" I say as Julien nuzzles my neck.

"Michel is out loading up the vehicle. He says you need to get ready."

"Okay." I push Julien off me and roll out of bed. He groans and tries to grab my foot and pull me back but I resist, giggling. "Julien!"

Finally, he kisses my foot and looks in my eyes, his expression sad. "Come back to me," he says, choking up. "Don't disobey Soren at all. Be a good girl. I don't want you to die. I couldn't go on if anything happened to you."

"Don't worry about me."

He shakes his head. "I do worry about you. You're far too head-strong for your own good. Michel is right about this, Eve. You must simply comply. Obey. I know you don't like it, but it'll keep you alive so we can be together again. Promise me."

I inhale and consider. I hate promising something I know I won't be able to keep.

"Promise me!" He frowns, his brow furrowed.

"Okay," I say and nod. "I promise I'll be so obedient, they won't believe I'm the same girl."

"Don't be too good, or Soren will force you to disobey just to get a reaction. As much as he might protest about obedience, I think he really likes those he can't completely dominate."

"It must be lonely being the only one of your kind," I observe. "There's no one like him, besides the Twelve."

Julien shakes his head. "Feeling sorry for him?"

"Not one bit," I reply. "I hate him. I want to see him destroyed. But still, I can't imagine being like him. That's why I don't want to ascend, Julien."

"It's not so bad. It would make you more immune to everything. You really should."

I dress quickly. "I can daywalk now. That's all I need."

He says nothing, watching as I pull on my clothes and smooth my hair back into a ponytail.

"I'm not sleeping with Michel again," I say to Julien when he pulls me between his thighs. "I can't forgive him, so don't be too jealous."

"I'll believe that when I hear Michel complain," Julien says. He kisses my neck, brushing a loose strand of hair from my face.

"I'm serious, Julien. I told him I wouldn't sleep with him again."

Julien nods, but says nothing. I know there's no way I can convince him otherwise so I merely kiss him, my hands cupping his face and stroking the whiskers on his jaw.

"I love you," I say when I see the expression in his eyes. "I'm coming back to you as soon as this is all over."

"I love you. More than you can know." He pulls me against him, his arms wrapping tightly around me. "Oh, God, Eve," he whispers against my throat. "I'm so afraid you'll never come back."

I smile. "I will."

We kiss once more. It's tender at first but soon turns almost desperate. He tries to pull me back down onto the bed.

"Stop it," I say softly, pushing gently on his shoulders. "I have to go."

He takes my face in his hands, his eyes locked on mine. "Come back to me."

He releases me and I leave him sitting on the bed, his head turned away as if he can't stand to watch me go. I don't look back when I close the door behind me, uncertain whether I'll ever see him again.

Downstairs, Michel is waiting for me in the car. Dylan helps me with my bag and I climb in beside Michel. Dylan leans in through the passenger door window and kisses my cheek.

"Be safe, sister. We'll meet again soon. Don't worry about Julien. I'll take care of him."

I nod, but am so choked up I can't speak, watching him as we drive off until he becomes a small speck in the distance.

THE TRIP IS UNEVENTFUL. Michel doesn't make much conversation and I don't try either. Both of us are focused on how to behave now that we're going to be playacting as lovers instead of really being together. I'll have to show Michel affection in front of Soren or he'll be suspicious and force the issue. I know what he's like. He wants me with Michel so he can torture us.

I watch Michel out of the corner of my eye as we drive down the back roads to Soren's compound. Every so often, I know he wants to say something but stops himself. I don't encourage him.

Maybe it's cruel of me, but I'm sick to death of all his lies. I'm tired of his refusal to be open and truthful with me about anything outside of his lust for me.

At least Julien tells me the truth.

. . .

I SNOOZE MOST of the trip, my head leaning against my bag on the side of the car. I'm jolted when the car goes over a large bump, and blink awake. We're almost there and my stomach is all butterflies, wondering what Soren will do once we arrive.

Will he be his usual charming self? Will he delight in his triumph and wallow in it? I have no idea what to expect. I'd think he'd want to kill me. He probably does, but is going to use me first then throw me away, like he threw Danielle over the walls of Carcassonne and onto the garbage heap.

I remember that scene from Julien's manuscript. It comes back to me as we drive down the streets towards Soren's mansion. Michel was broken over it, but he was forced to kill Danielle just as he was forced to kill my mother. I remember the description of Julien searching for Michel and finding him digging her grave with his bare hands, his nails torn off, his fingers bloody.

Then, what does Soren do to torture Michel even more? Creates me to torment him and bring him out of his self-imposed celibacy so that Soren can gain power and rule as a god.

I turn and look at him, my gaze moving over his profile, so beautiful with his square jaw, soft mouth, perfectly straight nose, and long, thick black lashes. His hair falls in waves down the back of his neck. God, he's so handsome…

Inside, I know he's an honorable man who has been forced to do dishonorable things because of the war he's fighting—and has been fighting—both with his own nature and with Soren. How he only ever wanted to be a priest and live a pure life serving his god. How the war between the Church and Catharism came between him and his brother. How he was taken by a heartless vampire who played with him, tortured him by forcing him into a sexual relationship with her despite his vow of celibacy.

How all of this was because of Soren. He's a fantastical creature of some kind, beyond a vampire but not quite an angel. I still don't know what he is, but he's spent his long life trying to become powerful. He wanted a stronghold in the Languedoc region of France eight hundred years ago and sent his Norse princess to find a way to gain that foothold. She realized Michel and Julien's family had the wealth and power to give Soren that foothold.

She died at Michel's hand because he couldn't stand to live another day as the monster she had made him. All of this—my existence, Soren's manipulation of us all—is revenge for her death.

Michel must feel my eyes on him because he turns, his expression hurt despite the fact I've said nothing. He must be thinking how much I hate him for lying to me about my father. It makes my heart break for him all over again and I realize he's only doing what he thinks will prevent Dominion and keep me alive.

He's so afraid Soren will kill me…

Everything he's done is to prevent Dominion and keep me alive… It hits home once more how wrongheadedly heroic he truly is. I can't help it. I reach out and take his hand, squeezing it. He glances down at my hand on his as if to try to understand what it means, but in a second he knows. The walls come down between us and he knows what I'm feeling and thinking.

At that moment, he knows and I know that despite it all, I still love him. That I see him for what he is—a man forced to be a vampire who is now only trying to do what is right.

He raises my hand up to his lips and kisses it, then turns his eyes back to the road, keeping my hand in his the rest of the way to Soren's.

A PHALANX of guards greets our vehicle when we pull onto the street that leads to Soren's compound. They're in full SWAT uniforms with visors and weapons drawn. Michel pulls up to the roadblock and one of them leans into the car to peer at both of us. He nods to Michel and then glares at me for a long moment. I can feel the hatred in his eyes. My cheeks heat under his gaze and I realize I'm the one who tried to kill his master. Finally, he stands back up again.

He must have known we were coming, knows who we both are, for not a word is spoken. It shocks me for a moment. This is all so well choreographed. Soren is waiting for us and we are merely obeying his and Blackstone's demands. I feel helpless, caught up in this little drama. My only consolation is that there is still a small group of rebels—vampire and human—who refuse to go along with either Blackstone or Soren. They've infiltrated both organizations and are just waiting to strike.

We drive along the street to the compound where even more guards with full-body armor and weapons stand ready. Security is intense and I'm taken aback at how they're just waving us through, given who I am.

Michel stops the car in front of the mansion and turns it off. "Get out," he says, his voice low. "Do what they say without hesitation." I start to remove my seatbelt, but he takes my hand in his, stopping me. "Without hesitation, Eve. I can't say that enough. You're still alive only because both Blackstone and Soren have a use for you. Otherwise, you would have been dead in the cottage the night Soren's forces attacked."

I force a smile. He's so afraid for me. I can feel it when he touches me, when we briefly connect, letting me in to reinforce his fear. In his mind's eye, I see an image of me on my knees before a gloating Soren, my hands and ankles manacled and attached to a chain that someone holds. Michel is standing beside Soren, watching.

"Is that a vision of what could be or what will be?"

Michel shakes his head as one of the guards opens my door. He removes his hand from mine. "Without hesitation, Eve. If Soren has to wait another generation to create another Adept with your genetics, he will. For an immortal, twenty years is a blink of an eye."

I nod and exit the vehicle, but as soon as my feet touch the ground, another guard steps forward and grabs my hands, pulling them in front of me and attaching manacles to my wrists. My instinct is to fall into fight mode, but I remember Michel's warning and force myself to relax. I won't resist. I'll let them do what they will and wait for whatever plans are in place to act.

Michel comes around the vehicle and watches as another guard attaches manacles to my ankles and slips a long metal chain through the rings attached to both sets.

Michel nods. "Bring her to Lord Soren."

The guard nods at Michel. "Yes, m'Lord."

What?

Michel acts as if he's brought me to them—as if he's the one responsible for my capture and custody. I catch his eye as the guard pulls me past him and he widens his eyes, reminding me to obey.

I hold his eyes as I pass, frowning. I know he wants me safe. I know he wants to protect me. I know he doesn't want any of this. So why do I feel like he's betrayed me once more?

I follow the guard into the mansion and through the main foyer to a room in the rear of the building.

The room is filled with what look like military men, standing around speaking in soft voices. When they see us, the men part and let us pass. I feel their eyes on me, their hatred and curiosity almost palpable.

Soren sits on a throne-like chair on a raised dais at the far end of the room, the throne large and carved out of wood with ornate arms and legs and a huge back. Behind it, stretched out on either side, are two wings made of huge pieces of wood, the carving so intricate I can almost see every feather.

It's amazing.

He's dressed in black leather with a sword in a scabbard on his hip. His chin rests on a hand and his eyes are closed as if he's deep in thought. His long platinum-blond hair falls around his face and glows like a halo in the light. He really does see himself as some kind of emperor. He's going to play the part completely.

The guard deposits me in front of the throne and pushes me so that I fall to my knees on the cold stone floor in front of Soren. I cry out briefly from the pain, my cuffed hands stopping my fall.

I glance up, but Soren's eyes are still closed. Michel goes to his side and stands to his right. Finally, after long moments pass, Michel bends down, his lips to Soren's ear. He whispers something and then Soren lifts his head, his clear blue eyes opening slowly, as if he's coming back to consciousness or from somewhere far away.

"My Lord," Michel says, his voice soft, "I've brought Eve, as you requested."

Soren meets my eyes and holds them for a moment before nodding. "Good, good," Soren says, his voice low and slow, as if every word is a struggle. "I'm glad my men didn't kill her. I was afraid they'd be a bit too enthusiastic in sending a message."

"She was never at risk."

"Wonderful. But you failed to get her to ascend, I see."

Michel exhales and catches my eye. "She refused."

"And you're so in love with her you didn't think to force the issue?"

"My Lord, I—"

"Don't say anything," Soren cuts him off. "I trust everything went well with Blackstone."

"Yes," Michel says. "She took the daywalking serum at least."

Michel's eyes widen when he looks at me and I know he's warning me not to speak or do anything until Soren asks.

"Well, that's one consolation. She's more useful now." Then he looks at me fully, his eyes open wide. "So, Eve, you're back and apparently a little less recalcitrant than usual."

I don't say anything because it wasn't a question. I merely nod.

"Because of your hijinks with Dylan, I've been out of sorts for a while. I'm very angry, Eve. Very angry."

I say nothing. What could I possibly say in response?

Soren rises slowly, like it's an effort, and steps down the dais so that he stands directly in front of me where I still kneel, my knees sore from the fall. I'm surprised when Michel takes his arm and helps him down.

He's obviously still affected by the virus. Perhaps still battling it. Michel seems unconcerned or surprised and I wonder if he's been in touch with Soren the entire time. I wonder if Michel went immediately back to Soren once he was free.

I have to keep telling myself that whatever the case may be, Michel hasn't told me because of his attempts to keep me safe. I have to keep telling myself that or I won't be able to go through with this.

I wait, with my head bowed, for whatever it is that Soren will do with me and to me.

"Look at me," Soren says, his voice hard.

I glance up and see that he's even more pale than usual. He looks thinner, as if he's lost weight.

"Yes," he says, his hand still resting on Michel's shoulder. "I am weak. I've been fighting this pesky virus you gave me and while I've been mostly successful in eradicating it from my system, it's not yet complete. I need your magic touch, Eve," he says and lifts my head by the chin so that I can't help but stare into his ice-blue eyes. I try to blank my mind; I know he'll be able to read me and know everything. Luckily, my knees are bruised and hurt like hell. Hopefully the pain will be enough so he won't be able to read my mind. He strokes my cheek almost affectionately.

"I need your special skill to regain enough power to clear it completely from my system and that of the Twelve, who are still all in stasis. They're not as powerful and couldn't fight it off enough to fully wake. Once I'm back in tip-top shape and the Twelve are restored, we'll continue on this little quest for godhood. Are you game, Eve?"

"You already know why I'll comply with you," I reply. "Blackstone has my father. But do you have my parents?"

"No, I don't," Soren says and smiles. "If I did, you'd be the first to know. I have no idea where they are, but if you want Blackstone to keep good care of your father, you'll have to help me gain power so I can calm the fears of the masses as Blackstone trots them into his feedlots to fatten them for slaughter."

I bite my lip hard to stop from responding. He's trying to get a response from me, testing me. I know he enjoys my resistance, but Michel said comply. Without resistance.

So I bite my lip. I bite my cheek until it hurts. Until my mouth tastes like copper and I know I've drawn blood. It will heal soon enough.

Soren smiles down at me. "Fighting so hard to obey. So unlike you,

Eve. I know it galls you to bow to a higher power. It's necessary for a while at least."

He turns to face his throne and Michel helps him back up. He turns once more and slowly lowers himself into the throne with tremendous effort. He sits back finally and closes his eyes as if the exertion was too much for him.

In a moment, he opens his eyes and regards me once more. "Tomorrow, we'll have a little ceremony and you'll give me back my powers. Then we'll make some grand plans—you, Michel, and I—about how we're going to save the world from this horror Blackstone has wrought. That ought to put me in the good books with the humans, don't you think? An avenging angel returned to stop the menace of science and technology that threatens to enslave all humans to vampires? It's epic. It will form a whole new religion in the ashes of the old. A new religion that will last a thousand years."

"You sound like Ozymandias," I say, finally unable to hold myself back any longer. "Remember what Shelley wrote: 'My name is Ozymandias, king of kings: Look on my works, ye Mighty and despair!'"

Soren laughs, his head thrown back as if he enjoys the reference. He glances at Michel and smiles. "I can see why you love her." Then he turns his gaze back to me, his expression one of glee. "'Nothing beside remains. Round the decay of that colossal wreck, boundless and bare. The lone and level sands stretch far away.'"

He says nothing else for a moment, but I can see what I quoted pleased him.

"Yes, I know my poetry, Eve. I'm pleased that you know yours. You see," he says and leans on one elbow, "I was alive when Shelley wrote his poem. Hell, I've been around since Ramesses II, to whom Shelley referred as Ozymandias. I was alive when Ramesses II thought he'd rule the world and said those words. I know that truth far better than everyone else, Eve, but you have to remember I'm not a mortal pharaoh. I'm an immortal. We really do stand for thousands of years."

He smiles at me for a moment, then waves his hand in dismissal.

"I'm tired. Take her away, Michel, and do whatever you want with her. Love her. Hate her. Fuck her. She's yours, as I promised. All I ask is that you get her ready for the ceremony tomorrow. You know what that means."

Michel nods and bows toward Soren as he steps off the dais. "My Lord." Then he points to the guard beside me. "Bring her."

At that, the guard yanks my chain, forcing me to stand.

I follow them both as they leave the room and make their way down the long hallway back to the main foyer.

"Take her to my rooms." Michel points to my chains. "Make sure she's restrained. We don't want any attempts at escape." He doesn't catch my eye and I wonder if this is all a performance or if he is on Soren's side in this. Who would he choose between Blackstone and Soren? I can't help but think it would be the fallen angel rather than the vampire tyrant.

"That's it?" I say, unable to stop myself. "You're just going to send me upstairs with no explanation?"

"Shh," he says and puts a finger to my lips. "Without hesitation."

I shut my mouth firmly, frowning. I realize I must get myself under control and see the larger picture rather than let my emotions cloud my judgment. Michel is putting on a performance. He wants all vampires dead and gone, including whatever Soren is. He's biding his time, making his own moves in an attempt to have things turn out his way—free of Dominion and all vampires. It's just that he does this performance so well, he has me convinced. I have to keep reminding myself that he's a consummate performer, able to hide his true emotions to the rest of the world even if he can't hide them from me when we connect.

I follow the guard up a flight of stairs to the second floor and the east wing. He ushers me into an opulent room fit for the palace in Versailles with its tapestry-covered walls, ornate canopy bed in white and gold brocade, and white leather furniture. The huge floor-to-ceiling windows have exquisite drapery falling in puddles on the floor. It even smells expensive, like sandalwood and fine leather. I could imagine Marie Antoinette here, sitting at the small dressing table or lounging on the gold and white brocade settee at the foot of the bed.

The guard leads me inside and shackles me to the post of the bed. I can move about four feet in any direction, so I sit on the side of the bed.

"What if I have to go to the bathroom?"

He turns his back to me. "Hold it." He leaves, closing the door behind him.

I exhale and glance around, wondering what will happen to me now that I'm under Soren's total control and when Michel will come to free me from these chains.

CHAPTER 12

"Take away love and our earth is a tomb."

Robert Browning

Hours pass and I fall asleep on the bed facing the door, my shackled hands held out before me, my head on the pillow. I only wake when blood hunger begins to gnaw at my veins. I need to feed. I hear a creak in the hallway outside my room and lift my head, hoping that it's Michel come to free me, but nothing. It was merely the guard shifting his weight.

Michel, I say in my mind, hoping our blood connection will work and he'll hear me. I need you.

I let my mind open, searching for something—anything—from him, but there's no response. Or if there is, I'm too weak to hear it. Where is he?

What is he doing? Plotting with Soren? Making plans for the ceremony so I can give Soren more power?

More hours pass, the sky darkening and then brightening as dawn approaches on this gloomy winter day.

Will he leave me like this forever?

FINALLY, I hear footsteps down the hall and muted conversation outside the doorway. It must be Michel.

Sure enough, the door opens and in he strides, his coat on as well as a pair of leather gloves. He enters and the guard follows. I sit up on the side of the bed expectantly, my shackled hands held out.

"Unfasten them," Michel says, pointing to my hands.

The guard complies, using his key to remove the heavy metal manacles. Before he leaves, Michel pulls him aside. While I'm rubbing my wrists, the skin red and chafed, with thin scrapes from the rough metal edges of the manacles, I hear him mention food and blood.

My stomach rumbles at the thought of eating.

The guard leaves us alone and I watch as Michel takes off his gloves and slips them into the pockets of his overcoat.

"Eve," he says. He removes the coat and lays it on the back of a chair in front of the fireplace.

"Michel." I hold back, waiting for him to say something even though I really want to ask him where he's been—obviously outside, for he's dressed for the cold.

Finally, he comes to the bed where I sit on the edge, my hands folded in my lap, and sits beside me. He takes one of my hands and examines the scrapes, clucking his tongue.

"Soren really must invest in some higher quality restraints. He's gone all medieval on us."

"How can you joke about this?" I ask, frowning.

He smiles at me, a guilty smile. "If you don't laugh, you'll cry?"

"Still…" I say, pulling my hand out of his. He takes it back immediately and kisses the skin where the rough metal edge scraped my skin raw, his wet tongue a brief, bright sting.

"Don't," I say and try to pull my hand away once more. I know what he's doing. He's reminding me of that day we met and how he licked my wounded hands, tasting my blood for the very first time.

"You're mine, Eve," he says, his so-blue eyes burning with a heat that surprises me so soon after he joked about the restraints. It's the blood; I understand how it affects us.

"I told you we weren't going to be together again," I remind him, but it sounds feeble. His expression—the look of pure possession in his eyes—does something to my insides. I know I could easily fall into his arms if he pushed a little.

"Of course," he says and rubs the skin, watching as it heals. Soon, the wounds are completely gone. It's not his saliva but my own vampire nature that heals them. I'm now immortal, or at least, very hard to kill.

He drops my hand. "The guard will bring us something to eat and then I must sleep. I'm exhausted."

"Where have you been?"

"Errands," he says. "Nothing that need concern you."

There's a knock at the door.

"Come," Michel says. He rises and goes to the door, holding it open as the guard wheels in a cart with covered plates of food. I see a carafe of some red liquid—it could be wine or blood. I'd welcome either, but I do need blood.

"Thank you," Michel says and closes the door behind the guard as he leaves us alone once more.

Michel inspects the food and then pours the liquid into crystal glasses etched with a delicate floral design. He brings them over to me on the bed and sits beside me once more.

"Here," he says, handing a glass to me. "Drink this. You look like you need it. I know I do."

I take it and sniff. Blood. I drink it down in one long draught and see that he does as well. It feels so damn good in my stomach—like relief. Now I know how an addict feels when they get their fix. A moment of euphoria sweeps over me and I sit with my eyes closed and enjoy the sensation. The taste of blood, its coppery tang, lingers on my tongue. I would like more but I won't be greedy. The amount I took is enough to keep me going for a day or so. I don't want to get used to drinking a lot. The guilt is too much because I know where this blood came from—Soren's and Blackstone's slaves.

"Better?" he says and as he smiles at me, there's a hint of guilt in his eyes. "Sorry to have left you for so long, but I had things to do."

I shrug and say nothing, too interested in the food I can smell from across the room. "Can we eat now?"

I stand and cross the room, peeking under the silver domes at the meal. There's some kind of roast with root vegetables and gravy. On another plate is fruit and cheese. A hank of dark bread and knife sit to the side. I fix myself a plate, barely aware of Michel standing beside me.

"You're hungry."

I say nothing, and cut a slice of the dark rye bread, slathering it with butter from a small ceramic crock. I sit on one of the wing chairs by the fire and dig in, intent on the meat and what looks like parsnips. They aren't my favorite, but my stomach is rumbling and the scent is amazing.

Michel fixes his own plate and comes to my side. Together, we eat in silence, the only sounds the clink of cutlery on fine china.

Finally finished, I lean back and sigh in contentment. I don't protest when Michel pours me a glass of wine. I take a sip. The wine mixes with the remains of the blood I drank earlier and while that would have turned my stomach only a few months ago, now I appreciate the mix of flavors. Michel pours himself a glass and leans back in his chair, his eyes on me.

I remain silent, waiting for him to speak.

"You're very quiet," he says, his own voice soft. "Are you never going to speak to me again?"

I meet his gaze, our eyes on each other. "Where were you?"

He shakes his head. "That's of no importance to you."

I sigh. "Will you ever tell me the truth about anything?"

He takes a sip of the wine and then carefully places the glass on the table beside him.

"This is the only truth you need to know," he says, leaning closer to my chair. "Everything I do, I do to save humanity from slavery. Everything."

I say nothing in response, for how can I respond to that? I could deny it and say he's doing it for his own benefit, but I know him too well. He's the most selfless person I know.

"I'm sorry that you have to suffer," he says, his voice solemn. "If I could have had things turn out differently, I would have. I would have had you in Boston University, completely oblivious to this world."

"That didn't work out so well."

"No, it didn't. My plans to keep you hidden didn't work. You can't begin to realize how that breaks my heart, Eve."

I sigh. He's right. I know he tried to change this fate. He did what he thought was right but I still resent how much he's lied to me about his role in my mother's death, about his relationship to my parents, his role in my life after my mother died—about so much. And then it comes to me. A realization.

"You found me on purpose," I say, my voice low. "You knew where I was. You were waiting."

He says nothing, and I know I'm right. I continue, figuring it out as I speak.

"You decided that when I went looking for the translator, you would come for me. You already knew I was immune to compulsion so everything that happened afterwards was a lie."

"I gave you every chance not to become a vampire hunter," he interjects. "You took every chance to do it."

"Did you know Franklin would abuse me?"

An expression of pure horror comes over his face. "Of course not! My, God, Eve…" He shakes his head slowly and I can see real pain in his eyes. "As soon as we learned the truth, we took you out of his home and put you somewhere safe. I had no idea. How could you even imagine…"

"You see the future."

"I had no gift of prescience then, just vague dreams of a future I didn't recognize as such. It was my ascension that brought out my precognition."

"But you did know where I was and knew I was intent on pursuing my mother's calling."

He rubs his eyes and is silent for a moment. "I gave you the choice. You didn't want to study music. You wanted to study science and become a vampire hunter for the Council. You were operating blindly with no contacts in the Council, so theoretically, you would have been unable to become a vampire hunter unless someone initiated you. You would have become a forensic scientist, but not one involved in the Council's work. That was good enough for me. It was your choice. When you started looking for a translator, I could see you were going to try to find the Council. I had to be the one to guide you in the life if that was the case."

"But you knew I couldn't be compelled," I insisted. "That's why you gave me the drug to wipe my memory of you killing my mother."

"No, I gave it to you because I assumed you could be compelled. I didn't know. I tried to compel you. Sadly," he says, adjusting his position, and taking another sip from his wine. "I was unable. If you had gone back to playing music, I would have been happier. If I could have kept you hidden, I would have, but you have such a strong will..."

"You wouldn't have had me as a lover if you had succeeded."

"Eve, I was celibate before you."

"So you say..."

He puts his glass down hard. "Why do you fight me in everything?"

"Because you're not honest with me," I answer, responding to the tone in his voice. "You don't tell me the truth. Not all of it. So now I never know when to believe you. If you had told me the truth from the start, I'd cooperate."

"No, you wouldn't," he says with an audible sigh. "You wouldn't have the heart to go on. I know, Eve. I've seen it. I tell you only as much as I need to. Any more and you'd give up."

"Then you must think I'm a coward."

"Not at all," he says softly. "I know you're very brave. Too brave. But your heart would be broken."

I shake my head. "So what am I supposed to do? Just blindly do what you tell me to?"

"Yes. Blindly. Have faith that I know what I'm doing and am doing what's best."

"I have no faith and you know it."

He nods. "I know. What else can I say? It's imperative that you obey me now. Trust me. This is the only way. The only way. Please."

I sigh, my mind plagued by doubt and confusion. Part of me knows that I have to obey, but it still rubs me the wrong way regardless.

"I'll try," I assure him. "But if you think I'm going to sleep with you, you're mistaken."

He shakes his head and says nothing in reply. He finishes his glass of wine, then stands up and straightens his sweater before coming to my chair. He bends down and before I know it, he takes my head in his hands and kisses me squarely on the mouth, his lips covering mine. I'm too shocked to pull back and the kiss goes on and on. Finally, he pulls away, his hands holding my face.

"You will," he says and looks deeply into my eyes. "When this is all over, you will. Happily. Eagerly."

I say nothing and wait for him to pull away. He kisses me once more briefly and then lets go of me, standing up straight.

I sit mute and watch him go to the armoire and begin undressing. He removes his clothes, leaving only his black boxer briefs. Then he goes to the bathroom and I hear the sounds of water being poured into a basin. He's washing up. When he comes out of the bathroom, his hair around his face is a bit wet, the long strands hanging in his beautiful eyes.

"You're so sure of yourself," I say as a stab of desire for him, even now, goes through me, warming my body. I respond to the sight of a nearly-naked Michel like Pavlov's dog to a bell.

"Not of myself."

I exhale. "Then you're so sure of me. Of me still wanting you after everything that's happened.

"No," he says and shakes his head. "I'm sure of what I feel. That I still love you and you still love me, no matter what happens."

I watch as he crawls into bed, pulling the thick duvet over himself. Silence passes between us, and I hear his breathing slow and deep.

"I'm not fucking you, Michel."

He turns over, the sound of the sheets against his bare skin audible with my enhanced sense of hearing. I hear him sigh.

"I won't touch you," he says quietly. "You can come to bed and sleep without any worries."

I sit in silence for a long while, fighting with myself. I don't want to seem like a petulant child, but at the same time, I don't like that he's sleeping in the same bed as I am. I'm afraid that we'll end up making love despite my promise to myself—and to him—that the sexual part of our relationship is over.

"Come to bed, Eve," Michel says, his voice tired. "You have a big day ahead. You have to help Soren gain power so we can play out this game."

I exhale in resignation. I am tired. Whatever I have to face tomorrow will be better if I have a good sleep. I relent and go into the bathroom and wash my own face and brush my teeth, using the remaining water from the carafe.

I remain in my clothes, refusing to put on the t-shirt I brought along to sleep in.

I don't trust myself. When I get into bed, I make sure to sleep on top of the sheet instead of under it so that if he does sleep beside me or against me at any time, I won't feel his naked skin.

I need all the help I can get to keep my promise.

CHAPTER 13

"NOBODY HAS EVER MEASURED, not even the poets, how much the heart can hold."

Zelda Fitzgerald

WHEN I WAKE in the middle of the night, Michel is, as I expected, spooned against me, but there's a thin sheet between us and so we don't actually touch. Still, there's no denying the ache in me from the feel of his body warm against mine, his arm around my waist over the covers, his head on the pillow next to mine. I say nothing and merely slip a little further away from him so that there's an inch or two of space between us. I'm instantly cold, for despite how little warmth a vampire's body creates, put two of them together and the effect is mutually reinforcing.

Now, I shiver all alone in the bed, and pull the thick coverlet more firmly around me. Beside me, I feel Michel shift and hear him breathe in deeply.

"Stubborn girl."

"I'm not a girl." I make a face, realizing that I'm being stubborn but I have to fight my base desires for him. He can't think that I'll just happily reestablish our sexual relationship after learning he put my father away in an asylum despite his being sane. I can't forgive him for that. Not now. Maybe not ever. Who knows how many lies he's told me and how much he's still keeping from me?

He grasps my arms and rolls me over so that I'm underneath him. The sheet between us can't hide his arousal.

"To an immortal who has lived eight hundred years, you're a girl." His gaze moves over my face and while he started out with an expression of frustration touched with anger, detectable in the downward curve of his mouth and the crease above his brow, as he continues to examine my face, his expression changes. His frown relaxes and his eyes soften.

Without my conscious consent, the walls fall between us. I feel his emotions well up and overwhelm him. And me.

"Oh, Eve..."

"Don't," I say and try to wiggle out from underneath him, but he's far too strong. "Don't force me, Michel!"

He doesn't let go, but his grip loosens and now I'm halfway out from under his body, the sheet still between us. His face is directly over mine, his eyes on mine, his mouth a few inches away. He blinks, his thick black lashes dark over clear blue eyes.

"I would never force you." Then he kisses me, and at first I don't respond, but it's impossible not to, my body quickening and my muscles tensing even as my flesh swells and throbs. I don't know any longer what my desires are, or his, because it's just one big mass of lust, one mixed up wall of need.

Before I'm even aware, I'm kissing him back, my mouth on his. I gasp when my tongue finds his, the warm wetness sending a jolt of lust to my core. When his tongue touches mine, he thinks of licking me, tasting me, the hard nub of my clit beneath his tongue, my scent in his nose arousing him, the soft moans I make as desire builds in me making him harder.

He knows how good it feels for me, and I know how much it arouses him to feel me hard and wet and responsive under his tongue.

I pull away, gasping. "Stop!"

He does, his breathing harsh. In truth, my body wants him, but my mind doesn't. I breathe slowly, trying to calm the desire I feel, and soon he relents and rolls off me, collapsing on his back beside me, a hand covering his eyes.

"Just because you can make my body respond," I say, squeezing my thighs together reflexively, "doesn't mean my mind has said yes."

"I know," he replies, his voice low. "I can't resist you." He turns over so that he's facing me, resting on his elbow. "I don't want to resist you."

"I told you I won't be with you again."

"You will be once more," he says and it sounds more like he's trying to convince himself. Reassure himself. "You'll come to me and extend your hand and ask me to make love to you."

I frown. "You've seen it?"

He nods and brushes a strand of hair from my cheek.

I turn over so that my back is toward him. "Well, it won't be today."

I hear him sigh. "No, not today."

He lies back down and says nothing for a while, but of course, now I can't sleep. I'm achy with need, my flesh still throbbing from the desire he built up in me.

What I want is to slip my hand down and get myself off quickly, but of course I can't. Instead, I try to breathe through my desire, hoping it will fade quickly so I can go back to sleep.

In a few moments, I hear him sigh once more and then he turns over, the bed covers rustling, and now there's more than a foot of separation between us.

This is going to be incredibly difficult. I don't know if I can do it.

"Soren will know we're not fucking," I say.

"He knows we will, eventually."

"Goddammit!" I say in frustration. "I hate this. I hate him knowing anything."

"Quit being so petulant, Eve," Michel says, and I finally hear real anger in his voice. "You're smarter than this. Accept what fate has chosen for you. This has to happen if the future both of us want is to come to pass. Give in."

"You know I don't believe in fate any more than I believe in God."

"Fine," he says, still angry. "Be a child. Fight it every step of the way. Make it more difficult for us all."

"Difficult for you."

"No," he says and rolls back over, turning my face so that I have to look in his eyes once more. "Difficult for you as well. You want it. Deny that truthfully. Your body needs it. If you weren't so rebellious, you'd make love with me now so we both could go back to sleep."

I close my eyes; I feel close to tears. He's treating me like a disobedient child and I'm responding like one. It's just so damn hard…

"I am who I am," I say, my voice breaking. "I can't."

He sighs heavily and lies back down. "You will. I can wait."

"Don't hold your breath," I whisper, but of course he can hear me no matter how quiet I am. I hear him make that sound in the back of his throat—that characteristic sound he made the first night I met him and he was expressing frustration with me.

Poor Michel. He thought I'd be his happy little slave girl, doing his bidding and salving his wounds from living so long, complying with his plans so he could have things go his way. Instead, I've been his brother's lover and have fought him ever since we met.

"I love Julien, Michel," I say, aware that it will hurt him, but maybe it will stop him from trying to get back between my thighs. "If I had known that you were responsible for putting my father away, that he was sane when you did it, and that you knew where I was all along and were waiting for me to come of age so you could use me, I would never have asked you to share me with him."

There. I said it, finally said it to myself and to him. I would have chosen only Julien had I known. If I had known, I would have hated Michel. How would things have turned out differently?

I don't know, and I try to block it all out of my mind. I turn over and wrap my arms around myself even more tightly, pulling my knees up almost to my chin, trying to clear my thoughts.

But I do know how it would turn out had I chosen Julien, if I'm honest with myself, for I've seen snatches of it in his mind's eye. If I had chosen Julien over Michel, Michel would have become hard and even more calculating and heartless. He would have pursued his ends with no sympathy for anything or anyone. He would have become the monster I saw in the park way back when we met, his wings extended, killing in cold blood like the dark, avenging angel that he appeared to be. His heart would have been so brittle it would have shattered, and the shards would have cut at him for the rest of his existence, which he would be only too happy to end once Dominion was vanquished and Blackstone defeated completely.

As his swan song, Michel would have arranged it so that Soren killed him as he was killing Soren, the two of them dying together in some tragic farce of poetic justice—the monster and his creature killing each other.

That possible future exists. I know for I caught a glimpse, a brief glimpse, when I was in Michel's mind, and when he lost control for only a moment.

What other terrible futures is he hiding from me?

I kick myself mentally, because I don't believe in his visions. I don't believe he's some kind of angelic being no matter how many times he extends his wings and performs miracle-like feats of mind reading, healing, and foretelling the future.

I don't.

Despite everything, despite my anger at Michel for lying to me, for deceiving me, for what he did to my father (however well-intentioned), tears fill my eyes that it has come to this between us and I have to bite my lip to stop from crying out loud.

I lie cold and alone despite Michel's proximity, silently wiping away my tears. Everything has gone to shit. Soren is alive, Blackstone is triumphant, the plague has sent the world back to the steam age, Dylan has betrayed the cause so he could protect his parents, and mine are missing, probably being held captive to be used as leverage by some other player who wants something from me. Michel is a bastard, and I may never see Julien again.

I don't sleep for the rest of the night.

~

MICHEL WAKES and sits up in bed beside me, his hair messy, falling in his eyes in that deliciously sexy way that I try my best to ignore.

"How did you sleep?"

I yawn and stretch. "I didn't," I say.

He shakes his head at me. "I could have put you to sleep if you weren't so determined to shut me out."

"I needed to think," I say, not willing to get into a discussion of our relationship.

He slides out of bed and pulls on his jeans. "And what did you think about?"

"How we're going to defeat Soren. How we're going to stop Blackstone."

I watch as he zips up and fastens his belt. He's regarding me thoughtfully. "You don't have to worry about that part, Eve. You only have to do yours."

I sigh. "Do you really think Soren won't be expecting us to take another stab at using the serum?"

"He'll be expecting it. That's the only way to destroy him."

"But if he's expecting it—"

"It will be a distraction from the real attack."

"Which is?"

Michel smiles guiltily. "I could tell you, but then I'd have to kill you."

I frown, unable to comprehend why the Council would go ahead with a plan it knows Soren will expect.

"So while Soren focuses on the Council plot, there will be another unexpected attempt?" I ask.

"Something like that. Now don't ask for any more details. You know I won't put you at risk. Others may want you for your strategic purposes," he says, running a hand through his hair, "but I want you for your other more endearing attributes."

I'd slipped out of bed but stop in my tracks at that. "Michel, I told you that I won't be with you again. Not as lovers."

He comes to me, standing before me in all his bare-chested faded blue jeans beauty. He leans down to me, taking my chin in his hand. "You will be. When this is all over."

"You can't be sure of that," I remind him, trying to step away.

He smiles briefly. "I'll do everything in my power to make sure it happens. I love you, Eve."

He kisses me before I can escape, but his kiss is brief. He turns away when he's finished and goes to the armoire, removing a sweater from a shelf. The muscles in his strong back flex as he raises the sweater over his head.

He's so beautiful.

Part of me wants a future with him, the way we were when I met him again, in that brief moment before I found my online journal and discovered the truth. Those weeks and that evening are some of the only happy moments in my memory. I don't have any memories like that with Julien. We have nothing completely free of stress or worry about everything—vampires, Dominion, Blackstone... I was blissfully unaware of reality for those weeks before I learned the truth. All I knew was that I had this gorgeous man following me, getting closer, and then becoming my lover. It ended far too soon and ever since, my life has been filled with too much reality.

It's selfish of me to want to go back to the brief time before I knew vampires existed. Before I was one. When I thought Michel was just a very pale European man with a soft French accent who loved stars and walks on the beach.

I DRESS and a servant brings in a tray of food. Michel and I sit and eat our breakfast of eggs, bacon, juice, and coffee. There's a carafe of blood, but despite my hunger for it, I cover my glass.

"No," Michel says, frowning. "You must. You need your strength today. Deprive yourself tomorrow if it makes you feel morally better, but today you have to be strong."

He catches my eye and nods as if to underscore the solemnity of what he says. I know he's right. If I'm going to perform as Soren's conduit, giving him power, I need to be satiated. I take a glass of blood from Michel and drink it down. Immediately, I feel better. The fog from lack of sleep clears. The blood heals me, revitalizing me after a night spent worrying about the future.

"What happens today?" I ask as I drink my coffee.

Michel wipes his mouth with a napkin and sits back. He takes his glass of blood and drinks from it. "A ceremony with a congregation in the cathedral. You'll do your part and help Soren regain some power so he can heal the Twelve. The real fireworks, as he calls them, won't be until he has recovered completely, but he needs to re-establish the Twelve as his disciples."

"He's really going to play up the whole religious angle."

"Of course," Michel says. "It's what he knows. I realize you don't accept any of this for what it is, but regardless, Soren will try to establish himself as an avenging angel come down to Earth in a time of need. He'll paint himself as a savior from the ravages of the plague. He'll call for order and cooperation so that the population complies with Blackstone's curfews and martial law."

"That makes me sick," I say, making a face. "How can you go along with this?"

Michel shakes his head. "You haven't seen the streets, Eve. They've been overtaken by roving bandits. Men are searching for food and weapons and killing each other over them. They're capturing women and using them as sex slaves and servants. Raping them. Killing the ones who fight back. It's chaos. We need something to reestablish order."

"Why not a human police force? Why does it have to be portrayed religiously?"

"Because," Michel says and stands up, finishing the last of his coffee, "people need to feel secure in the power over them or else they'll rebel. When they see Soren perform miracles, they'll feel comforted to think that an angelic being that powerful will protect them and intercede on their behalf."

"But he won't. He's enabling Blackstone's vision of Dominion. All

Soren will do is ensure that the herd is led quietly to its slaughter. They won't be protected from vampires."

"Eve," he cautions and scowls. He leans down to me, his arms on the armrests so that his face is just inches from mine. "What would you prefer? That the people are hunted like wild animals and killed, their throats ripped out? Because that's what will happen if there's no law and order and if vampires revert to our hunter nature without any restriction."

"You mean it would be all-out war? Maybe that's more humane, because then humans will at least have a chance."

"They won't have a chance. Without technology, they're weak. They can't fight us."

"But this? They're like cows in dairies, being milked of their blood or slaughtered and hung, their blood drained."

"It's either that or the hunt."

I shake my head and a sense of despair settles in over me. "Why couldn't vampires be happy with the Treaty? It gave us rights. We survived and were protected."

"Eve, there were factions in the Council working for the extinction of vampires. Your mother felt that way at first and there's still a group working to that end. Were vampires supposed to just let them continue their work? Eventually succeed? Or should they have tried to find another way?"

I sigh and play with my spoon, stirring my coffee slowly. Of course he's right. Some members of the Council were planning on finding a magic bullet to destroy all vampires. That was what my mother initially desired and what she worked for until she met Julien and Michel. I assumed that vampires would be in favor of the goal of curing vampirism, that they'd want to be free from this constant hunger. I want it.

I say nothing more, so Michel rises and leaves me sitting at the small table, my cup of coffee in my hand. I'm so conflicted. Will I be able to live with myself if I go through with this and help Soren?

Can Soren truly prevent chaos? Is being a forced blood donor preferable to being hunted?

Michel selects some clothing from the armoire and lays the ensemble out on the bed. Finally, he turns to me. "Time to get ready for the performance of your life, Eve."

I grip the armrests and grit my teeth. "And if I don't do it?"

"Your father will be tortured. Not killed right away, which would be a mercy."

"Can't someone rescue him?"

Michel holds up a long white gown, inspecting the neckline. "You saw security there. Do you really think we can just waltz up and capture him?"

"Julien could."

He shakes his head. "Not even he could."

"He escaped custody before."

Michel waves me over. I rise and go to his side, taking the gown in my hands. It's made of a white diaphanous material and looks like something a Greek goddess would wear.

"He had modern technology to help him. None of it works any longer. Besides, Blackstone is an expert in security and tactics. I doubt anyone could break into his compound and extract a hostage. Not even Julien," Michel says, emphasizing his twin's name as if he's amused. Or jealous.

"I hate this charade." I take the dress into the bathroom to change, not wanting Michel to watch me. I pull off my clothes and slip on the gown, but I can't reach the zipper.

I go out to the bedroom and turn my back to Michel. "Can you help me with this?"

He says nothing and comes up behind me, zipping up the dress. I adjust the single strap that goes over one shoulder, leaving the other bare.

"If you expect me to wear a laurel leaf crown, I'll rebel," I say when I go to the mirror and check myself out.

Michel comes up behind me and looks at me in the mirror. I can see a sense of possession in his eyes as they move over my image. "Put your hair up to expose your neck."

"Don't tell me Soren's going to bite me or something."

"No, but we all like to see the marks we leave on those we've turned."

"It's Julien's mark," I say. I touch it, remembering the journal entry that described how I got it.

"Only by default. It should've been mine, would've been mine, if Julien hadn't gotten himself staked."

I leave the mirror and go back into the bathroom, twisting my hair up into a bun as I go. I secure it with a few pins while Michel stands in the doorway and watches me.

Finally, I turn to him and smooth the gown. "Do I look the part?"

"Completely," he says, his arms folded. "Soren will be pleased."

I follow him, my stomach in knots about what will happen at the ceremony and if I can go through with it.

CHAPTER 14

Oscar Wilde

When I walk down the staircase to the main entry, Soren is waiting, dressed all in white, bent over a cane. He's so weak, but his eyes – his eyes are steely and filled with intelligence. His robe resembles something from Biblical times and emphasizes his pale hair, skin and ice blue eyes. He raises his eyebrows when he sees me and stands a little taller. I feel self-conscious under his gaze, for I remember wearing something similar to this dress, and of us together, in that brief glimpse of the alternate past Michel showed me. Soren will have seen it as well. It makes me shiver with disgust.

Was Vasquez sending me to Montana to tempt Soren into taking me as his concubine?

"Eve, lovely lovely Eve," he says, his voice cracking. He takes my hand, kissing it with a flourish, his eyes never leaving mine. "How hard it must be for Michel to lose you…"

I clench my teeth and try not to offer up a saucy retort but it takes up every ounce of energy. So Soren knows I won't be with Michel again. At least I don't have to worry about keeping up that ruse any longer.

We take a hydrogen-powered vehicle to the cathedral, a line of trucks with armed men standing on the sides flanking us. The streets are empty, but now and then I see a face in a window or a shadowy figure in a doorway. The people are in hiding as their vampire-angel overlord drives down the street, so I'm surprised when we arrive and see people streaming into the cathedral. I see armed guards with guns standing along the street, as if protecting those attending, but nowhere do I see a single vampire. The guards are all mortal. Still, the people are cowering as they walk down the street, in fear of the threat of violence. Like me, they're hapless pawns in this whole business.

We enter by a rear door. Soren walks slowly, using a cane, his body bent forward as if every step is an enormous effort. The guards form a human wall around Soren, shielding him from the eyes of the public. Is he afraid that they will see him like this, frail and weak and so very unlike an avenging angel?

We return to the small room off the side of the main altar where, once before, we waited for a ceremony to give Soren power. He sits on a chair, catching his breath. Is he even now still fighting off the virus?

Soren waves to Michel and me to come closer.

"Let me tell you how this is going to go. Eve," he instructs, breathless. "You're going to become my high priestess and restore me. Michel, you're going to get your wish. Both of you will illustrate my power to these mortals." Then, he points to Michel. "Go ahead. Fulfill your side of the bargain. Give it to her."

"What bargain?" I say and turn to Michel, but he doesn't meet my eye.

He nods to Soren and takes a small box out of his jacket pocket. I recognize it immediately as the box he tried to give me back at the safe house. Inside is a vial of clear liquid, the waters of life—the drug or compound that makes vampires ascend. Into what they ascend I still don't know, but I know one thing—I won't cooperate.

"If you think I'm going to take that, you're wrong," I say, stepping away from Michel. "I don't need it now. I've taken the daywalking drug."

"Blackstone's drug is temporary," Soren says, pointing to the vial in Michel's hand. "That is permanent."

I hold my hand out, palm facing Michel. "No."

"Make her take it," Soren says, waving at Michel. "Then let's get on with this."

I shake my head. "No, Michel," I plead when he steps forward, his brow furrowed, a determined set to his mouth. "Don't even think about it."

Soren makes a clucking sound with his tongue. "Force it between her lips and make her swallow if you have to. I told you I need her to be ascended for this to work. If you want to be mortal again, this is what you have to do."

"What?" I cry and turn to Soren. "Mortal again? Michel?" I turn back to Michel but he avoids my eyes.

"Just a little bargain Michel and I made," Soren says, his voice filled with gloating. He turns to Michel and smiles conspiratorially. "Go ahead. Fulfill your end of the bargain and I'll fulfill mine. I need something really spectacular to solidify my stature in my flock's eyes. A death and resurrection should do the trick."

"Michel!" I turn to him. "What does he mean, a death and resurrection?"

Michel steps closer to me. "Without hesitation, Eve."

"No, no," I beg, unwilling to cooperate now that I know the terms. "I am not drinking that."

I recall an entry in my journal about the way Soren resurrected a dead man after the bombing in the Middle East. Can he truly bring someone back to life? I remember Michel touching the dead bird we found on the beach, its lifeless body springing back to life, fully healed...

"Eve, I need to show them I can eradicate vampirism," Soren says.

"Michel will be the test subject. I'm going to kill him as a vampire. I'll resurrect him as a mortal. He'll regain his immortal soul and will become a true priest, my high priest. That's my promise to him."

"Why?"

"This is my pledge to the mortals gathered here. If they cooperate with me, follow me, recognize me as God's appointed angel on Earth, I'll rescue them from the evils of Dominion. Your ascension will give me all the power I need to do this, for, as an ascended vampire, your ability to channel their worship will be magnified ten-fold."

"You're going to destroy vampirism?"

Soren shrugs. "Eventually. It will take time, but Blackstone's research is now going to be put to good use. First, I need you to help me. You must drink the waters of life."

"No. I won't," I say again, anger making my voice waver. "I will not drink that. Not unless I have some assurance you won't just use it as a means to encourage Dominion by you and your Twelve."

Soren frowns. "Eve, I'm doing what you want. I'm getting rid of vampirism. Michel will be the first. Oh, and Julien, of course, since they're genetically identical. It's based on the original serum we developed that uses quantum entanglement, and the side effect is that Julien will become mortal as well. Won't he be surprised?"

"Does he know?" I say, a wave of panic filling me. "He doesn't want to be mortal."

"He has no choice. We haven't had time to make it specific enough so that Michel alone dies and is resurrected. Whether he wants it or not, Julien gets mortality as well."

I shake my head, moving back towards the door we entered. "You're going along with this?" I say to Michel. "Against Julien's wishes? He doesn't want to be mortal again."

"It's not his choice to make," Michel answers quietly. "In the end, he'll see that this was the only way."

"You'll lose us both if you do this. Julien won't forgive you. I won't forgive you."

"No hesitation, Eve," he says and his eyes widen. "Please trust me. This is the only way."

I head to the door, but a guard steps in front of it. I turn back to see that Soren has stood up and is leaning on his cane.

"Force her, Michel," he says, his voice low. "Or I'll kill her and wait another generation. I can wait. What's twenty years to me? But you and I both know there'll be a lot of death and pain in the interim."

Michel turns to me and I can see fear in his eyes. "Eve... This is what you wanted. What your mother wanted. What she died for. A cure for vampirism."

He pulls me aside and leans in close, his hands on my arms. The expression on his face is so desperate, I wonder if he's certain or trying to convince himself.

"This is what he'll do," he says. "This will be his promise—to protect humans by eradicating vampires. He'll stop Dominion."

"I don't trust him," I say, my voice low. I try to pull away, but he holds me firmly in place. "He can kill me if he wants. Maybe if he has to wait a generation to get another Adept like me, humans will have fought back. Have you thought of that?"

Michel shakes his head. "If we wait a generation, countless humans will die. Do you really want that decision on your shoulders?"

"If he has the cure, then it means we can find it as well. Why give Soren any power?" I whisper. "He doesn't deserve to have that kind of power. He's weak now. We should deny him when we can."

"Eve, every moment we waste is a moment that the plague spreads and Blackstone enslaves even more mortals, turning them into living blood bags..."

I shake my head, having finally made my decision. I am not going to give this monster any power. I glance over at him. He's weak. He can barely stand on his own. If I give him power now, we're back to where we started with the plague spreading and Soren a threat. Is Michel so determined to be mortal again that he's willing to take the risk?

"Do it," Soren says to Michel from across the room, his voice impatient. He steps down off the dais so that he's next to us. He looks so short and thin compared to Michel, as if the virus is taking all his energy and his body is wasting away.

"It's the only way you'll ever get to be mortal again, Michel." He puts a hand on Michel's shoulder. "Giving you back your mortality is more than I should do, considering what you did to Marguerite. No one can do this except me and you know it. I won't turn you unless you make her ascend. If you do, I'll turn you right now. I have the cure for you right here." He pulls out a vial and holds it out so Michel can see it.

Michel frowns but says nothing.

"Think of it," Soren says, his voice warm, one hand cupping Michel's cheek with clear affection. "You could finally get what you want. Be a real priest again. Administer to a flock. Die a natural death. I can turn you. You force Eve, she helps me get power, and in return, I turn you."

Michel can't take his eyes off the vial in Soren's hand.

"Michel!" I exclaim and go to his side, taking his hand in mine. "This could be a trap, playing on your desire to be mortal again. How do you know he won't kill you and leave you dead? Don't do this…"

"Eve…" he says, shaking his head slowly. His eyes are wet and I know he's close to breaking. "How can you ask me to say no to this?"

"Will you cure me as well?" I say to Soren.

"It all depends on how well you obey me, Eve. You tried to kill me just a few short weeks ago. You do what I need and I'll consider it."

I turn back to Michel. "Have you known all along this would happen?" I say, my throat choked with fear. "Is this what you've been waiting for?"

"It's one possible future. It's by far the best possible future. For all of us. This is why I'm helping him. He's the only way to prevent Dominion from taking hold completely. Believe me, Eve. If I could see any other way…"

I'm almost at the breaking point, shocked and horrified that he's choosing death and trusting that Soren will resurrect him.

"Michel," I say, squeezing his arm. "I don't want to ascend."

He blinks, smiling at me, but there's a distant look in his eyes. "It will all be okay, Eve. You don't have to trust Soren. Just trust me."

I turn, unwilling to stand here and not fight back, and try to escape. He motions to the guards, who grab me before I can fall into fight mode. I try to escape their grip, but they're obviously ascended and I'm helpless. Michel stands before me with the vial in his hands. He breaks the tip off and then points to one of the guards.

"Hold her head still."

The guard does as Michel commands, taking hold of my head while the other holds my arms. I bite down hard, trying to prevent Michel from opening my mouth.

"Plug her nose," Michel says and the guard complies, one hand holding my chin and the other plugging my nose. Soon, I'm unable to breathe unless I open my mouth. I try not to, holding out as long as I can, but finally I gasp and Michel pours the liquid between my lips, then holds my mouth shut so that I have to swallow. His cheeks are wet, his eyes and nose red, but his jaw is set firmly and I know there's no fighting him now.

When I finally swallow, Michel motions to the guards and they release me. I cough and sputter, spitting out whatever I can, but I've swallowed most of the liquid.

"You shouldn't have," I say and wipe my mouth on the back of my hand. "I'll never forgive you."

"Never is a long time."

"Oh, cut the theatrics," Soren says. He turns to me, his eyes widening. "You should be feeling it very soon." His face betrays real interest, as if he's excited that I'm now going to ascend or whatever it is that the drug does.

I stand horrified, scowling at Michel, who says nothing.

How could he? Forcing ascension on me so he can be mortal again? Making me into everything I always wanted to destroy, and he gets exactly what he wants? He must know this will drive a wedge between us. Does he really think this is the only way to save us all?

The look on his face says it all. From across the room, I can feel his emotions like we're touching. Hope. Excitement. But also guilt.

"You should feel guilty," I say to him, my fists clenched. "I'll never forgive you if anything bad happens to Julien."

"Julien will be fine, Eve. This has to happen," he says, his voice soft. "One day, you'll understand."

"Stop with the vision bullshit," I respond, tears in my eyes. "You just want to be mortal again."

"I do. But this will save us all."

While I'm wiping my eyes, I start to feel strange. It begins in my chest—a feeling of warmth spreads out and up to my face and head. A wave of euphoria, like a rush of some powerful drug, flows through me, making me gasp out loud. Everything becomes extremely bright all of a sudden, as if there's too much sunlight. It reminds me of those pictures of ultraviolet vision, the edges of every object blurring with a fuzzy, bright pink glow. I look at Michel's face and it shines as if it's made of crystal, his eyes two blue diamonds.

"Oh, God," I say and lean against the nearest wall for support, my legs feeling so wobbly I could fall to my knees. I'm breathing fast, panting as wave after wave of euphoria passes through me, spreading out from my chest with every beat of my heart, down my legs and then up to my head. I feel as if the very roots of my hair are standing on end. Gooseflesh covers my entire body.

I'm lost in this experience, unable to speak or do anything but feel whatever it is that is happening to me. I hear Michel and Soren speaking, but it's as if they're underwater, their voices muted, drowned out by these other overwhelming sensory experiences.

"Get her blood and then the guards will bring her to the altar. You can play your part afterwards."

Michel takes my wrist and cuts it with a sharp knife. The pain is brief and bright but overwhelmed very quickly by the strange sensations in my body. I watch, unconcerned, as my blood drips into the chalice. He takes the same knife and slices Soren's forearm; a few drops of his blood fall into the chalice to mingle with mine. Then Michel hands it to me, holding it up to my lips. I drink it down, no longer having the will to fight.

Two guards enter the small room, leading a woman in a gossamer-thin gown whose hands are tied with rope.

"Go ahead," Soren says to Michel. He points to the woman. "Drink your fill since it will be your last kill."

"I won't kill her," Michel says as he approaches the woman.

"Do it. I'll revive her in front of the congregation. You know—double their pleasure. Save an innocent from the monster who took her life, then take the monster's life in retribution."

Michel approaches the young woman, who cowers in fear when she sees him transformed into the hunter, his eyes bloodshot and his teeth long. "Don't be afraid," he says, his voice soft. "You'll be fine."

He leans down and she struggles for only a moment; his touch calms her. She leans back, exposing her neck to him. Michel bites down hard, drinking her blood. When he pulls away, blood drips down his chin, his teeth still sharp but now bloody. He hands the woman to a guard, who picks up her limp body. Another guard approaches with heavy chains and shackles in his hand.

I watch dumbfounded as the guards fasten the iron bands around Michel's wrists; I'm surprised that he complies without fighting. He tests the shackles and then nods in approval. Another guard comes to me and slips one of his arms around my waist, practically lifting me up and carrying me out of the room.

Our strange procession makes its way into the cathedral to the altar, the guard holding the dead body of the woman Michel killed, another carrying me, and finally, two guards pulling Michel in chains. I'm overtaken with awe when we enter the sanctuary and climb the stairs to the high altar. It's amazing, with high flying buttresses on all sides and gilded columns. The light streams in through arched stained glass windows that appear to me like a million prisms. An organ plays something soft and dreamy and I can feel the music vibrating inside my body.

The guard deposits me at the base of the high altar. Every sense is heightened and despite my horror at watching Michel kill the young woman, my mind is overwhelmed. I stand facing the rows of pews, looking at the people, their faces shining like beacons of twinkling light. I hear the voices of a choir floating on the air, making my throat choke with emotion.

I don't know what's happening around me, so high on whatever drug they've given me, but I can see people pointing at me, covering their mouths as if in awe. I feel it from everyone in the congregation—wonder and terror. They're all looking at me, pointing and whispering, and I feel so strange, as if I'm now completely different. I've transformed into something else, something otherworldly. I look around, watching what's happening with a detachment that surprises me, but I don't care to do anything at the moment except to experience it.

Soren enters like an emperor, carried on a large, ornate chair with gilded arms and legs. The congregation watches and soon they start to "ooh" and "ahh" when they see him for while he was a small, frail, pale man in the other room, he too, has transformed. He went from frail to mighty, from old and weak to young and strong and beautiful, empowered by sharing blood with me. I feel the congregation's amazement and it makes me even more emotional. As I watch, Soren actually enlarges before us, the bright light flowing from him even brighter, if that's possible.

The guards place the chair on the raised dais of the high altar and Soren rises, standing before the congregation, his huge white wings spreading out to full width behind him. I feel the link between all of us—Soren and the congregation—and the intensity almost makes me pass out.

He's an impressive sight, even to me.

The other guards pull a now resistant Michel into the room and he fights as if he doesn't want to comply. He looks a sight, the only one dressed in black, for everyone else is in white. I can barely stand to watch, but it's such a performance, I'm unable to look away.

My heart is beating far too fast. I see Michel on his knees facing the congregation, his bloody mouth and chin stark against his pale face. Soren stands tall before us, fully restored, wings blazing glory behind him. He comes to my side and holds my hand, looking into my eyes, and I see him now as he really is. Bright white light comes from him like he's lit up from the inside.

Do you feel it, Eve? Do you feel this bliss? he says to me telepathically, so only I can hear it. *I know you do, for I feel it with you.*

I can feel the bliss, but I know it's nothing more than the effects of a drug. It's the neurotransmitters in my brain lighting up, nothing more. I refuse to believe it's anything spiritual or based on faith, for I have none.

Then he turns me so that I face the congregation, saying words that I don't hear because another wave of elation flows through me. Whatever he says, it makes the people gathered release a collective 'ahh' like it's something miraculous. He calls me his new angel.

He turns back to Michel and motions to the guards, who drag Michel over so that he is now on his knees at Soren's feet. Soren lays a hand on Michel's head like he's giving some kind of blessing. I can't understand what he's saying but then I remember…

"See this beast before you. A vampire. See the innocent he killed, caught in the act brazenly flaunting his power." Soren nods to Michel and Michel lifts the tiny ampoule to his lips and drinks it quickly. No one but Soren and I can see him do it, for Michel's back is to the congregation.

Soren turns Michel towards them and Michel bares his bloody teeth, showing them he's a vampire and the many among the congregation cower, their faces fearful, and a murmur arises. I feel their fear from this distance.

"This is the threat before humans—the threat of vampire rule. I tell you this now," Soren says, his voice booming through the cathedral, "I am the only one who can save you from this threat. But in turn, you must swear your loyalty to me. To the Church."

He forces Michel to his knees and places his hands on Michel's shoulders. A bright light shines from his hands.

"I destroy you, vampire," he says, his voice theatric and full of emotion like some circus ringmaster or snake oil salesman. "I cast you out of this body and into the abyss!"

A huge flash of light brightens the interior of the cathedral so we're all momentarily blinded. Of course, I know that he's only pretending to do it with his power; it was the drug Soren gave him and Michel took that will have an effect. Soren wants the congregation to think he's responsible for "exorcising" the evil.

Enough sense has returned to me that I recognize the act taking place before me for what it is. Soren and Michel have conspired to make those gathered believe Soren is casting out a demon, purifying Michel. I turn to watch Soren, my mind now cleared. He's enjoying this performance. The more awe the people feel, the more power he gets directly through me.

He's a power-hungry monster.

Why is Michel going along with this?

Michel coughs after a moment and grabs his throat. Soren bends down to Michel and whispers to him, but I can't hear what he's saying. Michel's face is more pale than normal, and he's grabbing his throat as if he can't breathe. I'm momentarily afraid that Soren is killing him now that he got what he wanted—truly killing him. And why not? Soren has his power once more and a congregation in awe of him.

Soren hates Michel for killing Marguerite. He's been torturing Michel all these centuries in repayment for his loss. It makes sense that he'd want to kill Michel and use me to do it.

I cover my mouth and stifle a sob. Michel was so foolish to believe that Soren would give him what he wanted most of all. It would make Soren only too happy to destroy Michel and finally get his revenge.

Michel falls to his hands and knees, vomiting blood onto the ground before Soren, the stone beneath him stained red.

"Begone, monster!" Soren shouts, an aura of light around him bright as an acetylene torch, a crackling sound and scent of sulfur in the air.

"No!" I manage, but my voice is barely above a whisper. I reach out, wanting to go to Michel, to help him, but I can't move. The guards behind me hold me back.

The light dims and Soren kicks Michel's body over with a booted foot so that Michel is on his back, his eyes staring straight ahead, his lips bloody.

My heart squeezes. Is he dying? Is he already dead?

Before us, Michel lets out one last gasp and a black vapor is expelled from his open mouth, the mist rising up in the air and then evaporating before us.

Michel himself changes. At first, it's almost imperceptible, but then I can see with my vampire-keen eyes. His skin changes from pale white to flushed pink and then bluish-white in death. His teeth recede in length and before our eyes, he transforms from vampire to mortal.

"Is there a physician amongst you?" Soren says, his voice booming. "Come up and see the power I alone wield."

People turn and examine each other. Finally, a heavyset man with a beard and shaved head steps forward, urged on by others around him.

"And you are?" Soren says to the man, who approaches the raised altar.

"I'm a doctor."

"Check him and see if he's truly dead."

The man kneels down to Michel and presses two fingers on Michel's neck. He's still for a moment. Finally, he glances up at Soren and shakes his head.

"There's no pulse." Then, the man bends down and puts his hand on Michel's chest, his ear to Michel's lips. "He's not breathing," the man says, standing up. "He's dead."

Soren nods. "And the woman?"

The bearded man goes to the woman, who likewise lies on the red carpet on the altar floor. He checks for a pulse and signs of breathing but shakes his head again.

"She's dead."

"Observe, all of you who have eyes to see," Soren says and kneels down to the woman, taking her hand in one of his and then laying his other hand on her forehead. He closes his eyes, and soon a bright light emanates from his hand, passing into her. Soren's face is scrunched up as if he's in pain, struggling.

Finally, the woman's back arches and she inhales a long, gasping breath.

We all stand in mute awe at this. I don't know what to think, except that she must not have been dead.

She must not have been.

There's no other explanation. She must have been drugged with something that only makes her appear to be dead. There are medicines that mimic death, that slow the heart and respirations down so much that people have been mistaken for dead before. That must be what he used.

Still, the congregation surges forward, standing on the stairs leading to the high altar, crowding around them. They stare down at Soren, who is speaking softly to the woman, her neck healing from the bloody wound before our eyes.

Soren lets go of her hand and stands up fully.

"This is what I promise if you follow me," he says. "I will destroy every vampire in existence. I will protect those of you from their predation. You need no longer fear them if you follow me. Dominion will be defeated if we stand together. But you all must swear allegiance to me." He says nothing for a moment and a silence descends over the cathedral. "You must accept me as your only leader."

The guard helps the woman up and she stands beside a fallen Michel, who lies motionless on the floor. Soren isn't resurrecting Michel like he promised, and panic fills me. Michel's dead.

He's truly dead and Soren is standing over his body like a conquering warlord.

"Bring him back!" I manage to say, but my voice is hardly there; I'm still so weak from whatever drug Soren has given me.

I try to go to Michel, but I'm unable to escape and the guards easily restrain me, their hands gripping my arms. I stand there weeping, the realization that Soren has tricked Michel hitting me. He's betrayed him. Now Michel is dead, I'm an abomination, Soren has regained his power, and the people are kneeling down as a group before him.

The last thing I see through blurry eyes as they drag me away from the altar and out of the cathedral is Michel's dead body, his eyes staring lifelessly towards the ceiling, one of Soren's leather boots on his chest.

Above his dead body, Soren smiles.

CHAPTER 15

Honore de Balzac

The guard drags me to the vehicle and pushes me into the back seat, locking the door behind me so I can't escape. Now that my body has adjusted to the drug Michel forced me to drink, my mind is clearer and the realization that Soren has tricked Michel sinks in.

I weep, my face in my hands, giving in to sorrow. Soren's scientists must have developed a drug that destroys vampirism—the dream of my mother and of the Council, who hoped to end vampirism for good. Unlike the previous nanovirus, it doesn't destroy the vampire's body. It isn't a real cure, though, because it kills the victim.

If Soren has succeeded, there'll be no need for the Council or the Treaty of Clairveaux. There'll be no need for Adepts and the SCU. Michel and Julien and all the vampires in existence—me included—will be destroyed.

I should be happy at the prospect of no longer being a vampire, but all I can do is cry.

My mother hoped to develop a drug that would reverse vampirism, but it appears that Soren's drug kills the recipient and doesn't merely eradicate the vampire genes. I can see how that might appeal to the masses, who live in fear of vampires (and rightfully so). They've been terrorized for weeks since the plague spread and vampires finally felt safe enough to emerge from the safety of the shadows, but still...

The fear that must have gripped humans as they realized a long-held fear—vampires! Here!—was real...

I've always known of the existence of vampires and that I could die from one the way my mother did. But your average human thought they were the product of fantasy, of vivid imaginations and medieval ignorance.

Now they know better.

A side door opens and two guards carry Michel's body out of the cathedral. I cover my mouth in horror. Although I was furious that Michel was willing to turn me into an ascended vampire, I can't stand the thought that he's dead. I weep as I watch them load his body into the rear seat of the vehicle in front of me, laying him down uncere-moniously and closing the doors afterwards. They stand beside the vehicle and one lights up a cigarette, then passes one to his compan-ion. They smoke in silence, their eyes scanning the street and buildings.

After another few moments, the cathedral door opens once more and Soren exits, making his way toward the vehicle where the guards placed Michel's body. A guard opens the door and Soren sits in the front seat with a driver beside him. The convoy of vehicles parades away from Holy Cross Cathedral just as the front doors open and the masses begin to emerge. They're busy speaking to each other, pointing when they see Soren drive off. The reverence they feel for him is visible in the wideness to their eyes.

A murmur ripples through the crowd as they recognize him and even now I feel it flow through me, no doubt flowing directly into

Soren. They will go back to their homes and neighborhoods to tell the story of what happened here tonight—that Soren is an avenging angel come to rid the world of the vampire threat. That he destroyed a vampire before their very eyes and resurrected his victim. That he promised to destroy all vampires if the humans swore allegiance to him.

A new mythology will arise because of this night. That truth, the knowledge that I am a part of it, sinks in and horrifies me. The very last thing in the world I want is to be part of some cult that worships Soren.

I thought this plan of Michel's and Julien's would result in the defeat of both Soren and Blackstone. Now, I'm afraid it has meant the death of both twins.

We drive through the streets towards Soren's compound in silence, and when we pull up, one of the guards opens my door. I emerge onto the driveway behind Soren's vehicle, running to the car to try to open the back door, where Michel's body lies. He's still, his arms above his head, his eyes half-lidded. Soren gets out of the front seat and I turn to him, wanting to strike him, wishing I had some kind of weapon so I could kill him.

"You lied!" I scream and try to hit his chest but he grabs me easily, my wrists in each of his hands. "You said you'd make him mortal, not kill him!"

He's smiling but I can see an edge of anger in his eyes. "Cut the theatrics, Eve. I'm going to bring him back. I made a promise, and Michel delivered. So now I will as well."

Soren drags me away while one of the guards opens the door and pulls out Michel's body from the vehicle. Soren has wrapped his arms around me from behind, still holding onto my wrists, so that I'm restrained.

"You don't realize how much you love someone until they're gone, do you, Eve?" he says, his lips next to my ear. "Now you know how I felt when Michel killed my Marguerite. By all rights, I should leave him dead, but that would punish you instead of him. So I'll revive him. He still has a part to play in this little story."

We follow the guard with Michel's body into the mansion, through the foyer, and down the hall to Soren's study.

"Place him on the sofa," Soren says, pointing to an ornate sofa in gold and white brocade beside a wall of books.

The guards comply and lay Michel's body there. I don't want to look, to see his dead body, but I can't look away. What is he going to do now?

Soren turns and smiles conspiratorially. "Watch this."

He sits on the sofa beside Michel and motions me over. "Come here, Eve, and watch me resurrect your beloved. Oh, and this affects Julien as well, since the two of them are linked temporally by the serum."

I step closer, my heart racing.

"Check first, so you know for yourself that he is truly dead. Feel for a pulse."

I do, placing my two fingers on Michel's neck. I feel nothing. Then I take Michel's wrist and check for a pulse there. Nothing. His body is even starting to get cold, his cheeks cool to the touch. He's not breathing.

He truly is dead.

"Julien is dead as well? Right now?"

Soren nods. "They're linked. What happened to Michel also happened to Julien."

"You used Blackstone's serum?"

"Modified, but yes. Cooperation with your enemies for the short term is often beneficial."

I cover my mouth, my heart racing to think that Julien is also dead. I watch as Soren turns Michel's head to face him. He cups Michel's cheek in one hand and lays the other on his chest.

"Michel," he says, his voice soft. "*Nous revenir.* Come back to us." A bright light shines from under Soren's hands and he leans closer, repeating the words. "*Revenez à moi, Michel.*" He presses on Michel's chest and shakes him. "Come back to me."

Before our eyes, Michel takes in a huge breath, his chest straining and his back arching. His eyelids flutter and then he focuses on Soren.

"Yes, Michel. You're back. Good," Soren says and smiles.

Michel makes a face as if he's in pain and then tries to sit up. "What happened?" he asks, blinking rapidly. "I feel…" He frowns and shakes his head as if confused. He reaches up and touches his face, then looks at his hand like he's never seen it before. "Did you…"

"Yes," Soren says and I'm so shocked, I can't do anything but stand there with my hand over my mouth in disbelief. "You're mortal. I've given you your wish."

"And Julien?"

"Him as well, although I suspect he won't be nearly as happy about it as you are."

Michel turns and sees me. "Eve…"

I cover my mouth with both hands, tears blurring my eyes.

He's mortal.

I can see a flush in his cheeks for the first time since I met him, his color normal. He no longer has that pale skin I've grown accustomed to, and he looks even more beautiful, if that's possible.

"I'm mortal."

"Yes," Soren says, chuckling. "You're mortal. Eve still can't believe it, for she doesn't really believe I can do such things. But you know it to be true and that's why you agreed to my little plan."

"Yes," Michel says. "I know what you are."

Soren stands up, leaving Michel to slide his legs over the edge of the sofa so that he can sit up. Michel runs his fingers through his hair and down his chest, as if checking to see what it feels like to be mortal once more.

"Michel," I say, kneeling down on the floor at his feet, my joy that he's actually alive overwhelming my earlier anger at him for forcing ascension on me. "You're mortal."

He smiles. "I am." He takes in a breath and there are tears in his eyes. "Finally."

I can't help myself and I wrap my arms around him as I kneel between his spread legs. I bury my face in his neck and let myself cry, really cry, hard.

Finally, when I've regained control, I pull back. "I thought you were dead," I say, my voice catching. "I didn't believe he could do it."

"Now you know." Michel cups my face with his hands. "You have to trust me, Eve. You have to know I'm only doing what's best."

I nod and wipe my eyes, smiling through my tears.

He kisses me, his kiss tender. I kiss him back, needing to feel his arms around me, his mouth on mine. Of course, being so close to him, I smell his blood and it smells like heaven. For the first time, I know how he must have felt all that time when I was still mortal and we were lovers. The bloodlust is never far from the surface and it competes with my emotions.

I turn to Soren, wiping my eyes. "Make me mortal, too."

Soren shakes his head, his eyes half-closed. "Not in the cards just yet, Eve. I need you as you are."

I stand up and face him. "What do you need from me?"

"I need you to help me resurrect my brethren," Soren says. Then he turns to Michel. "Now you have your most fervent wish. You can become a priest once more, if that's your desire. And in my church, celibacy is optional, so you two can go back at it, if you so desire."

Soren wags his eyebrows at me suggestively and I make a face, turning back to see Michel's response.

Michel frowns. "Priests are celibate. You're not God, Soren, however much you'd like us to think so. If I'm a priest, it will be of the one true Church."

"Have it your way," Soren says, shrugging. "I'm starting my own church, or at least taking over the Catholic Church in America, and in my church, celibacy is optional. So if you choose it, it will be entirely your own decision. Eve can always go to Julien if she needs some lovin.'" Soren grins lasciviously at me.

"I understand," Michel says. "Besides, Eve has already chosen for me."

Michel looks in my eyes and of course, he's right. I did choose. I know that has been his desire for centuries since he was turned into a vampire. To be mortal again, to return to the priesthood and to die at the end of a life of service to the Church.

Now is his chance.

Tears blur my eyes.

"It's for the best, then." I wipe my eyes and stand up, leaving him seated on the sofa.

We'll see how long his celibacy lasts, Soren says to me in his mind, our blood connection still in action. *He won't be able to resist you forever, Eve, if you still want him.*

I turn to him and frown, but he merely smiles as if he's amused by the idea of me trying to seduce Michel to break his vows.

Soren passes me. *You're the only woman he's truly ever wanted. I doubt it will be too hard to seduce him away from the priesthood. If you really want him, that is. You do have Julien.*

He wags his brows briefly in that way that infuriates me.

I don't want to communicate like this with him. I don't want him to think I welcome this intimate connection.

"I'll respect his vows," I say out loud, unable to keep a touch of acid from my voice. "Unlike Marguerite. If she had, she'd probably still be alive. She had Julien as her slave. She didn't need Michel as well, especially considering his vows."

"She was a needy little thing," Soren says aloud, and I'm thankful he's given in to my refusal to do the mind-meld thing. He frowns at me, and I wonder if I haven't gone too far, but then he shrugs and speaks quietly with a guard standing by the door. The guard leaves and the three of us are now alone in the cavernous library.

The door opens and a servant brings in a trolley with a tray of food. "I've ordered some food for Michel. He must be hungry for something real now that he has no bloodlust."

Michel sits at the table, peeking under the silver domes to see the food. He wastes no time and starts to cut the meat and eat, a look of relish on his face. He smiles, and it's so full of pure joy that I can't help but smile with him. He really is happy to be mortal again, to live free of the burning need for blood that plagues us every moment of the day.

"After I'm done, I want to go for a walk," he says and shovels a forkful of meat into his mouth. He chews for a moment and nods. "I can't wait to see the stars. Feel the sun on my face."

"You'll need protection," Soren says, seemingly amused at Michel's newfound enthusiasm for life. "Eve can look after you. She's good with a stake and sword, or so I hear. Now that she's ascended, she's even more formidable. I know she'll protect you. Imagine that! Eve protecting a mortal Michel as he administers to his new flock. How ironic, considering that she's the one who tempted him out of his pseudo-celibacy."

"I didn't tempt him. He tempted himself."

Soren smiles. *Oh, don't tell me you didn't lust after him, Eve. Why, I know you did. He knew as well, which is why he broke down. It's silly, anyway—celibacy. Complete waste of time. A human ideal, not one of God.*

Michel is still busy eating, taken by his new existence free from bloodlust. "I wonder how Julien is," Michel says as he finishes a piece of meat.

It's then I remember that the serum Michel took would have changed Julien as well. I turn to Soren. "Is Julien mortal as well?"

Soren pours himself a glass of blood. "Whatever happened to Michel happened to Julien. I imagine he's waking up with a bad headache and no longer feels the need to bite whatever human he's near."

"You might want to check on him, Eve," Soren says matter-of-factly. "In fact, I insist. Hopefully, when he started to feel strange, he had the good sense to lie down or else who knows where you'll find him. Go get him and bring him to me. I'm sure the brothers would like to spend their first days as mortals together. But I want you back here for Friday mass. I'll send one of my guards with you on the trip."

"You took a big risk. What if he'd been doing something dangerous? Like driving a vehicle?"

"Seeing as he didn't see fit to come to me, that was the risk he took," Soren replies. "I'm aware of his ties to Blackstone and have been for a while now. You can't hide anything from me, Eve, so don't bother trying." With a wave of his hand, Soren dismisses us and sits down at his desk.

"Let's go," I say to Michel, who has finished his plate.

He looks at me expectantly. "I want to go to the cathedral first. Say a mass."

I can't believe it. "Michel… What about Julien?"

He exhales. "In the morning. He's fine, Eve. Soren has someone watching over the apartment. I have to sleep and so do you. We'll go in the morning."

I shake my head. He really is going to be a priest again. The thought hurts in a way that surprises me. It hurts to think he's so ready, and happy, to give me up and return to the Church. That being a priest is more important to him than I am.

I bite my cheek to stop the tears that sting the corners of my eyes and together we leave Soren behind.

Michel walks me to my room and leaves me without a word, but I hear the key in the lock when the door closes. He's locking me in to prevent me from leaving.

I lie back on my bed, staring at the ornate tapestry design of the canopy. Cabbage roses and vines and birds flying in the sky.

I don't sleep for one moment. Whatever has happened to me has made me too hyped up to relax.

CHAPTER 16

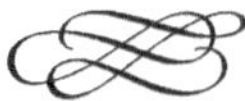

"In every living thing there is the desire for love."

D. H. Lawrence

I've been out of bed for an hour, when Michel returns.

He sits across from me, dressed in a priest's vestments, a wooden cross hangs around his neck on a leather strap. "I know you're not very happy with me."

"That's an understatement." I can tell he's treading carefully with me. I'd almost forgotten I'm ascended and it's because of him. I wonder if he's waiting for me to blow up at him.

"Are you going to ever speak to me again?"

I shrug, my emotions kept bottled up because I fear if I let up for even a moment, I won't be able to stop crying.

I stand up. "Let's go."

He sighs, as if he wanted to have it out with me, but I can't do it. I can't argue with him any longer.

We leave the mansion without another word and take the vehicle into Boston and the safe house where Julien is staying. Michel seems happier than I've ever seen him, watching the scenery as we drive as if seeing it for the first time.

"I forgot how beautiful everything is," he says, his voice reverent. "Without bloodlust…" He turns to me. "How beautiful you are."

Despite my anger, my heart squeezes at that. I find I'm as entranced as he is by the beauty of the scenery as we drive back to the safe house. He's seeing it again for the first time as a mortal. I'm seeing it for the first time with my enhanced senses as a monster.

Finally, I can't hold back. "What the hell am I, Michel?" I turn to face him. "I hate this. It means I'm an even more powerful tool for Soren. How could you go along with this? Just so you could be a mortal again? What about the rest of the world?"

Michel doesn't look at me. "I know you won't understand, so I won't bother arguing with you about it. Just know that whatever I do, I do for the rest of the world. Not me."

"I find that hard to believe, seeing as you told me when we first met that all you wanted was to become a mortal again and return to the priesthood. You said you'd do it in a second. Well, Soren gave you that chance and you've lost me because of it."

Michel sighs beside me. "Hadn't I already lost you? To Julien?"

I say nothing. What can I say? He's right.

"Tell me why you did it," I implore. "Make me understand."

He shakes his head. "I can't." He turns to face me and smiles, but it's not a happy smile. It's forced. "Back to the same old trap—if I tell you, it kills you. I don't want that. I don't want us to have to wait another twenty years for Soren to create another you."

"Maybe the next me will have a better life than I had."

Michel exhales loudly. "No," he says, his voice low. "She has a far worse life than you, growing up under Dominion, living in the dark corners of the world until Soren finds her and has her for his own pet. She and I don't meet until she's already his creature. We're never lovers."

"What about Julien?"

He stares out the window in silence for a moment. "She does meet him. Of course, they become lovers." Then he turns back to me. "But it doesn't end well for either her or me."

I move away from him, closer to the door.

He grabs my hand and squeezes. "Don't be too mad at me. It's only because I love you more than anything that I'm doing any of this."

As much as I would like to, I can't take my hand away because he's staring at me with those beautiful blue eyes and his expression is so sincere…

I believe him when he says that. I just don't believe that he can control the future the way he thinks he can.

We drive the rest of the way in silence, but he keeps my hand in his as if he can't bear to let go.

We arrive in the neighborhood that surrounds the safe house and Michel speaks with each guard we meet. None of them have seen Julien. They have heard nothing and assumed he was busy and waiting for our return. I'm impatient to get to the safe house and make sure Julien is okay. I want to run past the guards and into the building, but I have to wait. We have to spend time at each checkpoint.

When we're finally at the safe house, I rush up the stairs to the apartment ahead of Michel and bang on the door.

"Julien!"

Michel joins me at the door.

"He's not answering," I say, panic in my voice.

"Don't worry," he says. "Julien is fine."

I do worry, banging on the door, determined to break it down if Julien doesn't answer.

Michel finally takes out his key and opens the door. I rush in, searching the apartment, and find Julien on his bed on his stomach, pillows over his head. His skin is pink and warm when I touch him.

He's asleep. There's an empty bottle of merlot on the night table.

He must have been drunk last night, celebrating his newfound mortality. Or mourning his lost immortality. With Julien, I have a suspicion it was the latter.

"Julien," I say softly and sit on the bed beside him. I lay a hand on his naked back and he feels so vibrant, so alive. I can feel his heartbeat under my hand, slow and steady.

"Julien," I say again, louder.

He startles and rolls over, a gun in his hand. He must have had it under the pillow.

"Eve!" he exclaims and puts the gun down. He sits up and grabs me, pulling me into a hug.

I hug him back, my arms around his neck, my hands on the smooth, warm skin of his shoulders. He smells so good and feels so good… Of course, being so close to a mortal makes my bloodlust even more intense and I have to pull away, almost panting from it.

"You ascended…" he says and frowns.

I turn my head slightly and I see them—white wings with huge feathers. I find that I can control them with my mind and flex them, amazed that I hadn't noticed them before.

"I didn't call them up," I say. "Do they just materialize at random times?"

Julien shakes his head. "When you're emotional. You can also manifest them at will, if you want to impress someone." He grins at me and it's the old Julien—playful, cheerful, and flirty. "I suppose you want to bite me. It's wonderful to not feel bloodlust."

"I was afraid you'd be upset to be mortal again."

He shrugs. "I was a bit upset at first," he says and picks up the empty wine bottle from the bed. "It took a bit of the red stuff to convince me mortality was acceptable." He puts the empty bottle back on the side of the bed and turns to me. "Besides, Michel said this has to happen."

"Michel told you that Soren would make you mortal?"

Julien glances at Michel, who's leaning against the doorjamb, his arms crossed. Michel's face is unreadable.

"Michel told me a few possible versions of what was going to happen," Julien admits and a moment passes between the twins.

"This," Julien says and holds out his arms, "was one of the possible futures. Of course, I didn't believe him. I guess I was wrong not to." He shrugs again. "I'm okay with what has to happen. I believe him now."

"I thought you'd want to be a vampire again."

"Not now," he says, sighing. "Maybe in the future."

"So you know what's going to happen as well?"

"We only know a few possible outcomes," Michel says from the door. "Now that I'm mortal, I don't see anything. It's probably better that way. I know some threads of what could happen. I know what choices I have to make. But I can't control anyone else, so I'm as blind as the rest of you."

I sigh and take in a deep breath, examining Julien, who sits beside me, naked except for his boxer briefs.

"I need some blood," I say.

Julien gives me a half-grin. "I'd let you drink some of mine, but now that I'm mortal, I'm kind of partial to it. There's some in the refrigerator."

I get up and pass Michel, who follows me into the kitchen. I take out a bottle of blood and remove the metal cap, drinking it down without stopping. I'm going to need all the blood I can get to stop the craving I have to bite both of them.

When I finish, I drink a glass of water to clean my mouth and turn to see them both standing in the doorway to the kitchen, watching me with interest.

"So, how does it feel to be mortal again and not need blood?" I ask.

"Amazing," Julien answers, smiling. "I didn't think I'd be happy, but I am. I'm going to get dressed and go for a run."

"We have to take you back to Soren," Michel says. "He wants you with us there."

"I don't think so," Julien replies, shaking his head.

"You have to," I say, my voice pleading. "If you don't, Soren said he'll kill Michel."

Julien takes in a deep breath. "Fuck." He stands with his hands on his hips for a moment, staring out the window. "All right," he says and then turns to Michel. "So this is the way you're going to play it?"

Michel nods. "Has to be this way."

Julien nods slowly, thoughtfully. "Okay. But I can at least go for a run, breathe in some fresh air? I need it after last night. I'll be quick." He jogs for the bathroom, leaving Michel and me alone.

Michel turns to me, staring at me. "Things are going to happen that will shock you, Eve," he says. "You'll understand everything once they do."

I shrug and move past him. "Good. Finally. I've been kept in the dark—deliberately—for too long." I go to the living room and sit on the sofa, relaxing as the blood goes through my system. The euphoria from it makes my heart race.

Michel follows me. "If I had a real choice, I would have taken you to Wales long ago, Eve. None of this was my choice. It's what's necessary."

"So you keep saying."

"You'll finally know the truth. All of it."

"I'm waiting," I say, impatient with all the talk, distracted by the way the blood makes me feel. "I want to believe you, Michel, but I can't. I need evidence."

He smiles without speaking and goes to the window, looking out at the street below. "It'll take years for the world to recover," he says after a while. "To reverse the effects of the plague. Things will never be the same, though. It will be a new world. Hopefully, better."

"How can it be better after so many have died? That has to leave a scar on those who survive."

"People are resilient," Michel replies. "Each new human starts out fresh. Their goodness will resurface. I have faith."

"I don't. Things can actually get worse."

Michel sits on the sofa beside me. "I have faith, even if you don't." He smiles at me softly.

What can I say in response? Of course he has faith. That's Michel.

Julien emerges from his room, dressed in sweats and a hoodie. He bends down to lace up his boots. "These aren't the best to run in but there are no sneakers anymore because they all used plastic or latex. I might be able to find some old sneakers in a shoe museum but until then, these old military boots will have to do." He laughs, standing up. His gaze passes between Michel and me. "I'll be back."

"You'll do that thing I asked you?" Michel asks quietly.

Julien nods. "It'll be done."

"What thing?" I say and turn to Michel.

"Just a security thing."

"Be careful," I say, turning back to Julien, realizing that he's mortal now and can die with frightening ease.

"I'll be fine," he assures me, that grin starting, his blue eyes twinkling. "In case you forgot, I have handlers."

He leaves us sitting in silence.

"So now what?" I say to Michel after a moment.

He turns to me, his expression intense. He's resting his head on his hand, watching me.

"Now we do our duty."

"I wish you'd tell me."

"You'll know soon enough."

I sigh and stand up, not wanting to sit so close to him. Despite the blood I just drank, I still want him. I have this craving to pull him into my arms, take all his clothes off, and feel his warm skin next to mine. I want to put my mouth on his neck, feel the pulse of blood beneath his skin, and bite.

"I have to be alone for a while."

He nods. "I understand, Eve. Now you know how I felt being alone with you all this time, being your lover. How Julien felt."

"It's hell," I say and stand in the doorway, looking back at him. "But at the same time, irresistible."

"You can see how it was practically impossible for me."

I nod. "I know."

He looks so devastatingly beautiful sitting there on the couch, his dark hair a bit messy, his skin flushed and full of blood. I leave him in the living room and go to the bathroom, closing the door behind me. I sit on the side of the tub and take a few deep breaths to calm myself. I want to take a hot shower, hoping that the heat will warm me a bit and remove the thoughts of a naked Michel from my mind, but it will take too long to heat the water. A cold scrub with a washcloth will have to do.

Did both brothers go through this with me for all this time?

No wonder they couldn't say no to being my lover once they found me again...

I undress, glancing at myself in the mirror before I take a cloth and wet it in the cold water. My skin is so pale it appears almost flawless, as if the waters of life have perfected me. There are only very thin, pale lines where Julien cut me when he saved my life that day in Blackstone's boardroom. The bite mark on my neck is barely visible.

While I wash, I think about the waters of life. Whatever this substance is, it clearly isn't natural. It has to have been engineered. Who or what engineered a substance that alters DNA to remove flaws and perfect the genome? Thousands of years ago, humans had no knowledge of DNA or inheritance.

It's while I'm rinsing the cloth, my eyes closed, thinking about the Knights Templar, that I hear a sound and turn. Julien opens the bathroom door, completely naked, his eyes half-lidded with desire. He stands behind me, his eyes on my reflection in the mirror.

"Perfect timing," he says, that lopsided de Cernay grin starting when his eyes rake over my naked body.

"Julien!" I scold, my heart racing at him being so close and so naked.

"I want to fuck you as a mortal, Eve. It's been eight hundred years..."

"But Michel's just down the hall..." I protest when his hands rest on my hips and he pulls me tightly against him.

"I told him to get lost for a while so you could scream my name out loud when you come."

"You did no such thing," I say, frowning and stepping away from him despite my desire for him. Then I see his smile and know he's joking. "Julien!" I hit him playfully on the chest. "Is he still in the apartment?"

"No, he really did go downstairs to load the truck. I told him I was going to wash up and he said you were already in the bathroom. I told him to take a walk around the block. I didn't need to say anything else."

Julien washes himself off quickly, as if he can't wait to be with me, soaping the cloth and washing off his sweaty body. I can't help but watch him, enjoying the spectacle of a beautiful Julien, wet, naked, and soapy. My body responds, my flesh swelling, my breath quickening.

I want him. I need him.

My own body responds to everything with ten times the force of a vampire, which is already ten times that of a human. I need him and I swear that I'm so aroused, I'll come in only moments of him entering me, no foreplay necessary. But I'll take the foreplay because it will feel fantastic as well.

When Julien is finished rinsing off, he takes a towel and begins to dry himself. I enjoy the view, especially how he's so obviously aroused and wanting to feel what it's like to fuck as a mortal again.

"Don't connect with me at all," he says, his voice husky. "I want the whole thing to be entirely inside of my own body. Is that okay with you? I know you like to join together, but give me this once, please."

I nod, barely able to think, let alone talk at this point. He finishes drying himself off and kneels down before me, taking my leg and draping it over his shoulder. I lean back, my hands resting on the edge of the counter, and watch as he begins to kiss all around me, my inner thigh, my hip, my mound.

"Oh, God, Julien," I whisper, my breath catching when he finally places his mouth over me. "I don't think I'll last…"

"Don't try," he says and everything is such a blur of intense pleasure that's almost too much. I'm lost to the sensations, my pulse racing, muscles tensing. When I emerge momentarily from my erotic haze, Julien is inside of me and begins to thrust, watching where our bodies join, and then he meets my eyes. I drop the wall between us so I can feel what he's feeling, and it's perfect, so hot and needful and elated. He can't feel me at all, and it's a good thing because I feel like the top of my head is going to explode, the pleasure building in my core.

Then I'm over the edge, pleasure ripping through me, my muscles tensing, my body shaking with each deep thrust. He's not far behind me and I force my eyes open to watch him come the first time as a mortal. His first time in eight hundred years.

His face is red, his eyes squeezed shut, teeth gritted as if he's in pain, but then his face slackens into pure bliss as he ejaculates, again and again…

"Oh, God!" he cries, his eyes almost rolling back into his head. Then he collapses against me, his face in the crook of my neck, his breath coming in quick gasps as he recovers. "Oh, God, that was good."

We rest for a moment, leaning together, me sitting on the counter with my legs wrapped around his waist, his face in my neck, my fingers running through his hair.

He pulls back and cups my face with his hands.

"I love you, Eve." He kisses me, his mouth covering mine. Our tongues meet and caress each other. My heart feels like it will explode out of my chest, I love him so much.

"Was it good for you?" I say, smiling coyly when he pulls away. I run my fingers through his short black hair, then stroke his chin with its perpetual three-day growth of beard.

"Was it good for me? Are you kidding?" He smiles and leans closer, kissing me again forcefully. "God, Eve. It's so different fucking without any connection. You're totally into your own sensations. But as much as I liked it, it is better as a vampire. Especially as an ascended vampire. What do you think?"

I nod and kiss him briefly. "Much better. A thousand times better. Almost too much, but not quite."

"I know," he says. "But there's something to say about being totally in your own body now and then. I guess it's what I'm stuck with for a while at least."

"What do you mean, for a while at least? Will you become a vampire again? Do you want to?"

He doesn't meet my eyes and instead plays with a strand of my hair, twirling in between his finger and thumb. "Who knows what the future holds?"

"You know," I say. "Or at least you know what Michel plans. Tell me!" I demand, hitting his shoulder.

"No can do," he says and grins. "You know better than to ask, Eve. Do I have to spank you? I remember doing it once before and it didn't turn out well, so don't push me!"

"Sorry," I say, smiling. "I don't remember you spanking me, but I do remember reading about it."

He pulls me tightly against his body and kisses me again. His kiss is so sweet, his lips so tender against mine, that I don't push. I clear my mind of any thoughts of the future and enjoy him.

After a long moment, we pull apart and I wash off before dressing once more. Julien follows me into the hallway and then goes to his own room to dress.

"I'm going out to run an errand," Julien says. "Michel's got me doing some security thing. I'll be back later."

I frown. "It's not safe for you any longer, now that you're mortal."

"I want to do it. I want to get out and enjoy the weather. Don't worry about me. I'm with an Adept."

I shake my head. "I don't like it."

He comes over to me and grabs my shoulders, kissing me playfully. "You are so cute when you worry about me. But remember, Eve, I was a knight before I was ever a vampire. I know my way around a sword and gun." He grins and the look in his eye makes me smile.

"Okay, but don't be too long. Soren wants you to come back with us."

WHILE I'M PACKING up my things, I hear noise at the front door and think to myself that Julien must be back from whatever he was doing, but I hear a sound like a woman's voice.

I leave my bedroom and find someone standing in the doorway

dressed all in black, wearing a long black coat with a hood. I don't know who it is, but then a gloved hand pulls back the hood and I see a petite woman with long hair and vampire-pale skin.

For a moment, I don't understand who she is. Michel turns to look at me, his face expectant. She's standing there beside him, two large men with weapons behind her. When her eyes come to rest on me, a jolt of recognition goes through me, sending my heart racing.

I know who she is.

My mother...

CHAPTER 17

Elizabeth Barrett Browning

THE ROOM IS silent for a moment and I shake my head, as if somehow I can shake away this crazy scene in front of me.

"Mom?" I manage to say, my voice small, childlike. I cover my mouth with a hand for if it is her, and I'm certain it is, she stayed away from me for years.

All those years…

"But you're dead," I say, and even to me it sounds ridiculous—she's standing here in front of me, as undead as undead can be. She did die, but was reborn as a vampire.

The one secret Michel was able to hold on to all this time.

"Where have you been?" I ask, my throat choking up.

She walks closer, her brow creased. She tries to smile but I can see it's forced. Tears fill her eyes. "I'm so sorry, Eve. It had to be this way."

"What do you mean, it had to be this way?" I say and shake my head, confused. "Why did you never come for me?"

She reaches out to me as if she wants to embrace, but there is no way I'm letting her touch me. There's only one conclusion to draw from her absence all these years.

She abandoned me.

"Don't touch me," I say, stepping back from her. I rush to my bedroom, slamming the door behind me; my emotions are overwhelming and I have to cover my mouth to stop from crying out loud.

My mother's alive? She's been alive all this time and never once came to see me? To speak to me and explain what happened?

All this time, I've thought I was motherless, my mother dying in her office at the university at the hands of a monster. Then I learn it was Michel who killed her on Soren's compulsion. Now I have to accept that she's alive and has been this whole time? She didn't die when I was eleven? She's a vampire?

Michel comes into my bedroom alone, closing the door behind him. He stands in the entry, his expression dark.

"Stay away," I warn, covering my face with my hands. "I don't want to talk to you. You've lied to me ever since you met me. Everything you've said to me has been a lie."

Michel sits beside me, taking me in his arms despite my protests, and after a moment I finally relent and let him hold me. I cry against his shoulder, unable to process it all.

"I gave her some of my blood before she died," he begins. "After they took you, I went to the hospital and brought her body back to my house. Soren couldn't know she was alive, Eve. He couldn't know where you were or he would have taken you. Your mother and I knew that the only way to save you was to hide you." His expression is pained, his brow knit, his eyes pleading. "She didn't want you to see her as a vampire."

"She wanted me to join the Council? Be an Adept?"

He nods and takes my hand. "She realized that it was the only way to stop Dominion. You and Dylan—you're key. That's all I can say for now."

I try to accept it all, fighting with my heart, which hurts like I've been stabbed. All those years I mourned her... All those years I was a motherless child.

"Why couldn't you have told me? I could have kept it secret."

"We couldn't risk it. If you ever fell into Soren's hands, he'd know or find out."

It's all too much to take in, so I just sit, my hand still in Michel's. I need his warmth right now. My body feels like ice.

"I don't know if I can see her," I say, biting back tears.

"You'll regret it if you don't." Michel moves closer to me, taking my face in his hands.

I don't want to look in his eyes, because I think I'll break down in sobs if I do, so I close mine and listen to his voice.

"Think how hard this must have been for her," he says, his voice imploring. "She was a vampire, the one thing she taught you to hate more than anything. She was afraid you'd never accept her."

"She should have given me the option."

He pulls me into his warm embrace and I lay my head against his shoulder. I let it out, crying without control, and he rocks me softly back and forth.

"Oh, Eve," he whispers. "I'm so sorry. I'm sorry that all of this had to happen to you."

"If my mother was alive, why didn't she stay with my father?"

Michel pulls away and brushes hair off my forehead. "You should talk to her about that."

"Tell me! You never explained why my father was put into an asylum when he was clearly sane."

"Eve, your father and mother didn't agree on your future. Your father was pushing things and..."

At that moment, my mother walks into the room. I glance away, turning my face towards Michel's shoulder, not wanting to deal with her now.

"Eve, I heard your question," she says, her voice just like I remember, clear and melodic. "Let me tell you what happened."

I squeeze my eyes shut. I know it's childish of me, but I can't help it. My heart feels as if it will break any moment. I want it all to go away.

"Eve," she implores. "We have to make sacrifices for the greater good. Your father...he didn't want to make the sacrifice that was required of him. He didn't want to let you go to your fate."

I pull away from Michel, catching his eye when I do. He nods softly.

"What she says is true," he confirms. "Your father wanted to run away with you back to England. He insisted that you would be raised outside of the Council and trained as a pianist. But however well you play, you were meant for a much greater purpose than playing Chopin."

"That should have been my choice," I remind them both.

Michel frowns, so I glance away. My mother stands a few feet away. I look up at her slowly, worrying it will hurt to see her face. She's beautiful, just as I remember her, with lustrous hair and large eyes with thick lashes. She holds her arms out to me.

"Eve, won't you come to me and let me hug you? I've wanted to so badly." Her voice cracks. "My arms ache to hold you."

"You could have had me all this time."

"No," she says, shaking her head. "I couldn't have. I had to go into hiding. If you'd stayed with me, both of us would be dead now and Dominion fully in place."

"You can't know that."

She pulls a chair over and sits directly across from the bed. She leans down, her elbows on her knees. "Eve, I believe Michel can see the future. I know he can."

"How do you know?"

"He was waiting for me when I decided to rejoin the Council. He'd already seen it. It was him who brought me back in."

She reaches out and tentatively takes my hand. At first, I want to pull mine back, but I resist. I let her hold my hand. She strokes it, her fingers fine and delicate. She has a dancer's body—lean but strong. I inherited the ability to dance from her, my musical talent from my father. But my mother also gave me the desire to understand the world around me, to find a way to destroy the very thing that she and I have become.

"Mom," I say, overcome once more with emotion.

She sits on the bed beside me, putting her arm around me. Michel takes this as his cue and gets up from the bed. I let her pull me into her arms and stroke my hair the way she used to when I was a child, my head on her shoulder.

"Oh, Evie," she says, her own voice choked with emotion. "I'm so sorry. So sorry."

Michel stands in the bedroom doorway, his hands in his pockets. I glance at him and see an expression of understanding in his eyes. Empathy. I'm reminded once again of his own loss. He lost his mother as a young boy and was sent to live with his father, who had married properly and didn't really want his bastards to live with him. The twins were treated terribly by the man and by his wife, their stepmother, who never accepted Michel and Julien as her sons.

At least I had foster parents who genuinely cared for me and even loved me. After I left Franklin, I was cared for properly, and lived in a middle class neighborhood with middle class parents who raised me well. I went to a good school, and there was money and scholarships for college.

Everything was going along well, with my plans to study medicine and become a research scientist studying vampirism for the Council—if I ever found it—then the university released my mother's files, some snag in bureaucracy finally settled. That day changed my life. If I hadn't received the file boxes…

I turn to my mother and frown. "Did you have anything to do with me getting your research files?"

She bites her lip and I can see it in her eyes—the truth. I turn to Michel.

"And you? Were you in on this with her? Both of you deciding when it was time to bring me into the fold?"

Michel glances away. "You had just turned twenty-one. We knew you wanted to find the Council. We knew you'd go stumbling around, trying to find someone with connections to your mother's past work.

We wanted to make sure it was us and not anyone else. Not Blackstone. Especially not Soren."

I frown at him. "Julien told me I was meant for him. Why did my mother work with you instead of Julien?"

He gestures to my mother with his chin. "Your mother will tell you. It was her decision." His expression is hard to describe—worried, like he knows what she tells me will upset me.

"Eve," my mother begins, "Michel and I were in agreement on how things should proceed because we knew that if we didn't involve you, you'd die. Dominion would not be defeated."

"Why not Julien?"

Michel glances away as if he feels guilty over it. My mother looks at the floor.

"Tell me!"

My mother glances at Michel.

"Julien was going to help your father escape with you," he says quietly. "He had to be stopped."

"What?" I frown, trying to figure out what he means. "How was he stopped?"

"I compelled Julien to leave the Council and work for the Church instead. It was the only way we could move forward with our plans."

Michel compelled Julien?

I take Michel by the arms, staring up into his blue eyes, which are hooded as if to protect himself.

"I don't understand. You compelled him to get him out of the way?"

"There was no other way, Eve. Julien wasn't going to cooperate. He would have helped your father. You would have died…"

Exasperated, I turn to my mother. "Tell me. I won't cooperate until you do."

My mother doesn't meet my eyes. "Julien was…" she says and watches Michel where he stands with his back to us. "He was going to prevent the Council from accepting you as an Adept on the grounds that you hadn't been properly trained and would be a liability rather than an asset. Most Adepts are trained at an early age, but your father and I kept you out."

I frown, making a face, anger welling up inside of me. "So you did what? Compelled him into submission to get him out of the way? And you sent my father—your husband—to an insane asylum where he was mistreated and neglected?"

"Just until you could be trained, Eve," my dear mother says. "He wasn't technically insane, but he wouldn't listen to reason. With me dead, Julien wanted you to live with your father and study music. Your father and he…they were going to prevent you from your destiny. Michel compelled Julien, made him give up his desire to save you, and he joined the monastery. It was the only way we could keep him out of the SCU and Council business."

I can barely believe what I'm hearing. No wonder there has been so much animosity between the brothers over me. I thought it was because they didn't want to share me, but it was fundamentally an issue of how to use me—or whether to use me.

Everything I thought I knew about the brothers is backwards. It was Julien who wanted me to study music. It was Michel all along who wanted me to become an Adept.

They actually compelled Julien to keep out of Council business. I thought he chose that because he was tired of fighting. I thought he had given up on fighting Dominion.

"My father's life has been a living hell all this time because of you both!" I explode. "Julien was compelled—forced!—out of the Council and SCU to shut him up?

I get up from the couch and go to my room. All I want is to find Julien and slip my arms around him. My head is pounding, my heart is pounding. I need some time. I stop at the door to my bedroom and turn to them.

"I want to be alone for a while. I need to think."

With that, I close the door, leaving them behind. I crawl under the covers, pulling the coverlet above my head, and cry my eyes out.

"THE FIRST MAGIC of love is our ignorance that it can ever end."

Benjamin Disraeli

I STOP CRYING after a while and my mind goes over everything I've just learned. In the end, I know I have to make a choice. But I have to speak with Julien before I decide anything.

After washing my face off in the bathroom, I return to the living room, where my mother and Michel sit on the sofa. They turn when I enter the room, their expressions expectant.

I sit on a chair across from them. "Where's Julien?" I ask.

"He's still out. I knew your mother was coming and couldn't risk him finding out she's alive."

"He doesn't know?"

Michel shakes his head. "He's compellable. If he knew, Soren would know. Blackstone would know."

"Michel, you have to tell me what's going on. Tell me what you can about what's going to happen."

Michel glances at my mother and she nods to him. He exhales and rubs his chin, as if it hurts to have to explain. "I know this is hard for you, but time is becoming extremely precious. We don't have a lot of it. We have to help Soren so he'll stop the plague as soon as possible. That's all we can safely tell you. No more questions."

"How is it that Soren doesn't know that my mother's alive? He'll find out if he doesn't already know."

"He has some blind spots," my mother says. "He doesn't see us, Eve."

Michel holds out his hand. "No, Natalia. Don't."

She looks at him, her expression frustrated. "It's the only way to convince her."

Michel holds his head as if he has a headache. "Now you've played a card that you can't take back," he says to my mother, a note of resignation in his voice.

She turns back to me and shrugs. There's a determined look in her eyes, as if she's made her decision and is going through with it. "He doesn't know my mind. Or Michel's. Or Dylan's. Or your mind," she says. "We're opaque to him and so he doesn't see us."

"No, you're wrong," I say, shaking my head. "He's been in my mind before. I know it. He's spoken to me."

"Only when he shares blood with you can he access your thoughts, but the ability fades once the blood leaves your system. The rest of the time, you're a blank. He can't get into your mind, he can't see you or your role in events. We're all blind spots. Adepts are invisible to him."

"But Michel can be compelled as well. If he knows you're alive, why doesn't Soren?"

Michel shakes his head. He glances away, as if he can't meet my eyes. A look passes between my mother and Michel. She nods and then turns back to meet my eyes.

"Michel isn't compellable. He never has been."

"What?" I frown and look at my mother and then back to Michel, who keeps his eyes averted. "But all that time… I read the manuscript. It said you both were compelled to stay with Marguerite. She forced you when you were with her to do all kinds of things. Then when you were with Soren, he forced you to kill my mother. You said it was only after you ascended that you became immune to it. You were never compelled?"

He shakes his head, staring at his hands. "I'm like you and Dylan. And your mother."

"But Julien… You're twins. Your DNA is identical."

"Eve," my mother says. "Think of epigenetics. Twin studies. Take twins separated at birth. Both twins have the 9-Repeat DAT gene for antisocial personality disorder—psychopathy. One is abused mercilessly while the other is raised in a loving environment. One becomes a criminal, the other is non-violent. All four of us have something in common. We're all Adepts who had violent or abusive experiences at a critical time in our development. It makes us uncompellable."

Michel sits up at that. "My father beat us. For some reason, Julien was more resilient. My father always saw something different in him and maybe favored him more. Julien stood up to him while I didn't. It's the experience of trauma that makes us immune. It makes us adept."

"But Dylan…"

"Dylan's first foster home was like yours," he says. "His foster mother was a drug addict and he lived in neglect and abuse until the Rhys family adopted him. Natalia grew up in the rough neighborhoods of Hungary during the occupation. You were abused by Franklin…" Michel takes in a deep breath. "Julien's still compellable and that's why he can't know that your mother is alive. Soren would know."

"So you sent Julien on some errand to get him out of the way so my mother could come by?"

Michel nods. "He can't know, Eve. It would put everything at risk, Julien's life included, so if you truly love him, don't tell him."

I sit in silence for a moment. "Soren can't get into my mind?"

"His telepathy is one way, unless he shares blood with you. He can get into your mind and talk to you, but he can't read you," Michel says. "That's why he needs you to connect him to the others. That's what they lost. They lost their ability to connect with each other. It's a one-way link only but you give them the ability to reconnect."

"I'm sure he can," I say, remembering the times he's said things that were too close to what I was thinking. "He's read my thoughts before."

My mother shakes her head. "No. He's just very skilled at reading you as a person and he watches for your response. I'm certain of it. We've tested him. You'll go back to Soren, cooperate, and when the time is right, we'll make our move against him," my mother says. "If all goes as we plan, Soren will stop the plague, then he'll be destroyed, and we'll re-establish the Council and enforce the Treaty. We'll make our move against Blackstone. Then we'll eradicate vampirism."

"Soren already has a cure. Or, should I say, a poison that kills vampires."

"He also has the antidote to the plague," my mother points out. "Once he deploys it, we'll kill him. Then vampires will be history."

"What about a cure? I thought you had changed your mind about killing them all."

"At this point, that's not possible," she says. "Our only hope is to stop both Soren and the plague. Vampires will have to die off completely. Lord knows we've wrought enough pain and death against mortals that we don't deserve to exist. We don't have the time to spend finding a way to cure vampirism without killing them."

I frown. "But that means you'll die. And Dylan. I'll die as well."

"You won't die if we're successful," she points out. "By cooperating with Soren, by giving him power and helping him in his little power play, he'll turn you back into mortals, if you want. It's then that we'll act against him."

It's too much for me to take in at once. "I want to ask Julien what he thinks of all this," I say to Michel.

"You can't, Eve," Michel reminds me. "Julien is compellable. The first thing Soren will do is force Julien to tell him everything he knows.

I cross my arms. I hate that I can't talk to Julien about this. "I don't trust Soren to do what he promises," I admit. "You two think you can see the future, but so does Soren. He knows each and every possible future as well."

"He doesn't know all the parts we each play in those ends," Michel says. "And he can't see the four of us. Dylan, you, Natalia, and me. That's the key. And that's all I can say without messing up the future."

"So, I'll know the plan when I need to and not before? Is this more of what was done before? I know the plan without knowing I know it?"

Michel shrugs. "I can't say."

I sigh, exasperated, trying to understand it all. I turn to my mother. I should feel ecstatic that she's alive and here with me. Instead, I feel only betrayal. "So I should cooperate?" I ask.

"If there was any other way…" she says, reaching out to touch my hand. "We don't have much time, Eve. Every day the plague spreads. Now, are you with us?"

I glance at Michel. "Yes."

"Good. You have to go," she explains. "Take Julien back to Soren. Play along with him. Things will be put in place when the time is right."

Michel is still really upset. "There is another way, Natalia," he says, his voice shaky. "I wanted this as a last resort."

"That way took too much time. We have to move and soon."

Michel glances at me, his face haggard. "I'm sorry, Eve. Please know that this wasn't my choice."

I shrug, not knowing what he means. "I'm past forgiving you, Michel." When I say it, I see him cringe. I turn to my mother. "Let's do it."

My mother smiles, but Michel is not nearly as happy. He seems as if there's a huge weight on his shoulders.

My mother stands up. "I have to leave, now, or I'll see Julien on the way out."

She comes to me and pauses, a pained expression on her face. I know she wants to be my mother again, but there's still a part of me that refuses to let her in.

"I'm sorry it had to be this way, Eve," she says softly. "Believe me, if

I could have wished this all away, I would have. We all have to do our duty."

"You could have come to me. If Soren can't read us as you say, there was no reason to stay away."

"Soren might not see me, but others can. I had to stay completely out of your life so there was no trace of me."

I nod, but don't make a move to hug her. The door closes with a heavy thud behind her.

~

MICHEL and I sit in silence for a while, nothing but the sound of wind outside the windows.

"Are you never going to speak to me again?" he asks, his voice sounding hurt.

"Give me one good reason why I should."

"Because I love you and you love me, in spite of it all."

I close my eyes and take in a deep breath. I'm not even going to argue with him about this. I don't know if I love him any more. How could I after everything?

There's a knock at the door. "Come," Michel says and a guard opens the door and pokes his head in.

"You asked to be notified when Julien returned. He's downstairs in the parking garage.

Michel nods. "Thank you."

The guard leaves, closing the door behind him.

"What do I say to him?" I ask. "Unlike you, I hate lying."

"Go ahead and tell him everything, Eve, if you really want to," Michel says, waving his hands. "It will kill him. Maybe all of us."

I shake my head and fist my hands to stop from responding.

"Go get him," he says with a weary sigh. "It's time to leave."

~

I SPEAK WITH THE GUARD, who tells me that Julien is now in the building's lobby, answering some question about security. I take the stairs and find him standing in the storefront, watching the street, his arms crossed. I tiptoe up behind him and wrap my arms around his waist, my head resting in his strong back.

I hear his intake of breath, and then he lays his hands on mine. "It's time to go back," I whisper. "But I really wish you and I could run away from all this. Go somewhere and forget about everything."

He turns around and wraps his arms around me, pulling me against his body. "Me, too," he says, his voice warm. "You don't know how many times I've thought the same thing."

"I'm so tired of this life, Julien. All the lies, the deception. The tragedy in my life. The secrecy. I feel as if I've never had any happy moments in my life."

"You've never been happy?"

I shake my head. "Not completely. There's always been this sense of impending doom, even when I've been momentarily happy with you."

He pulls me more tightly into his arms. "I'm so sorry about everything that's happened to you. I wanted none of this, but this is what we have to face. War asks a lot of us."

"I guess I thought I'd be doing research, not any of this," I say, frowning.

"I know. You thought you'd take over where your mother left off. Maybe you can one day. Maybe it's just a matter of time."

"I don't think so," I say, wishing I could confide in him but afraid that if I do, what Michel says will come true and Julien will die. I can't stand to have anything happen to him. We can't discover the key to immortality soon enough for my liking and the first thing I'll do when Soren and Blackstone are defeated is look for it.

I've made up my mind.

"What do you think Soren wants from you?" I ask.

"More torture, no doubt. He'll want to make each of us jealous of the other. Compel me to be with Gabrielle to make you jealous. Put you with Michel to make me jealous. His usual MO."

"He loves to see people struggle. It's like he can't feel things himself so he needs to watch others feel for him," I say, laying my head against his chest.

"I never thought of that," he comments. "Makes sense, though. I figured it was just having all that power. It corrupts, and I believe it. Soren's always been tougher on Michel because he knows I didn't want to kill Marguerite, that I spared her the agony of burning to death by staking her. If I could have seen what the consequences would have been, I would have fought Michel harder to keep her alive. But he was desperate."

I squeeze Julien more tightly, wishing we could have just thrown Soren back into one of the tanks. "We can't see the future," I remind him. "All we can do is make decisions based on the evidence we have at the time. That's all, Julien."

Julien sighs. "I wish..." he says and strokes my cheek with the backs of his fingers. "I wish we could run away. All I want is for us to be together, but we have to see this through. We have to stop them both—Soren and Blackstone."

I nod and stand on my tiptoes to kiss him softly, hugging him more tightly to me.

When we pull away, he kisses the top of my head and we stay like that for a long moment. Who knows when we will get the chance to embrace again.

WE COLLECT Julien's possessions before returning to the vehicle. Before we get inside, I slip my arms around Julien, pulling him down to kiss him in front of Michel. I don't care if Michel sees me, because I will never, under any circumstances, be with him again. I want him to realize that I'm with Julien now.

Whatever we had is over.

Julien holds me in his arms and kisses me back. Then he gets inside the vehicle. Before I can get in, Michel comes to me and pulls me aside.

"What do you want?"

He shakes his head slowly, an expression of regret on his face. "I know what you're trying to do, Eve. I'm sorry you had to learn all this. I'm sorry for my deceit. I don't blame you one bit for giving up on me. I expected it."

I shrug, not wanting to concede anything to him. I turn to the vehicle and see Julien through the window. He's watching, his brow furrowed. "You've lied to me so much, I'll never know whether to believe you again."

Michel looks a bit desperate, his lips pressed thin. "I lied only to protect you, Eve."

I turn back to watch Julien, who is looking at me with such warmth in his eyes, such affection and sympathy that I don't want to look away.

"This is a lot to take in," Michel says. He sounds so tired. "Give yourself some time. We were only doing all of this to protect you and to prevent Dominion."

"The road to hell," I mutter, wiping my cheeks. "I don't know who to trust anymore, except Julien. I'm not sure whether to cooperate with you or fight you."

"Don't do anything right now," he whispers. "Give it time before you decide what to do."

I turn and examine him. I can see pain in his expression, in the wideness of his eyes and the way his mouth is turned down in the corners. His eyes are bloodshot as if he too could cry at any moment.

His telling me the truth is a bit too late for me to forgive him, and for me to be with him again. I'm surprised at how much it hurts my heart to think that I could ever stop loving him, but right now, I have.

CHAPTER 19

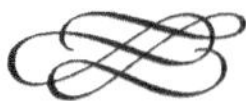

"The course of true love never did run smooth."

William Shakespeare

We take the vehicle back to Soren's compound. As usual, the streets are deserted and except for an occasional face in a window, I don't see a living soul. The winter is cold and a light snow falls as we drive through the streets. Here and there are the burnt hulks of buildings that were razed to the ground. With no firefighting capacity and no water service, fires burn themselves out, leaving the charred corpses behind.

It makes me sad to see the city this way. I love Boston's cobblestone streets and old buildings. I love the new parts of the city and the harbor. Now it's a mess. I wonder how far the plague has spread and how long it will take for this plan to make a difference. How much of the world can we save?

Can we save it or will it all fall into the steam age?

We approach Soren's compound once more, and are met by armed guards who examine the vehicle's occupants and wave us by. We're expected.

When we get to the driveway in front of the mansion, two guards come to the vehicle and stop us. They haul Julien out and put manacles on his wrists and ankles. Julien resists initially, but then Michel shakes his head.

"It's just show," Michel says. "You know how Soren loves a performance."

Julien gives in and holds his wrists out so they can cuff him in the old metal shackles. My heart squeezes, because I'm sure Soren will be gloating to have Julien under his control once more. He'll show Julien his power in the hopes of striking fear into Julien's mortal heart.

I follow with Michel as the guards lead Julien down the long hallways to Soren's study. We find Soren sitting at his desk with the blonde Gabrielle sitting on his knee, dressed in a revealing gown of blood red that highlights her pale skin. He's nuzzling her neck with affection.

I remember what Soren said to me about losing someone you love and feeling one hundred times the emotion a mortal feels

A memory of the dream I had of him crucified comes to mind and regret stabs through my heart. Michel is misguided. He's an idealist willing to do very bad things for the end he thinks is right. He's dangerous, as all extremists are, but even now, even after everything I've learned about Michel, I still don't want to see him dead.

The guard hauls Julien into the room, his chains clinking and jangling. Soren looks up from Gabrielle and sees us, immediately smiling, his expression one of triumph.

How I hate him.

The guard shoves Julien to his knees in front of the desk.

"Well, well, well," Soren says, sitting up and pushing Gabrielle off his lap. "What have we here? The brave knight himself." He rises and comes to stand in front of Julien.

For his part, Julien keeps his face impassive. If he feels any fear or hatred towards Soren, he says and does nothing to show it. He's stoic in the face of all that gloating.

"Are the shackles necessary?" Michel asks, his voice tired.

Soren frowns. "Questioning my decisions are you, Michel? Remember, now that you're human, you're vulnerable. I could crush the both of you with my hand. Crucify you upside down like St. Peter." He catches my eye briefly and a chill goes through me, making the hairs on the back of my neck stand up.

I just thought of that image only moments before... But my mother and Michel assured me that Soren couldn't read my mind.

"You'll do it if you want no matter what we do," I say, my fight to keep myself under control lost before even a moment has passed.

"You're right," Soren says, turning to meet my eyes, his voice filled with self-importance. "I will. If I want to. Right now, I don't want to." He turns back to Julien. "But I do so like to see Julien on his knees. You do as well, don't you Eve?" Soren turns to me again and winks.

What the hell?

Is he referring to what happened between Julien and me in the bathroom? But Michel and my mother said...

No, he didn't see what happened between us. He couldn't have. But he knows we're lovers and is trying to make me believe he sees everything.

How pathetic.

He's probably furious that he can't read us and does everything possible to make us believe he can.

He did plant the image of Michel crucified in my mind, knowing it would upset me and that he can bring that up any time with the same result. But the reference to Michel being crucified upside down like St. Peter coming so soon after I thought it... Is Soren able to get into my mind and read my thoughts? Are my mother and Michel wrong?

He's inserted himself into my mind so many times. Recently, when I learned he was free. When I was in Montana. In the Middle East.

He can get into my head, but can he read my thoughts when he does or is it one way? I'm desperate to test what Michel and my mother claimed, but can't think of a way at the moment. I feel helpless, waiting for others to put a plan in place that they say will work and that I can't know.

I only hope this plan works better than the last one.

"I know you were all hoping to see me permanently in stasis, or better yet, dematerialized," Soren says, "but the best laid plans…"

He winks at me again and then I know he must be able to read my mind. They're wrong about him.

Fuck you, I think, testing him.

You'd enjoy angel sex, Eve. Don't tempt me.

Crap. Every ounce of blood I have in my body freezes at that.

Soren strides over to where I stand and stops in front of me, smiling. He tilts my face up so that I have to look in his gloating face, into his eyes, which are amused.

We have a direct line now that you're ascended and we shared blood. Adepts are different like that—it brings out the capacity in you that we angels once possessed but no longer share without your direct intervention. Michel doesn't know and neither does your mother. I won't tell anyone if you won't, Eve. I was surprised to learn it myself, for I've never, in all my days, been faced with Adepts like you four. There never have been Adepts like you. I'll let Julien live if you keep our little secret. It's not something I want to become general knowledge.

"Good to see you again, Eve," Soren says out loud, his lips curling in a feral smile. "Now, we have work to do. I need more power so I can restore the Twelve to their former glory. You're going to give it to me."

He returns to Julien, who is still on his knees, his shackled hands in front of him. I'm so busy trying to sort out what Soren's revelation means that I only give him half my attention.

He can read my mind because I'm now ascended. Is my mother ascended? Dylan is. If that's the case and he shares blood with Dylan, he'll be able to read Dylan's mind as well. I know what I have to do—I have to prevent Dylan from sharing blood with Soren.

While I stand there, trying to figure it all out, Soren motions to a guard who brings forth a metal collar of some medieval design. It's thick and about an inch wide, with a loop wide enough for a chain to pass through.

"See this, Eve?" Soren says to me. "It's quite an ingenious design.

There's a spring-loaded blade in the inside. All you have to do is insert a special key and—" He inserts a tiny key into a slot on the outside of the collar and I hear a twang. A thin metal blade springs out, about an inch long and only millimeters wide. I can see that it's polished, sharp, and deadly.

"You position the blade over the external jugular. Death takes about two minutes. I don't like to use it, because why waste all that perfectly good blood, but I like the medieval nature of this beast. It will remind Julien of his origins."

"Please don't," I say, my voice choking with emotion. "I'll comply with you. No hesitation."

"Oh, so sweet," Soren says, making a childish face. "You love Julien so much, you can't bear to put him at risk of a hemorrhage."

Soren places the collar close to Julien and glances at me, raising his eyebrows questioningly. "Should I?"

"Please..." I whisper.

"What's really going to freak you out is this," he says and reloads the latch that holds the small blade in place. He motions me closer and I step forward with reluctance. "Watch this!"

I watch the collar, frozen, as Soren waves his fingers in front of it.

"Abracadabra and alakazam, and all that," he says. The latch slides aside and the blade springs out on its own with an audible thunk.

Soren can manipulate it with his mind.

"Please," I say louder.

He smiles at me. "Don't worry your little head off, Eve. I'm not going to put it on Julien. I want you two to fuck like bunnies and you can't relax and enjoy if you have the threat of death by exsanguination hanging over your head, now, can you?

Soren takes the collar over to Michel and before any of us can react, he places it around Michel's neck, closing the two sides of the collar and fastening the lock.

"It's Michel who will be the true test of your willingness to cooperate. Julien's far too easy. You'd do anything to keep loverboy alive. But Michel? You two have had a recent falling out, I suspect, so you won't be fucking, will you?" He turns to me. "Am I right?"

I say nothing, my throat choked from emotion.

Soren adjusts the collar on Michel's neck and dusts off his shoulders. "Not quite the collar you were expecting, Michel? How does it feel to be collared? Must be hard for someone like you to have the shoe on the other foot..."

Michel says nothing. His face is serene, as if he's ready to die, and that scares me more than I realized.

"You've always wanted to get revenge on Michel for Marguerite's death," I say, unable to stop myself. "Who's to say you won't do it anyway, no matter how much I cooperate with you?"

"Oh, I love it when you get all rebellious on me, Eve!" Soren says and shivers dramatically. Then his demeanor changes. "Marguerite's murder, you mean. If I wanted revenge, I could kill him with a thought," he says, his voice filled with menace. He frowns down at me for a moment and then smiles. "This is just far more fun! You'll never know if or when, so I'm counting on you to make the right choice when the time comes."

I'm furious, my fists clenched, tears in my eyes. He has Julien in chains and Michel in the kill collar.

I hate you.

Hate. Love. Two sides of the same coin, Eve. Intense emotion. I'll take whatever you can give.

I refuse to respond or look at Soren, and stand there, fuming.

Now he knows everything.

Everything, Eve. Remember that. If you let your fellow conspirators know, I'll use the kill collar on Michel, so don't let on, now, okay?

Michel fingers the collar on his neck, as if adjusting to the newfound menace he has to live with. He seems unconcerned. Does he believe Soren won't use it? Does he see a different death for himself? Or is he resigned to it?

At that moment, despite everything, despite all the lies, the deceit, and the manipulation, I realize I still love him, deep down inside of me. I can't believe it's possible, but I do. I'll do whatever I can to prevent Soren from using that collar. I'm sure Soren knows that, and that's why he's put it on Michel.

He knows I won't let him use it, and that it will cause me tremendous stress.

I'm so tired of it all, so weary from the constant threat we face from the uncertainty, from the sorrow at all the loss. All I want is to return to my little cottage on the beach and sit on my patio wrapped in a blanket and watch the sunset.

"Take them to their rooms," Soren says, dismissing us. He goes back around his desk and sits on his chair, pulling Gabrielle down onto his lap once more. He kisses her.

We're forgotten.

WE FOLLOW the guard down the long hallway to the other wing and up the stairs to a large room. There's a king-sized canopy bed with ostentatious bedding in the center. The furniture is Louis XIV or some number, white and gilded. A sofa and two wing chairs surround an ornate coffee table by a fireplace. Two huge arched windows look out over the grounds.

"Are we all staying here?" I ask when the guard ushers us inside.

A servant brings Julien's bags, such as they are, and places them on a low seat at the foot of the bed. I see that my spare items are also in the room, as are Michel's.

Soren is going to force us to stay together. I imagine he wants to force the threesome.

It won't happen. I promised myself after reading the manuscript that I would never be like Marguerite and be with them in front of each other.

Never is a long time, Eve...

Damn him.

Will you never give me a moment's peace?

Never is a long time, Eve!

I sigh and watch as Julien drags his chains around, inspecting the room. Finally, he plops down on the sofa, his shackled hands in his lap.

"At least he had the decency to shackle me with my hands in front," Julien says and cracks a grin.

How he can smile while sitting there with his hands and ankles in chains I'll never know, but that's my Julien. A surge of love for him flows through me and I want to kiss him and stroke his cheek, but of course I can't.

I have to keep my own promises to myself about the twins. Just because Michel and I will never be together again, doesn't mean I'll be with Julien in front of him.

Never is a long time, Eve.

I want to shake my hand in the air and curse Soren for intruding on my mind once more, but instead, I stand in the center of the room and squeeze my eyes shut, clenching my fists and gritting my teeth. There has to be a way to keep him out of my mind—some kind of pain I can experience that will be low and constant so he can't insert himself whenever he feels like it.

I glance around, looking for something—anything—that might do the trick.

Don't even try, Eve. Remember the collar. I want access.

I sigh and stop what I was doing.

It's hopeless. There's nothing I can do except cooperate with him. No matter what I do, he can kill either of the two men that I love— one I love passionately and one I still love, despite everything he's done to me. I can't let anyone know that Soren has direct access to my mind or I'll be nothing more than a direct line to their plots and plans.

It infuriates me, being so helpless.

"I need a drink," I say. "Is anyone else hungry?"

Julien smiles. "I could use a bite to eat. It's nice not to crave blood. But a nice slice of juicy venison would do fine."

I go to the door and crack it open. The guard steps forward and bends down to me.

"Can we get something to eat?" I ask.

The guard nods. "I'll tell the kitchen to send something up."

"Thank you."

I close the door and turn back to the room. Michel is seated on one of the wing chairs and Julien is facing him, examining the old cuffs on his wrists.

"Soren must enjoy the prospect of us being together," I say. "Let's not give him any reason to rejoice. I don't want to fight with either of you, so let's agree to get along while we're here."

Julien laughs. "If I know Soren, and believe me, I do, he'll be disappointed if there's no drama."

"Julien's right," Michel says, a half-grin on his face. "Soren lives for drama, especially the kind he creates. But I agree, Eve. No need for drama between us."

"He expects us to stay together in one big bed?" Julien says, gesturing to the canopy bed with his cuffed wrists.

"We'll sleep in shifts," I suggest, going to the bed and lying down. "I'm first."

I pull back the coverlet and creep in, pulling the blanket over my head so I can block out reality.

It's not much, but it's the best I can do.

CHAPTER 20

"LOVE IS, above all, the gift of oneself."

Jean Anouilh

MERCIFULLY, the brothers let me sleep for hours, and I'm so exhausted from all the stress and revelations and tears that I don't even wake up when the servant brings the food in. It's a dreamless sleep, luckily, so Soren must be too busy with the enchanting Gabrielle to bother me.

When I wake, Julien is standing at the window with his cheek resting against the glass. He looks lost, like he's given up all hope. For a moment, it alarms me. If Julien has lost hope, what hope do we have? Michel is sipping coffee and reading a newspaper—one of the only papers still in print, the newsprint recycled many times and the ink made from vegetable dye. It's hand pressed and set, and looks like something an English gentleman in eighteenth-century London would read with his tea.

"Did you have a good sleep?" Michel asks when he sees me sitting up on the side of the bed.

I nod and pull back my long hair, braiding it loosely to the side. His eyes linger on me a bit too long and I know that he still wants me. The priest in him has not yet strangled the hot-blooded man. The need in his eyes still has the power to affect me, despite how I feel about him. He was my first real lover, the first man to make me feel desire and lust. It's hard to see him and not think of him that way. It's hard not to love him, despite everything that's happened between us since we met.

He drags his eyes away from me and I glance away as well, taking in a deep breath to cleanse my mind of thoughts of us as lovers. It's Julien who should hold that place in my mind. He's been the true lover to me since we met—always telling me the truth when he can—when he's not compelled to hide it. Now he's in chains and we're with Michel and so there will be no lovemaking with him…at least for a while.

I rise and go to Julien's side, touching his shoulder. He turns to me and smiles, affection for me in his eyes. "Sleep well?" he asks, his voice soft. "I felt an incredible desire to join you, but it's such a turnoff to have a priest in the room while you make love."

I glance at Michel to see if he heard, but he seems absorbed in his paper and coffee.

"Julien…" I chide. "Get that off your mind. Nothing's going to happen while we're here, so don't get your hopes up."

"I'm always up for you," he says and grins, his voice husky and suggestive.

I can't help but smile back and punch him lightly on the shoulder. "Your cuffs and chains might get in the way."

"There is no obstacle that can't be overcome by someone determined to overcome it."

"Who said that?" I ask, wondering if I've heard it before.

"Me," he says and grins at me. He sneaks a peek in Michel's direction and then leans down to quickly cover my mouth with his, slipping me a bit of tongue before he pulls away. He wags his eyebrows.

"You are so bad."

"I'm so bad I'm good."

We smile at each other, leaning in a bit closer, and I'm just about ready to sneak another kiss when there's a knock at the door. I pull away when Michel puts down his paper.

"Come," Michel says, and the door opens to admit one of the guards.

"Lord Soren wants you," he says to Michel. "Alone."

Michel frowns and puts his cup down on the coffee table. He rises and glances towards us as he passes. "Probably getting instructions for this event Soren wants us at."

Julien nods, his face suddenly serious.

Michel leaves with the guard, but he takes a look back at us before he closes the door, his brow furrowed. As soon as the door is closed, Julien wastes no time and raises his arms, threading them around me and pulling me against him.

"About damn time," he says. "Kiss me. I've been deprived for too long."

"Julien!" I struggle in his arms half-heartedly. "Michel could come back at any moment. I told you nothing will happen in front of him."

"He's not here now," he says, his voice low. "Kiss me like you mean it."

I stop struggling and look in his eyes. There's a playful grin on his face, but his eyes say something else entirely, as does his body. He pulls me closer and bends down so that his lips almost touch mine. He hovers there, his breath warm on my lips, his eyes open. He's waiting for me to kiss him like I mean it, this hunk of man that I want to lick and bite and suck and ride all at the same time.

"I don't think we should," I say and he moves lower, kissing my neck, licking the skin over his bite mark, which is barely visible now that I've ascended. It sends a jolt of lust through my body right to my core and I clench as if I had him inside of me. "Julien, no," I whisper, but it doesn't sound convincing.

His hands slide down my back to my buttocks and he grabs them, pulling me against his erection.

"Oh, God," I moan, inhaling when he rubs his hard length against me. "Stop."

"Michel will be gone for a while," Julien says. "I need you. Let's go into the bathroom."

"We had sex only a while ago," I say.

"Too long," he replies. "This fucking as a mortal is better than I remember."

Julien has my blouse open and is struggling to grab my breast with his cuffed and chained hands, his mouth practically devouring my neck, when Michel returns.

I don't hear him at first, so focused on what Julien is doing that I fail to notice the door opening. Then, I see him standing in the doorway with the guard behind him. Both of their eyes are wide.

Michel is dressed in black vestments with a blood red stole and a huge wooden cross on a string. The metal collar—the kill collar—is visible beneath the jacket he wears. He wears no cap, so his head is bare, his longish hair falling down the back of his neck. He's a devastatingly beautiful priest. Michel turns on his heel and walks away, out the door and down the hall. The guard follows, closing the door slowly.

"Julien," I whisper, pushing him off me.

"What?" he says and frowns.

"Michel saw us."

Julien turns to the doorway. "I didn't hear anything."

"He's gone now," I say, adjusting my blouse. I straighten my hair and leave Julien at the window.

He follows me, sitting down across from me, an expression of frustrated humor on his face. "Fuck Michel," he says. "He's a priest now and wants this celibacy thing, Eve. There's no reason why we can't be together. He had his chance. He made his choice."

The door opens once more and Michel enters, barely looking at us. He stands by the fireplace and takes out a poker to move the logs around. "You're to get ready, Eve," he says, his voice quiet. "Soren wants more power so he can revive one of the Twelve. It will take a lot to revive them all and he wants to start tonight. We're going to the park where there's a makeshift stage set up under a tent."

"Sounds evangelical," I say. "I hate to be a part of that, Michel."

Michel exhales in frustration. "This is necessary for the time being. Just be patient." He sneaks a look at Julien and then goes to the door. "You have ten minutes to get ready. Julien, you're to come as well."

"What about these?" he says and holds up his wrists with the shackles and chains.

Michel shrugs. "You know how Soren loves to show off his power over people."

Before I know it, Michel is gone. Julien and I rise and stare at each other for a moment.

"We're finishing off what we started the first opportunity we get, Eve," Julien says, pointing at me, his chains jangling, a lopsided grin on his lovely mouth. "Fair warning."

"Not if we're anywhere near Michel and he can walk in on us," I point out.

"Eve," Julien says, his eyes narrowing, "I'm asserting property rights since Michel gave up his."

I laugh and step closer to him. "In case you're forgetting, I'm the one with property rights now that you're mortal."

"Well," he says and raises his fingers to my cheek, "I'm asserting rights as property—yours." He grins and I smile back, glad that at least he still has his sense of play, despite everything that's happened.

THE DRIVE to the park is slow, with a phalanx of security vehicles spread out back and front. People walk together in small groups to the park for the ceremony. They point and wave when they see the central vehicle with Soren just visible through the window. No doubt he arranged things so that people could see him.

I sit between Michel and Julien across from Soren. I'm wearing a white gown that Soren's guard brought to me and my hair is up the way Michel likes. Soren seems pleased that we're all together again and while he waves to the passing crowds, he speaks to us.

"This is how it's going to go. Eve, you and I will share blood. I'll suck up as much adoration from the crowd as possible, and then I'll resurrect one of the Twelve. I've brought along Kael. He and I always saw eye to eye on things. He'll be useful to have back first."

Kael. Is he referring to fallen angels?

"Which one are you?" I say, trying to keep my voice from sounding patronizing. "Obviously, Soren is just your human name."

"Wouldn't you like to know," he says. "Besides, you don't really believe, so until you do, you can guess."

I turn away from his too-piercing gaze and watch the crowd. He wants us to think he's an angel. I'm not going to argue with him. He could kill Michel in a second and I'd be helpless to do anything but watch him die…unless I turned him. But he wouldn't want that.

I'm acutely aware of being in between the brothers. Of course, Soren arranged it that way so he could gloat. He loves to see the three of us in close proximity, probably feeding off the angst we all feel in such close quarters—the suppressed desire, the jealousy. I can almost sense his triumph across from me.

"Oh, Eve, Eve, Eve…" he says, smiling. "I always love a doubter who has a conversion on the road to Damascus. So damn compelling. I can't look away and will love so much the moment when you finally believe."

"Don't hold your breath," I mutter.

He says nothing else as we drive through the streets.

I see a white canvas tent in the distance when we arrive at the park. Beside the tent, a crew of men are busy digging in the dirt. A small crowd of people dressed in winter clothing have flocked to the tent and mill around, speaking in groups, forming lines to get inside under the cover. There might be fifty or sixty people in all, and they walk down a path lit by fiery torches. They seem happy, their breath visible in the chilly air as they speak to each other.

Does Soren really give them hope? I imagine he's far more of a comfort than the usual religious officials, for none of them can do miracles. Soren has resurrected the dead and executed the guilty with ball lightning. If I didn't know it was all projection and some kind of mass hysteria, I'd be impressed as well.

~

WE EXIT the vehicle on a side road to the north of the tent and a line of guards forms a narrow row that Soren walks through, dressed in a white robe, his pale hair long and shiny, his skin white. His wings unfold behind him as he walks through the rear of the tent and a collective gasp moves through the crowd when they see him in all his glory.

I hear sighs, weeping, and stifled cries.

He knows how to put on a show.

We follow him through the flap in the tent and inside. There's a full marble altar at the head of the tent, surrounded by tall candles. Religious statues and artifacts stand behind the altar—an angel bending over the virgin with the baby Jesus, a crucifix with Jesus looking up to the heavens, a medieval painting of John the Baptist baptizing Jesus. Michel stands at the altar and moves a collection of items around that I don't recognize—reliquaries, chalices, and a huge Bible opened with a silk ribbon down the center.

A guard positions me beside the altar and I stand and stare at the congregation, aware of their adoration and awe of everything they see. Soren is formidable, sitting on a huge marble throne behind the altar, his wings spread out to their full width. What must people think when they see him?

They truly must believe this is the apocalypse and Soren is God's angel come down to rescue the faithful. With the technological plague destroying modern civilization and vampires roaming the streets at night, unafraid of retribution, I can understand their fear and their desire to turn to the Church, though I don't share it.

Of course, it's not the apocalypse, not in the biblical sense. It's humanity battling vampires and vampires battling each other. It's more akin to something out of Mary Shelley or Bram Stoker than the Bible, angel wings notwithstanding.

While I wait for the blood ceremony to begin, I notice that men are moving portable metal barriers into place around the tent in sections of chain link fence five feet tall and at least ten feet wide. I wonder why. Is it to prevent people from coming in during the ceremony?

Several guards wheel in one of the cement tanks from the SCU's underground facility—I recognize it immediately. In it is one of the Ancients—Kael, from what Soren said. I see him as he passes. Lying beneath the liquid that keeps him in stasis is a very strange and other-worldly-looking man with the same white skin and fair hair as Soren. Nordic in heritage, probably chosen for their distinctive appearance, well aware of humanity's preference for genetic rarity. It's a show, nothing more.

The ceremony progresses without any fanfare. Michel goes to Soren with a knife in his hand and cuts Soren's wrist, angling it so that the blood trickles into the chalice. He collects blood from my wrists and holds the chalice high above his head as if asking for a blessing of the contents. His eyes are closed and he's whispering something to himself. I can barely make it out, but it's in Latin.

"*Accipite et bibite, ex eo omnes. Hic est enim calix sanguines mei.*"

Then he repeats it in English, his voice loud enough for the entire crowd to hear. "Take this, all of you, and drink from it; this is the cup of my blood."

He passes the chalice to Soren, who takes a drink. I shudder to think about how Soren has perverted this rite. Do the faithful understand how they're being manipulated? How Soren is using the Church, its teachings, history, and rites to gain followers so he can increase his power?

They don't know and I'm sick that I'm part of this perversion. I hate that everyone— Michel, Julien, my mother, even Dylan—expects me to accept that I can't be told details of the plan to destroy Soren and that I must go along blindly. When did Dylan accept what Michel says as gospel?

I take the cup from Michel and drink, squeezing my eyes shut because I know I'll be assaulted with the emotions of the congregation once I drink. Before I've finished, it happens. Our blood mingles and whatever abilities I have as an Adept and as an ascended vampire meld together to amplify the usual effect this sharing of blood has on me.

I feel as if a shroud of adoration has engulfed me. It takes my breath away, choking me with emotion. My knees weaken and Michel has to grab the chalice out of my hands, taking one of my arms and leading me to a chair on the dais beside Soren. I slump into its plush cushions and watch what happens from beneath my half-closed eyes, drugged from the endorphins and unable to move.

Soren stands on the dais beside me, his body glowing with an unnatural white light. Or is that my vision, affected by the blood? I can't tell, but he appears to grow in size, his wings expanding to almost fill the space around him—twenty feet around.

The people cower in awe when he stands to full height, stretching his arms above his head. I feel the crowd's fear and awe even more intensely now and I expect that was Soren's purpose in showing them his magnificence. He walks to the tank where Kael is suspended and stands beside it, staring down at the contents.

"Behold," he says in a booming voice. "Mine enemies would destroy me and my kind in the hopes of preventing the birth of a new world, but they have failed. If you believe, if you truly believe, I will resurrect my brethren and together we will rid the world of all vampires and usher in a world of peace and prosperity for all." He glances at the crowd as they gather at the foot of the dais, watching him with a mixture of eagerness and fear apparent in their blanched faces and wide eyes. "Do you believe?"

A few nod, but most of them appear too afraid to speak.

"I said DO YOU BELIEVE?"

"Yes!" they respond as one, and the wave of emotion they emit collectively knocks the air out of me.

Soren reaches into the tank and I can see from where I sit that he's touching Kael's body to stop the nanovirus and help him fight it off so he can regain consciousness.

The light surrounding the two increases in brightness, almost blinding me with its brilliance. There's a crackle in the air like electricity in a light bulb, an audible hum as if from a generator, and the scent of sulfur burns my nose. Before us, Kael rises out of the gel that has encased him in the tank and steps out with Soren's help, his body dripping with goo. He's naked, the perfection of his body and its pale whiteness striking, his wings soaked with gel. Some internal heat warms the gel so that it evaporates, steam rising off his body as if he's burning from an inner fire. It leaves him clean and dry and perfect. His wings spread out and the mortals surrounding the tank gasp and step back in fear.

Each time the crowd gasps or responds, I see that it gives Soren even more power, the light surrounding him brightening appreciably.

"How are you, my brother?" Soren says once Kael is completely dry and standing beside him a few feet from the crowd.

"I feel as if I could eat the whole world," Kael says in a deep, mellifluous voice.

"We will," Soren says, smiling. "But first, you can start with them." Soren turns to the crowd and waves his hand. A jolt of fear goes through me.

What does he mean, start with them?

Kael strides over to the closest man and grabs him by the scruff of his shirt, lifting him up by it before biting the man's neck. He feeds like a wild animal, almost growling as he does; it takes barely a few seconds for Kael to drain the man. He discards the body to the floor and turns to the woman beside him.

She screams and tries to flee, as do the others now that they know their purpose, but Kael is fast and there are armed guards and a high metal gate surrounding the tent, preventing any escape. Before us, Kael moves from one mortal to the next, draining each one efficiently before throwing the bodies unceremoniously to the ground. I try to sit up straight, but I'm still under the influence of the crowd, whose only emotions are fear and dread and panic. My heart races in my chest. If anything, the fear and dread and panic feeds Kael and Soren and they both appear almost gigantic, eight feet—ten feet—tall if not taller, the mortals in Kael's grip like children as he holds them up to drink their blood.

I turn to Michel, barely able to speak, finding his face as white as a vampire despite him being mortal, his cheeks wet with tears. His grimace tells me everything I need to know—he hates this as much as I do. Beside him, Julien stands mute, his face dark, his fists clenched.

I had no idea I would be helping Soren resurrect Kael only for the monster to kill dozens of humans.

"Michel!" I cry, reaching out to touch him from where I sit. "Did you know?"

He only shakes his head, unable to meet my eyes—probably out of shame. His shoulders shake, but he makes no sound. Or if he does, I can't hear it above the shrieks and screams, the tat-tat-tat of automatic gunfire as the guards shoot those who try to scale the fence to escape.

It's a massacre.

"Julien, do something!" I yell, but Julien is like a statue, shackled in chains watching everything that happens without acting. "Julien!" I scream, but it's like he can't hear me, or if he can, he can't respond.

Has Soren compelled his compliance?

When the last mortal is dead, the bodies in a heap in the center of the tent, guards appear and drag the bodies out. I watch through tear-blurred eyes as they dump the bodies into the large pit they've dug just outside the tent.

Kael appears to have drunk his fill. He's ten feet tall and spilled so much blood that it stains his chest and abdomen and legs.

He's the kind of being described in the Book of Enoch. As I watch in shock, trying to take it all in, I remember reading a passage from the Book of Enoch while searching through my mother's files..

"And they became pregnant, and they bare great giants, whose height was three hundred ells: Who consumed all the acquisitions of men. And when men could no longer sustain them, the giants turned against them and devoured mankind, devouring one another's flesh, and drinking the blood."

He is Nephilim.

～

MICHEL PULLS me out of the tent towards the waiting vehicle and I fall into his arms. He has to carry me, so weakened by the horrors I experienced while watching Kael kill more than four-dozen humans. There's no way he drank all their blood—even though he appears to be ten feet tall, he couldn't have digested all that blood.

Julien follows us, dragging his chains behind him.

"Michel," I begin as the car drives off, leaving the scene of carnage behind, "you never said anything to me about this. Did you know this would happen?"

"People die in war, Eve." He doesn't look in my eyes when he speaks. "In every war it's the same."

"But it's my fault!" I cover my face with my hands and weep, horrified that I enabled that bloodbath. "Soren would never have been able to resurrect Kael without my help. Their deaths are my fault."

Michel puts his arm around my shoulder, but he knew this would happen and he let it! He let me help Soren resurrect a murderer.

"Don't touch me ever again." I push him away, barely able to see through my tears, and move towards Julien, who slips an arm around me.

I move as close to Julien as I can, wiping my eyes with the sleeve of my gown, unable to bear seeing Michel's face,.

"I mean it, Michel. I can't forgive you for this. I can't forgive myself for trusting you."

"It had to be this way. To get where we want to be, we had to go through this. I know it's horrible," he says and shakes his head slowly, staring at his hands, which are open in his lap, "but this leads directly to other events that must take place if we're to rid the world of him and the others like him. Eve, you have to trust me. You'll know in the end that I was telling the truth."

I say nothing. There's nothing possible to say in response to that. Either he's right and I will know or he's crazy and I'll know that as well.

We drive the rest of the way to Soren's mansion in silence.

CHAPTER 21

"ONLY THE BROKENHEARTED know the truth about love."

Mason Cooley

I RUSH up the stairs to my room in Soren's mansion and slam the door before throwing myself onto the bed in the darkness. I weep inconsolably, pulling the covers over my head, horrified with what I've been party to. When Julien and Michel enter the room and Julien comes to the side of the bed, I wave him away and turn my back to him, not wanting to face either of them now.

"Eve," Julien says, his voice filled with pain. "I'm so sorry. There was nothing I could do. I literally couldn't move or speak the entire time."

I don't respond and finally he gives up and joins Michel. The two brothers sit by the fire, facing each other, and wait while I regain control over my emotions. I try to shut out my mind, to blot out the images from the slaughter, but I can't. I keep coming back to the image of Kael standing tall with blood dripping down his face and chest like the Nephilim mentioned in the Book of Enoch.

An apocryphal book of the Bible, Enoch references the Children of Irin, offspring of the fallen angels. According to Enoch, the fallen angels mated with human women and produced a race of monsters who ate the flesh—and drank the blood—of humans.

Supposedly killed during the great flood, a tenth of them survived to remain as demons, tempting humans until the Day of Judgment.

My mother once wanted to understand their powers, to understand what caused vampirism, and to use science to eradicate them. Now, instead of fighting them, I have taken part in the resurrection of one of their most powerful members.

I'm sick to death, and when I remember the pile of bodies, the victims' necks torn and bloody, I feel nauseated. I pull back the covers and run to the bathroom to vomit. I cough and gag, my stomach far too empty to produce much more than saliva and stomach acids. Julien comes in and kneels down behind me, stroking my shoulders as I retch, my face wet from tears.

"You're okay," he says, handing me a wet cloth when I'm finished. "You're okay."

I wipe my face off and try to catch my breath, not meeting his eyes out of shame. "I can't believe it," I say, my voice quavering with emotion. "I can't believe Michel let me do it, knowing what would happen. I'll never speak to him again."

Julien threads his shackled arms around me and pulls me into his embrace. I don't fight. I need his warmth and comfort and I press my face into his chest while he rocks me.

When we return to the other room, Michel is gone.

"Good," I say and curl up on a chair by the fire. "I don't want to even look at him right now."

Julien sits across from me, his hands on the armrests. He looks exhausted, his face haggard and his eyes bleary. "Don't be too hard on him, Eve. He was as horrified as I was at what happened. I don't think he knew that Kael was going to kill everyone there. Besides, I didn't think you believed Michel has visions. Had visions."

I wrap my arms around myself more tightly. "I don't know what I believe anymore. Kael," I say and turn to Julien, "he was some kind of monster. A giant."

Julien nods. "Nephilim. One of the originals."

"Who is Soren? Or should I say, what?"

Julien shrugs. "Grigori. Fallen angel."

"You believe that?"

He rubs his chin and jaw, which are covered with thick whiskers. "Yes. I don't know what they are or where they came from, but they're obviously real."

I watch the flames flicker in the hearth for a moment, unable to get the image of a blood-covered Kael out of my mind's eye.

"They're real," I confirm. "We have to find a way to destroy them. I won't help Soren resurrect any more of them. I'd rather die fighting than bring another one of them back."

"My thoughts exactly."

I look at Julien and nod. "We have to find a way to escape. And then we have to find a way to rescue my father from Blackstone."

"Soren will want to bring back others right away," Julien says, his expression haunted. "We have to act fast, whatever we do."

"You're former special ops. How would you escape?"

Julien shrugs and watches the fire for a moment. "I've been watching security while I've been here, looking for weaknesses. Noticing procedures and processes. I might be able to come up with some kind of plan."

An ache fills me, the craving for blood strong despite the ghastly scene I witnessed earlier.

"I need blood, but I don't want to ever drink it again."

"I know how you feel, Eve. It's heaven not to need to feed. But you need your strength."

Julien is right. I have to feed, no matter how much disgust I feel at the prospect. I stand up and go to the table where a crystal decanter of blood sits beside three glasses. I pour myself a cup and drink it down quickly. Immediately, the blood makes me feel euphoric and washes away the pain and horror of the day. I look at the glass, stained with the remnants of someone's blood, filled with incredible guilt that I know I'll never completely get over.

I cover my eyes with a hand and bite my lip, trying not to start crying again. Julien comes over and threads his arms around me and rocks me slowly, his voice soft and soothing.

"Shh, shh, it's okay, Eve..." He kisses my forehead and pulls me closer, his warmth finally piercing the chill that has enveloped me since the events of the evening. "It's going to be all right."

When he finally pulls me to the bed and begins to undress me, I don't fight. I need him. I need to overwrite the memories of the night, replace them with the touch and taste and scent of him. The feel of his naked body on and in mine, of me on him, momentarily wipes away the darkness inside of me.

MERCIFULLY, Michel stays away so there's no uncomfortable discovery of me with Julien. I lie in silence, alone in the bed while Julien washes up in the bathroom, trying to sort through the events of the last few days.

My father is not insane. He's been kept a prisoner in an asylum to keep him from taking me away and out of the Council. Right now, he's being held captive by Blackstone as insurance to make me comply with his plans.

My mother is alive and a vampire. Michel turned her and she's been in hiding ever since, waiting for the day she could return and fight with me and the twins against Soren. She thinks Soren can't see into her mind and isn't aware of her existence, but she—and Michel— are both wrong. He can.

Michel is not compellable and never has been. He thinks Soren is unaware of it and has pretended to be compelled by him ever since. This means he wasn't compelled to kill Danielle but did so because he would rather it have been him take her life than Soren. This means he was not compelled by Marguerite either and became her lover willingly. I really should find the manuscript—all of it, including the parts Michel removed—and see what else I can learn.

Blackstone is cooperating with Soren to share power, with him controlling the streets and Soren controlling the pulpit, but both plan on ultimately defeating the other and are jockeying for position.

The Council has been infiltrated for a long time and has to be reconstituted with those who we know are not compromised and who share the goal of destroying both Soren and Dominion.

Most important of all, Soren can read my mind and the mind of anyone with whom he has shared blood. That means me, Michel, and Julien. He knows everything that has transpired among us since that first time we shared blood. I cannot reveal this to either twin since Soren can read my mind any time he wishes and will kill Michel with the kill collar. Happily.

I don't see how I can ever conspire against him.

I feel incredibly helpless at this moment, for I realize now there is nothing I can do. Nothing. I am the window through which Soren can watch everything. Blackstone. Michel. My mother. Julien.

I close my eyes and fight tears.

Julien emerges from the bathroom and comes over to the side of the bed when he sees me wiping my eyes. He frowns and sits down, stroking my hair. "What's the matter? Did Michel come back? Did he say something that upset you?"

I shake my head, wishing I could confess to him, but I can't. "No, Michel hasn't returned. I have no hope anymore, Julien. There's no hope."

"Shh," he says and leans down, wiping away my tears. "There's always hope. Sometimes you just can't see it." He smiles, but it's forced. "At least we have each other." He bends down and kisses me on the lips. I let him, needing the comfort. Michel will soon be back and so I want to get every moment of comfort from Julien that I can before he does.

"I better get up," I say and slip out of bed, smoothing my messy hair and pulling on a robe from the foot of the bed. "I'll go get dressed. Can you order us some breakfast? We never ate a meal last night."

Julien nods and I go freshen up.

~

WHEN I RETURN fifteen minutes later, there's a tray on the coffee table laden with fresh bread and cheese and some fruit. A carafe of coffee and a teapot sit to the side with cups, cream, and sugar.

My stomach grumbles at the sight, and I sit with Julien while he fixes a plate of food.

"We have to talk," Julien says, looking at me from under his eyelashes as he sips a cup of tea. "I won't be part of this any longer."

I glance up at him from my cup of coffee and frown. "What do you mean?"

"I've been thinking about what you said. I don't want to cooperate any longer. I know you don't either. If that means I die, so be it."

"I know how you feel," I say, afraid that Soren is listening and will know what Julien is going to do. "But maybe we should sleep on it for a while. Soren will kill Michel if you leave."

"I've thought about it long and hard. My cooperation leads to too many deaths. All those in the tent…they're as much on my conscience as on anyone's because I did nothing to stop it. There will be thousands more. How can I stand by and let people die through my actions —or inaction? I can't."

"You're mortal now. You can die so easily."

"Some things are worse than death," he says and I can hear the resolve in his voice. "I'm finding a way to leave and I'm taking you with me, if you want to come."

"Soren will kill Michel," I say again. "He said he would if either of us fails to comply."

"Soren will kill thousands of others if we do cooperate. At least if I leave, I can help fight him," he points out, stirring his coffee thoughtfully. "I know how to fight. If I can rally enough people before Soren gets too much power, maybe we can prevent him from bringing back the Twelve. If Soren kills Michel…" He pauses, staring into the distance. "So be it. We're all dead anyway. Someone else can take the responsibility for sending people to their deaths. I'm through being passive. I'm going to fight." He turns to me, his blue eyes piercing. "Will you come with me?"

"My father…"

"Eve, do you really want to resurrect the rest of those monsters? Think how many people will die. Is one person's life worth a thousand? Is your father's life and Michel's life worth a thousand other lives?"

I wring my hands anxiously. I know that whatever Julien says to me is pretty much saying it to Soren.

"I can't," I say, feeling trapped. Helpless.

There's a knock at the door. Julien glances at it, his jaw set. "That's probably Michel."

So it is.

"What do you want?" I say, opening the door and noting he's still wearing vestments. He looks every inch the priest he always wanted to be.

Michel looks me up and down and then he peers inside and sees Julien. "I want to speak with you—alone."

"I've said everything there is to say to you."

He closes his eyes for a moment. "Eve, please…"

"What is it?"

"Just give me a moment."

I pop my head back in the room. "I'm going to speak with Michel for a bit."

Julien frowns. "What about?"

I can see the disapproval in his expression. He's jealous of every moment I spend with his brother.

"I have no idea," I admit. "I'll be right outside. He has something to tell me in private."

Julien nods, but I can tell by the tightness of his mouth and jaw that he doesn't like it. I close the door behind me and go to stand with Michel, my arms crossed. The hallway is dim, but I can see his face in the light from a lantern that hangs in the hallway. He's frowning.

"Well?"

He takes in a deep breath. "Eve, I've come to say goodbye."

A shock goes through me. "What? Not you as well?"

"What do you mean?

"Your brother said he was leaving, too," I say, my stomach in knots. "You can't expect that Soren will let you live if you leave. He'll use that," I say pointing at the kill collar.

"Maybe," he says, his expression dark. "Maybe not. He has no one else besides the Twelve who are even near his age. He'll get lonely for the old days. That's why he always has us around. We're his only link to the past."

"Where are you planning to go?"

He shakes his head. "One of my properties, if anything is still standing."

"You know Soren will find you and bring you back or kill you."

"He could kill me if I don't go. Besides, I'm not cooperating any longer, Eve. I can't accept this path your mother has put us on."

I'm scared now. He has this look in his eyes, distant and resigned. Resolved. Like he's doing something big. Like he's made a final decision.

"You and Julien are both mortals now," I remind him. "He can kill you both with a thought. Stay. See if there's some other way…"

"I can't help him any longer," he says, his eyes haunted. "I can't stand by and watch it. I'm a priest. I'm supposed to save souls, not take them.

"Michel," I say and step closer, "I don't want anything to happen to you. I could turn you and you'd be protected. As a mortal, you're so weak…"

He cups my face with his hands. "Eve," he says, his eyes huge, "I'm free of hunger for the first time in eight hundred years. Can you even begin to understand that? No bloodlust. No raging desire to feed. To kill. I'm finally free to be a priest again. Julien might have been happy being a vampire, but I could never be."

I shake my head, my eyes brimming. "How can you be a priest after everything that's happened? How can you give up the life we had? We could spend eternity together, if you and Julien could get over your jealousy."

"You told me we would never be together again. Have you forgotten that?" He smiles, but I can see the hurt in his eyes. "Besides, the priesthood has been my calling since I was seventeen. Maybe even before. You knew I'd return to it given the chance. You asked me that when we were first lovers; I was honest from the start."

He strokes my cheek with the backs of his fingers as he speaks, as if he can't deny his desire for me. His love for me. At that moment, I can't imagine existence without him.

"Don't worry about me," he says, his eyes filled with resolve. "I don't care any longer what happens to me. If I have to die in order for Soren to be destroyed, it doesn't matter. All that matters is that Soren will finally be destroyed. He won't have a chance to proclaim himself savior of everyone. That would be unacceptable to me as a true believer, and even death is worth the price to stop him. So, Eve," he says and furrows his brow, "just let me go now, please. It makes it all the harder when you try to stop me."

He leans down and kisses me, his mouth soft on mine, lingering a little longer than his newfound classification as a priest would deem appropriate. I do nothing, standing unresponsive while he presses his lips against mine, but then I can't hold back and throw my arms around his neck, pulling him against my body, kissing him back with a fierceness that surprises even me.

I love him. My love is all mixed up with bloodlust and desire, but it is love I feel for him in this moment. I do still love Michel, despite everything. Despite how he lied to me from the first moment he met me and ever since. I love him in the way you love someone despite their flaws, knowing them, accepting them...

I realize now that, in his mind, every lie was for the greater good and every lie hurt him, but he felt he had no other choice. Although it broke up our relationship, he felt he had to lie and do everything he did to save the world.

I can only hope that whatever vision he has seen of the future comes true and that all his lies and all the pain he's caused me and that he's experienced as a result have been worth it.

Michel indulges me for a moment as I kiss him, but then he pulls away, prying my arms from around his neck. I'm afraid that this will be our last goodbye. I'm afraid that I won't ever see him alive again. That the next time I see him, he'll be dead.

"Michel," I whisper and he slowly pushes me away, straightening his vestments and running a hand through his messy hair. Tears blur my eyes. "Michel…"

"Don't cry," he says, shaking his head, smiling softly. "I'm happy. We'll both be happy, Eve. Trust me. It will all be okay."

I want to stop him and tell him that Soren will know he's leaving because Soren can read his mind. But I can't. Soren will kill Michel if I reveal it. Michel turns away and leaves me standing in the hallway outside the bedroom. I watch him walk away, a hand covering my mouth, waiting for Soren to realize it and kill him with the collar.

Inside, Julien waits for me. I should go back to him; he'll want to know what Michel had to say to me. But I can't. I have to be alone and cry, and I don't want Julien to see how much this hurts me because I still do love Michel. I don't think I'll ever stop.

I slide down the wall to sit on the floor, covering my mouth with my hands to stop from sobbing. If I could wipe out the memory of Julien, I know I could be happy with Michel. We would live by the beach in a cottage near St. David's on the Pembrokeshire coast and have that quiet, happy life we had for a brief moment of time, fixing dinner together and watching the stars rise over the ocean at night, playing music for each other and making love.

If I could wipe out the memory of Michel, I could be happy with Julien. Together, we could travel and stay in exotic places, do new things I've never done before. We could practice our fighting skills together, walk along the trails that snake through the cities we visited. Drink chocolate milkshakes and eat cheeseburgers in retro diners on the road. We'd laugh in each other's arms and roll around on the bed, pleasuring each other.

But I can't selectively erase the memory of either of them, so I must live in a world where I have one but lack the other. A world where I miss the other every day, the one twin never quite filling the hole where the other might have been.

It is my curse.

CHAPTER 22

"COURAGE IS LIKE LOVE; it must have hope for nourishment."

Napoleon

AFTER A FEW MOMENTS, Julien opens the door and sees me sitting there, crying as silently as I can. He bends down to me and takes my face in his shackled hands. His expression is so empathetic.

"Oh, Eve… What did he say to you?"

I shake my head, unable to speak. He slips one hand under my arm and helps me up, trying as best he can to comfort me. I break down as soon as we're inside the room and the door is closed. I don't care if Julien sees me crying. I cover my face with my hands and weep. He threads his arms around me.

"Michel's leaving," I whisper, barely able to speak. "Soren will kill him."

"Shh, shh," he whispers, rocking me softly in his arms. "It's okay, Eve. Michel knows what he's doing."

He holds me while I cry it out.

~

LATER, I watch as he packs a small knapsack with his few personal possessions.

"Where are you going?"

He fastens the zipper and glances to where I sit by the fire. "There are a few weapons and things stored at Michel's mansion in Cambridge that I need," he replies, his tone light, "but I have a few places to hide out from my days undercover. You should come with me."

"You think you're just going to walk out of this place?"

"Yes," he says. "I've watched the security and I know their patterns, when they change shift, how many people patrol and where. I take out one, use his weapon, take out any others who come to respond, and then I leave."

"Sounds like a suicide mission."

"If they have orders to kill me, Soren would do it eventually himself. Why wait and let them use me as a tool for Soren to gain more power?"

I sigh in frustration; he sounds so determined. "What changed for you?"

He shrugs. "Kael. He changed everything. I had no idea he'd kill so many people. I thought maybe one or two to quench his thirst, but that many? If Soren resurrects the rest of the Twelve, it'll be hundreds. Maybe thousands." He shakes his head. "Not doing it." He jams something small into a pocket on the knapsack. "You should come with me, Eve. Now or never."

"Soren will kill Michel if I do."

Julien tilts his head and regards me. "He'll kill Michel if you stay. If you come with me, at least we'll die fighting. Put your Adept skills to use. Slay a few vampires on the way out. Doesn't that sound better than sitting here waiting for Soren to use you and then kill you when he's got what he wants?"

I know he's right—even though Soren can read my mind when he wants, I realize that fighting sounds better than compliance. If I die, he'll have no way to resurrect the Twelve on his own. It will be him and Kael. Maybe Blackstone can fight him. Maybe humans can find a way to destroy him using the nanovirus, if it's engineered properly. He has to have a weakness.

I get my own bag and gather my few possessions. "If we survive, we have to find a way to destroy Soren. The nanovirus may be the only hope we have."

Julien comes over and stops me, taking my hands and placing them around his neck. "I know we're taking a huge risk, but I can't stand by and let this happen, no matter what Blackstone thinks he can do to stop Soren down the road. I can't live with this. I won't." He bends down and kisses me, his fearlessness giving me strength. "Now, get your sweet little ass in gear and let's go. Time's a wasting!"

I pack as fast as I can, then follow Julien out of the room, glancing back to see if I've forgotten anything. I see the two wing chairs and remember seeing both Michel and Julien siting there. I wonder if we'll ever be together again.

We make our way down the hallways to the rear exit of the mansion. We pass through the kitchen to the scullery exit, and Julien stops to grab an apple off a tray, winking at the cook as he passes.

"You don't mind if we take a few pints of blood, do you?" he says to a cheery-looking woman of wide girth wearing a cook's white apron and cap, her cheeks rosy. "We're going to have a moonlight picnic."

She smiles at him, motioning to the icebox, letting him go and remove three bottles without complaint. I wonder if he's already been here and charmed her.

Julien adds the bottles of blood to the backpack and fastens it once more. We pause in the doorway. Across from the scullery exit is a path to the fence that circles Soren's property. There's not a guard in sight.

"Let's go," he says and takes my hand, pulling me behind him.

We make it to the fence. There's no one on the path, and apparently, no one's seen us. I climb the chain-link fence and throw a coat over the top coil of barbed wire. I climb over and drop to the ground. Julien follows close behind me, throwing his pack over first, which I catch, and then jumps down, landing on all fours, the chains that shackle his hands making it hard to maneuver.

"That was too easy," I say, and Julien nods.

"My exact thoughts. Do you suppose he's letting us escape?"

"Why would he? He wants me to help resurrect the rest of the Twelve."

Julien grabs his bag and leads me through the small copse of trees that borders the property. We emerge on the other side and there's nothing between us and the city of Boston except other Brookline properties that provide ample cover.

"The first thing we're going to do is find some way to get rid of these," he says and holds up his cuffed hands. The foot-long chain that links them is wide enough that he can use his hands, but it's definitely hard to do anything requiring dexterity.

We run, threading our way past Leverett Pond, through back alleys, down narrow paths between huge houses, and under a highway overpass. We don't stop until we've run about two miles, pausing to lean against an outbuilding that is part of Hall's Pond Sanctuary.

"I didn't see anyone following us," Julien says, catching his breath. "I can't believe we weren't caught on the video surveillance system."

"I don't get it," I comment, still not willing to tell Julien that Soren can read my mind. "All that security and yet, we were able to escape so easily. It seems like a trap to me."

"If so, I guess we'll find out," he says and stands up. "Let's go. It's a good walk to Michel's place."

We pass an abandoned service station and Julien finds a set of bolt cutters behind some boxes in the service bay. I use them to cut the chains and then the bolts that secure the manacles to his wrists. He rubs his skin once the manacles are off.

"Free at last," he says and smiles and once more I'm amazed that he can be so cheerful despite the reality we face.

We walk down the deserted streets of Mission Hill, up Essex Street to Park Drive and the Charles River, which we will cross to get to Cambridge. I'm aware that there may be people watching us from inside the buildings, but no one tries to stop us or contact us. Julien is silent as we walk, but he holds my hand in his, and now and then, he glances over at me and smiles.

I think of Michel and wonder if he's already dead. A surge of sadness goes through me at the thought. I imagine him bleeding to death, lying on the floor with his vestments on, a smug Soren standing over top of him.

Would Soren really kill Michel? A part of me doesn't believe it. Although he has reason to, even I can sense that Soren loves Michel. I don't understand it, other than it must be incredibly lonely as an immortal. Finding someone else who has lived a long time and seen so much, shared so much history, done so much, must be a comfort.

We cross the Charles River using the Boston University Bridge and make our way north and west to Michel's Brattle Street home.

THE MANSION IS DESERTED when we finally arrive. I remember it being surrounded by guards and lit with torches, but now it's an empty hulk, dark and cavernous looking from the street.

"Why is nobody here?" I ask as we walk behind the building through a narrow alley bordered with tall bushes and a brick and wrought iron fence. "Did Michel abandon it?"

Julien shakes his head and stops at the back driveway. The huge doors of the detached garage are open and the petroleum-fuelled vehicles sit empty and impotent. Wind moans through the trees, the dry leaves that remain on bare branches crackle like paper. A few brown-yellow leaves blow around the yard, dark against the white dusting of snow from an earlier flurry.

"Looks like he closed up shop and left," Julien says and shrugs. "I thought he'd leave someone here to protect the property from squatters and looters. We should be careful in case someone's in the house."

My muscles tense as we approach. The door is locked and all the windows appear unbroken, so perhaps people have left the city in search of food. Julien breaks the window in the kitchen door and opens it from the inside. The room smells of dust and dried coffee.

The house is silent other than our footsteps on the hardwood and tile floors.

Julien lights a lantern fueled with vegetable oil and we wander through the house in search of intruders, but it's empty. Julien even takes the stairs to the basement but finds no one there so it's just the two of us.

"We should keep our light low during the night in case we attract attention," he suggests. "Seems that people have left the biggest houses alone, probably thinking there's better security in place. There's canned food in the kitchen and lots of staples, so we can take some with us." He stands and surveys the living room. "Soren will come looking for us eventually. We should get weapons and supplies and leave as soon as possible."

"I'm going upstairs to find some of my things from the apartment."

Julien nods. "Do you need a lantern?" He holds it out to me.

I shake my head. I can see almost as well in the dark as I can in the light.

Julien cracks a smile. "I forgot. Human again," he says and shrugs.

I climb the stairs to the second floor and go to the dark paneled room where Michel kept my things. After sorting through a few boxes, I pull out a few pieces of clothing to bring with me. It's hard to know what to bring since I'm not sure where we're going or what we'll need.

I almost trip over a box of my mother's files. I open it and there on the top is the manuscript and the file on the prophecy of St. Therese of the Reeds. I scan the page, my eyes coming to rest on a section in italics—a quote from the original document.

And when I turned, I saw a being with wings of grey dressed in a uniform with leather breastplate and helmet, a huge sword in its hand. Behold, an angel of The LORD, an Archangel, come to bring news of the end of days. His skin and hair was as white as snow, and his eyes were like blazing fire. His face was like the sun shining in all its brilliance.

I fell to my knees before him, my eyes burning from the brightness of his countenance. When he touched me, I saw a vision of the future and fear was in my heart for a rain of blood fell from a cloudless sky and all was cold and dark. One would come, the Angel told me, who would take over the holy Church and fight those who would enslave the Children of God across the world. He would wield one weapon that could save those who faced the blood tribulation—a double-edged sword of dark and light. The one who wields the sword must be pure of heart, for the blade is a harsh mistress and he who wields her should regret the day they raised it not in service of The LORD.

I exhale as I read it, for it seems preposterous. No sword is going to save anyone against Dominion. A sword can't kill Blackstone—only a stake can. A single sword won't turn back the plague or stop vampires and Soren from ascendance.

The only thing that will stop the plague is some kind of engineered nanovirus that will shut it off. The only thing that will destroy Soren is a more potent nanovirus than we tried last time. We haven't come close to that yet because our ability to develop a new virus has been harmed by the spreading plague and loss of technology. Everything in a modern lab uses plastics in some part of its construction. All of it runs on electricity and most of that electricity came from coal-fired power plants, which are nothing but empty hulks now.

I put the document down. I'd really like to take the manuscript with me, but it's heavy and bulky. It would take up too much room in my backpack, so I return it to the box. These items will probably be safe here from looters, who likely will have no interest in old documents filled with prophecies foretelling humanity's doom.

I return to the main floor and find Julien packing up some canned beans and stew into a large backpack. He turns when I enter.

"Got everything you want?"

I hold up my backpack and nod. "I wanted to bring your manuscript so I could read it, but I figure it'll probably be safer to leave it here. If we return someday, I can read it then."

He smiles. "You could have the story right from the horse's mouth, so to speak. Ask me anything."

I nod, but I know Michel's probably compelled him not to reveal anything he doesn't want me to know. "I'll take you up on that. Where are we going, anyway?"

"Northwest," he says and jams another can into the backpack. "We need to get as far away from Soren as possible. There's a small cell of like-minded people from the old Council hiding out at Fort Devens. We should contact them. The group includes a couple of my old army buddies. We could stay with them for a while, formulate a plan."

"What about Dylan?"

Julien shrugs. "What about him? He pretty much betrayed you, didn't he?"

"He has his reasons. I'd do a lot to protect my father."

Julien finishes packing the backpack and stands. "Let's go," he says. "I don't want to stay here any longer than we have to. Are you okay to travel? Do you need some blood?"

"Maybe a bit."

"I'd let you bite me, but I need to conserve my strength." He grins and hands me a bottle of blood. It's preserved blood, rather than fresh, and I grimace as I drink down a half-bottle, replacing the cork once I do. It tastes off, and instead of the usual euphoria I feel when drinking blood, I feel only the bloodlust fade a bit into manageable background noise.

He puts the bottle back into his pack and refastens it.

"Feel better?"

I nod. "Able to face the rest of the trip at least," I say and force a smile. "Preserved blood is pretty awful."

"It is, but it keeps you alive. And me." He turns back and grins at me.

I can't resist him and smile back for real. "Julien, you know I'd never hurt you, don't you?" I say, only half serious. I do feel desire for his blood, but I feel more desire for him.

"I was just kidding," he says and takes my hand. "Let's go."

CHAPTER 23

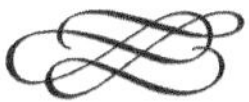

Aeschylus

Julien is laden with several weapons—ancient rifles, old handguns, leather holsters with bullets, and several swords of varying length. I carry a few swords and my backpack. Together, we walk until we reach the stables where Julien's friend keeps a horse and wagon for his use.

Julien speaks with the man and I see money change hands. Julien also gives the man two of his swords and a few cans of food, because that's the real currency. The man glances at me, his brows knitted together, and takes a puff on the cigar clamped between his teeth. I listen carefully to hear what they're saying, because he doesn't look pleased.

"I hope none of your trouble blows back onto me," the man says. "I'm not choosing sides here. I'm trying to stay alive."

"You have to choose sides, Nick," Julien says as he takes the horse's reins. "You already have by giving me the carriage and horse. Don't kid yourself. Soren won't see it any other way. He's not one who believes in the neutrality of capitalism."

Nick shrugs and takes out his cigar, using it to point at Julien. "Don't mention my name to anyone. The fewer people who know who I am, the better."

Julien says nothing more, but claps Nick on the back. Nick sneers at me and then turns away. Julien leads the horse and a flatbed wagon out and I place my backpack in the rear next to Julien's. The cache of Julien's weapons is hidden under a horse blanket. There's a sack of feed and a bale of hay for the horse, and an old barrel that sloshes as the cart moves—must be water. There are a couple of sleeping bags, too, and a crate of tin pots beside the bale. We're going to be roughing it for a few days.

It's practically like the Wild West. The only thing missing are the Stetsons and cowboy boots.

I hop up onto the seat beside Julien and we're off, taking a narrow road that runs north.

"How far is this place we're going? How long will this take?"

Julien glances over at me. "It's about fifty miles. A couple days, give or take, depending on the road, the horse, and how well-maintained the wagon is."

I nod and shake my head, amazed that in only a few short weeks, we've gone from being able to travel that distance in an hour to taking a few days to make the trip.

We drive northwest, taking Highway Two. The first day we plan to make twenty-four miles to Concord and find an abandoned motel on the outskirts of the city. After a few hours, my ass is sore from sitting on the hard seat, the wagon pounding over the road. I can only imagine how I'll feel at the end of the day.

While we drive, Julien answers my questions about the manuscript, filling me in on why he wrote it and what parts Michel must have taken out.

"I was taught to read and write by my father's tutor, who was grooming us for the priesthood. I liked to write, liked to read. You wouldn't think I'd be the one to write. After all, I was the fighter, the swordsman, the one who took risks. It was Michel who was the studious one. Our tutor, Gerard, used to reinforce how important it was to preserve the gospels for posterity, transcribing old records from Church history so they wouldn't be lost. It made me want to record what happened to us when we met Marguerite. If there was ever a story that needed to be told, it was me discovering that evil existed and walked the earth in human form. How we became that evil."

"You sound like a fanatic. Do you really believe in evil as in the devil? Satan?"

Julien shakes his head. "Oh, most definitely. I saw evil the other night when Kael killed all those people. I saw evil when I watched Soren. He enjoyed it."

We drive on for a while, me ruminating on the manuscript.

"What did Michel take out of the manuscript? What was so bad?"

He says nothing for a moment. "He did some bad things, Eve. We both did. Back then, it wasn't always possible to find the dying and take them. We did kill." He glances over at me. "Innocent people. A lot of them. I imagine he didn't want you to read any of the more gory details or how much he seemed to love it."

I find that hard to believe. Michel seemed to have such distaste for killing.

"Did he love it?" I ask, doubtful.

Julien nods. "He seemed to. He seemed to go all in while I was still struggling with it. Oh, I didn't fight being a vampire, but I never loved it—not at first. Not until I grew immune to death. After a few centuries of killing to stay alive, you grow hardened to it. Especially as a warrior. I thought it would be harder for Michel to become used to hunting and killing, but it seemed easier. Maybe it was all the beatings."

I make a face, immediately feeling sympathy for Michel. I don't really care anymore what either of them did back when they were first vampires. I understand now what it means to have this never-ending and overwhelming hunger.

"Why is Soren letting us go?"

Julien sighs heavily. "Maybe he isn't. Maybe Michel's dead and Soren is waiting to strike. I always thought I'd know if he died, because we're identical twins, but we haven't always been close. I've given up trying to second-guess Soren. I have to fight. It's what I know."

I feel a stab of pain at the thought that Michel might be dead, knowing it might be true. I watch Julien, thinking about the valiant knight he was back when he was a mortal the first time, fighting to protect his family's estates from the Church and dying for his father's lands despite hating him. Now he's willing to die for mortals in general to stop Dominion and Soren.

"My brave Julien," I say and take his hand, my eyes brimming, "how I love you."

He smiles and leans over to kiss me. "Not brave," he says and winks at me. "Foolish, probably. Stubborn, no doubt. Unwilling to be Soren's or Blackstone's slave, most certainly."

We drive on down the lonely road in silence. I'm lost in thought about the past and future and what we'll find when we reach Fort Devens.

WE STOP JUST AFTER MIDNIGHT, traveling for hours after sunset, our path on the road illuminated by the full moon. The motel we choose is one of those single story white plaster buildings with a dozen shabby rooms that look like they haven't been used for months. Dust is everywhere, but there are no bugs to be seen (it's too damn cold), nor any running water. Julien opens a garage door at the back of the motel, which has a service station attached, and puts the horse and cart inside, feeding and watering the beast and covering it with the blanket so it's warm enough.

We take the room closest to the garage. It's a standard room with two double beds, a desk, an old television, and a small bathroom. It's dilapidated due to the effects of the plague and anything with petroleum products has disintegrated, including the housing of the television, the phone, and some of the materials used in the bedding, the shower curtain, and the shampoo bottles. But it's shelter from wind and not too cold.

We spread out our sleeping bags on top of the beds. I'm not willing to get under the covers, despite them looking relatively clean. We use some of the water from the barrel to wash up and each eat a can of cold beans. It's not very appealing, but I'm hungry. I choke down the rest of the bottle of preserved blood and help tidy up. Julien checks once more on the horse and seeing that he's okay, returns to the room.

I've finished washing up for the night with the cold water from the barrel, and am waiting to see how Julien plans to spend the night. Will we both sleep or will we take turns keeping watch? We have no lights, no heat, and light no fire, but someone could be watching us, ready to ambush us in the night.

"You get some sleep," he says, coming to where I'm standing by the bed and pulling me into his arms. "I'll take the first watch. Then you can get up and take the next. Four hours each. That will have to do because I want to get to the base before dusk."

"Are you sure? I'm the one who can't be killed. I'll stay up and you can sleep. I can sleep in the cart during the day while you drive."

He shakes his head and strokes my hair. "Nope. I'm wide awake for some reason. I couldn't sleep now if I tried. You sleep. You're still adjusting to this new life."

I give in and kiss him briefly before crawling into the sleeping bag. Julien zips it up around me, tucking me in before kissing me once more, tenderly.

He goes to the window and cracks open the curtains, checking the street for any sign of movement on the road.

I close my eyes. It doesn't take long before I doze off, snuggled down deep in my sleeping bag, Julien sitting by the window, his own sleeping bag draped over his shoulders.

~

THE REST of the trip is much the same, with us traveling without stopping except to use the toilets at gas stations or houses that are abandoned and easy to reach from the road. We talk about France during the crusades, Julien's early life as a knight, and his reasons for leaving the Church. I haven't had this much time alone with Julien, just him and me, with a chance to talk—really talk about his life and his relationship with Michel—ever. It's wonderful.

He loves Michel, that's certain. They're brothers who have survived together for eight hundred years. No matter how each has treated the other, there is a bond that events of the day cannot completely destroy. Michel has deceived Julien. Julien knows it or at least suspects as much, but I don't say anything to him. He's been compelled and probably wouldn't hear what I said anyway.

AFTER ANOTHER DAY on the road, we arrive just outside Fort Devens an hour before sunset. We find a deserted house outside the base, with an old corrugated metal shed beside it where we can stable the horse.

We eat some more cold canned food; I have stew and Julien eats another can of beans. I'm eager to find a kettle and fire so I can have some hot food and especially some coffee or tea. Hopefully, Julien's comrades will have some. I don't think I've ever wanted a cup of something hot to drink more than I do now.

"Who are we going to meet?" I ask as we pack up our things.

Julien unrolls a sleeping bag. "Some of my old army buddies."

"Are they vampires?"

"Yes. They were in Blackstone's program as well. Now they're trying to fight him."

"How do you know they're not with him?"

He glances up at me, his expression serious. "Because they hate what he did to them as much as I do. We thought—we were told—that we were protecting the Treaty, not preparing to overthrow it. They want him stopped as much as I do."

He says it with such conviction that I know he really believes it. It's one of the things I love about Julien. He doesn't lie or deceive. He tells the truth. He seems as if he can't lie, unlike his brother, to whom everything and everyone is a part in some big cosmic chess game.

We finish unpacking our things and Julien brings the horse and cart out of the garage. After unloading the cart, I hop up beside Julien and we drive off to Fort Devens and whatever is waiting for us there.

It takes only half an hour, driving past Mirror Lake to the garrison at Fort Devens. Up Sheridan Road, we come to a line of buildings and go to one at the far end of the street. I expected to see guards along the perimeter, but there are none. At least none I can see. Perhaps they can see us. I expected that there would still be heavy security in place here, but it appears as abandoned as the rest of the countryside.

"Where are all the soldiers?"

"Deployed elsewhere, at the borders probably, keeping people inside. Those who haven't been killed or captured, at least."

We drive past a track, several tennis courts, and basketball courts to a white office building. Julien ties the horse to a bicycle rack and we enter, the interior cold and quiet. The walls are beige, the floors tiled in battleship grey. It appears to have been an administrative office.

"Are you sure this is where they are?" I question, getting a distinctly creepy feeling. It's far too dusty and silent.

"I was in contact with someone only last week."

"You were planning this already?"

Julien nods. "We agreed to meet up here—our old stomping grounds. They're probably checking us out. Wondering who you are. I never mentioned bringing a woman."

We stand in the middle of an empty room, the furniture and desks moved to one side, the floor bare but dusty. Our breath is visible in the chill air.

"Chris?" Julien says, going to a door of a side room. The interior is empty as well.

We walk down a long hallway. On each side are a series of offices with the desks and grey filing cabinets, bookshelves, and cardboard file boxes. Everything is covered in dust, as if people just picked up and left when the plague hit, abandoning their work. We enter another larger room that must be a reception area. As we step through the door, I feel something hard and cold press against the back of my head.

"Hold it right there," a gruff voice says. "Don't move."

I see an arm reach out to Julien with a long-barreled handgun in the hand, but dare not turn my head to see who is holding the gun.

"Whoa," Julien says, holding his hands in the air. "Steady. It's me, Julien de Cernay. I'm here to meet with Chris Robertson.

"Turn around. Slowly," the man orders.

Julien and I turn and we're face to face with a lone gunman, all-American in his white blond brush cut and fatigues, a gun in each hand still in our faces. He grins and lowers the weapons.

"Nice welcome, you sonofabitch," Julien says with a laugh and then throws his arms around the man, whom I take to be Chris Robertson. Tall, well-muscled, and square-jawed with white-blond scruff. They embrace, clapping each other on the back.

"You're looking very human, Julie-boy," Chris says, stepping back, eyeing Julien up and down. "Bummer."

"Yeah, wasn't my choice," Julien says and stands with his hands on his hips, staring at Chris. "You're looking like a Ranger who needs a serious blood transfusion. Don't get any ideas, okay?"

"Julie-boy?" I say, cracking a grin. I turn to Julien, who shakes his head, smiling widely.

"Chris is one of those nickname givers. All designed to humiliate to maximum effect."

"I always say if you can't humiliate your friends, who can you humiliate?" Chris replies. "Come on in and have a seat. I've got everything ready and some coffee brewing. Got a portable hydrogen cell battery we're using for power. An old hotplate, ancient coffeepot. I've been hitting all the antique stores and thrift stores for stuff that works and was made without any fossil fuels. It's not easy."

We sit at a table and while Chris and Julien catch up on the whereabouts of their former team members, I'm extremely happy to listen to the old percolator hiss and pop.

Chris retrieves a glass jar of cream and a bowl filled with sugar cubes. "That's fresh," he says as he puts the cream in front of me. "We have access to a farmer who keeps a couple of dairy cows outside the base. He's got chickens and goats too so now and then we get some good meat and eggs. No bacon, though. I really miss bacon."

Julien relates what happened in Boston with Soren and the Twelve, going over the whole story of their stasis and Soren's resurrection. Chris eyes me with interest when it comes to my part of the story. I can't help but feel guilty, especially when they discuss the resurrection of Kael and how Blackstone has a way to neutralize the plague.

Chris leans closer, his arms crossed on the tabletop. "We've infiltrated Blackstone's lab. We have someone inside who will help us when the time comes."

"Good," Julien says. "We have to stop the plague before it goes completely global."

They survey a map of the world and Chris points out the infected areas and shows how far the plague has spread in the weeks since its release. The map shows that the only parts not yet affected are huge tracts of Russia and the former Soviet Republics, China, the Middle East, Central Canada, and Central Africa.

"How fast is the plague spreading?" I ask while leaning over Julien's shoulder to examine the map.

"Depends on the prevailing winds, which help it spread, but it moves on its own," Chris explains. "There's been no additional release of the plague entity, so it looks like it will slow down and stop eventually. We don't know how long this most recent release will last. Blackstone was strategic in releasing it in areas that aren't rich in fossil fuels. I think he'll stop the plague before it's all destroyed, but not until the whole economic system collapses."

The map confirms that most of the developed world has been affected, with the exception of a small sliver of land running up

Central and North America. Right where the Oil Sands are located in Western Canada.

"If we could stop the plague in time, there'd still be lots of fossil fuel left. We could rebuild," Chris says. "If we're going to act, we have to do it soon."

～

THE COFFEE IS FINALLY ready and Chris pours us each a cup. It smells so good, I'm eager to get drinking, my focus on the way the cream mixes into the dark rich liquid.

We're just starting to relax when all hell breaks loose.

A noise and flash blind and stun me, my hearing dulled and my vision all sparkles. I feel Julien pulling me away from the table where we were sitting as my vision is finally clearing. Having vampire-sensitive eyes is not a good thing when a flashbang goes off. I'm still squinting against the pain as we run from the room, ducking down when we hear the tat-tat-tat of small arms fire.

"Here," Chris says, opening a side door and waving us through. "There's a stake truck just outside. Take cover."

Julien leads me out while Chris returns fire, providing us with cover so we can run behind the truck.

When Chris joins us, crouching down beside Julien, he reloads a magazine into his weapon.

"What the fuck is going on?" Julien asks, his voice low.

Chris shakes his head. "No idea. We have guards posted all along the perimeter. I don't know how anyone slipped through."

Chris peers around the vehicle's bumper and is rewarded by the sound of a bullet whizzing by. I manage not to scream.

"Damn," he says, turning to Julien. "We need some ground support or we're not getting out of here."

The sun is rapidly setting and darkness claims more and more of the base, the sun disappearing beneath the line of trees that circles the perimeter.

"Who is it?" I ask, wondering if it's Soren or Blackstone.

Chris shrugs. "Hard to tell. We've got to get to a better location and quick. You two go along the wall to that dumpster and I'll provide cover. If we can make it to the front, we can use the cover of the forest to escape."

Julien nods and motions to me to take the lead.

"On my count," Chris says and counts down from three, two, one.

I run along the wall just as he lets go a few rounds towards the door we left, pumping the bullets out in rapid succession. I make it to the dumpster and then Julien covers for Chris, who runs along the wall to join us.

"Go to the front, by the guard house," he instructs. "It's only a short run to the trees."

We nod and Chris covers us while I run for the guardhouse, Julien behind me.

"Keep going! Run until you get into the cover of the forest," Julien calls to me as he turns and provides covering fire.

I follow his command, running low and fast past the guardhouse and into the forest. It's dark inside, the moonlight filtering down from the tops of the fir trees providing a little light.

I run as fast as I can, crashing through the undergrowth, the bare branches scratching my face. There's something familiar about the scene; I have a strong sense of déjà vu all of a sudden. I stop to catch my breath and turn to see where Julien is, but he's not following me. I hear the crack of gunfire, several shots one after the other, and then return fire.

I keep running, my vampire vision having returned to normal after the flashbang. I can make my way quite well in the low light, running through the underbrush and between the trees. I hear someone behind me, the sound of leaves and branches snapping under foot and so I stop, turning back to see who it is. I expect to see Julien and Chris, but when I catch sight of the person behind me, my heart squeezes, for it isn't Julien's dark hair I see, but long white hair and a smiling face.

The smiling face of Soren Lindgren.

CHAPTER 24

Antoine de Saint-Exupery

"You didn't really think I'd let you just walk out of my compound, did you? How foolish."

I try to run around him, but then several of his guards appear all around us and I have nowhere to go. My fight sight doesn't provide me with any advantage nor does my ascended status, for they're all ascended as well. All I can do is fight with one, and with less experience, I'm unable to best him, ending up on the ground with my face shoved into the wet earth.

"Let her up," Soren says, and the guard drags me up to my feet and shoves me in front of Soren. He stands before me, his hands on his hips, a look of triumph on his face. "So, Eve," he says, an edge of anger in his voice despite his smile, "you thought you could escape?"

"I wasn't going to help you restore the other eleven. Not after Kael's killing spree in the tent. Julien felt the same way, as did Michel."

He waves his hand, dismissing me. "That was nothing. Just a snack."

I make a face of disgust and glance away, but not before I see him smile.

"Oh, and speaking of Michel, he's been taken care of already."

Horror washes over me and I remember the kill collar. It's then I catch sight of something in the distance—the strange shape is barely visible through the dense brush, but it looks familiar...

I start towards it, drawn to it, a large wooden circle about ten feet high. Inside is an upside-down cross.

"Michel!" I cry out and run towards it, but a guard stops me. We wrestle, but I can't seem to get away and he soon has me in a headlock.

"Let her go to her precious Michel," Soren says and waves his hand. "She has some hard choices to make."

I run to the cross and find Michel nailed to it, his hands and feet bloody. It's as I saw in my dream. Everything is the same except that Michel is still alive, although wounded and in pain. He's breathing fast, his face pale in the moonlight.

"Michel," I whisper and kneel down beside him, cradling his head in my hands. "Oh, Michel. I'm so sorry."

He says nothing, his teeth gritted, his eyes squeezed shut. I check his neck—the kill collar has been deployed. There's a small wound in his neck and blood is oozing out of it. He'll die if I don't apply pressure. I reach into my pocket and remove a tissue. It's not much, but I have nothing else. I push the blade back into its recess and press the cloth against his neck, between the collar and his wound, trying to stem the flow.

I panic, glancing around in search of Julien and Chris, hoping they've escaped and are even now rounding up some of Chris's men for a counterattack. I'm desperate to help Michel, but at the same time, I know I can't do anything with five of Soren's guards and Soren himself just a few feet away.

"Like I said, you have a choice, Eve," Soren says. "You either help me resurrect my brethren, or your beloved twins die."

"Don't do it, Eve," Michel whispers beside me through gritted teeth. "Don't help him."

I turn and look in Michel's eyes, which are half-open now. "You'll die if I don't."

He shakes his head slightly, breathing rapidly. "Don't. Not for me."

I hear gunfire in the distance, several different kinds, and know there is a firefight. One Julien probably won't come out of alive.

"Michel, I don't want you to die."

I remain kneeling by Michel, one hand pressing on the wound, the other pulling the kill collar away from Michel's neck. If I agree to help Soren temporarily, he won't kill Michel, and maybe Chris and Julien will be able to counterattack and rescue us. I'll do anything to keep Michel alive. I'll agree to anything.

Several guards join us where we stand around the cross, and I see that they are dragging Julien, their arms supporting his limp body. They throw him down to the ground in front of Soren.

"Ahh, there he is!" Soren cries. "The man of the hour. Valiant Julien, leading me so very conveniently to a rebel cell planning to fight me. What a fool."

I leave Michel briefly to crouch down and check Julien, whose eyes open and close as if he's close to losing consciousness. He has bullet wounds, one in his left shoulder and one in his lower abdomen. Both are bleeding profusely.

"Julien!" I cry, taking his face in my hands. "Julien! Stay with me!"

His eyes roll in his head and so I slap his face and he blinks and meets my gaze.

"Stay with me," I repeat. "Don't close your eyes."

I know I have to stop the bleeding, and rip off my coat, removing my blouse so that I'm wearing only a thin t-shirt. I tear the blouse up into strips and use it to pack the wound in his side, pressing to stop the flow, but it's a large exit wound, the flesh ripped away, and I know it's likely fatal.

The blood is fresh and hot and steams in the chill air.

"Do something!" I scream at Soren, who stands watching, his arms crossed.

"I said you'd have a choice to make," he reminds me. "If you agree to help me resurrect the rest of the Twelve, I'll let you save one of them. One. Who will it be? Julien, your brave knight in shining armor, or Michel, your soulful priest who can't keep his vows?"

I turn to Soren, my hatred of him so great I could explode, my eyes blurry from tears.

"Don't make me choose."

"But you have to. You have to choose which one will live. I need one of them for the ceremony. Michel would be my first choice, as he's my high priest, after all. But if you want Julien…well, you'd better decide quick because he looks as if he's not long for this world."

"If I save one, won't the other be saved as well?" I say, remembering how they were both made mortal at the same time.

Soren shakes his head, smiling at me. "No, sorry. Good try, but that was the serum. You know, spooky action at a distance? You're going to have to turn one of them to save them. It will be your first, no?"

"Not me," Michel says, and I briefly make eye contact with him from where I kneel beside Julien. "Please, Eve. Let me die as a mortal."

I wipe my eyes, knowing that it has been his fervent desire all his existence as a vampire. "You promised we'd all be together again," I say to him, unable to stop my tears. I know I can't turn Michel. Not if it means Julien will die.

"I'm sorry," Michel whispers, his face contorted in pain once more.

I kneel down to Julien, whose eyes are still open, but whose pulse is so fast, I know he's close to death. "What should I do?" I whisper to him.

He swallows and struggles to speak, his body shaking and cold. "I don't want to die."

I take one last look at Michel, whose eyes are closed against his pain, then bite my own wrist and place it over Julien's mouth. I feel his cold lips against my wound, feel his feeble attempt at sucking, and relief floods through me that at least a few drops of my blood and its potent virus have made it past his lips.

He'll die, but will wake up in a few hours, vampire once more.

"Take him down," Soren says, motioning to the guard, who goes to Michel and lays the cross flat.

Michel is still conscious and groans in pain. The guard wrenches the huge spikes out of Michel's hands and feet. Michel trembles but is silent. Soren bends down and unlatches the kill collar with a click and then, as we watch, he lays a hand on Michel's neck, covering the wound with his hand, healing Michel with his powers.

He meets my eyes and smiles, his expression smug. "You didn't really think I'd let Michel die for good, did you?" He turns back to Michel, whose face is a grimace of grief. "Fool wants to die now as a mortal, but I want him to suffer a little longer. Besides, I need him. I knew you'd save Julien. So did Michel, although I'm sure it still broke his heart."

Michel doesn't look at me. His eyes close and he gives in to his fate.

I hate Soren. I hate him with all my might. I hate that he forced me to choose, but at the same time, I'm so glad that he saved Michel. That will always be between us. Michel will always know that I chose to save Julien over him. Yes, he asked to be allowed to die, but the fact I went along with it says everything. I met Michel first, and I loved Michel first, but I would have let him die.

Deep down, I was afraid that if I saved Michel, Soren would let Julien die. For whatever reason, Soren seems not to care about Julien except as a means to make Michel jealous.

Is it really because Julien is compellable? Does that make us different, less malleable, and therefore more equal?

The guards pick up a dying Julien and haul him through the trees back to the base. I follow in Soren's wake with Michel beside me, surrounded by several of Soren's guards, their weapons drawn. As we approach the road bordering the base, I pass by several fallen rebels, including Chris, who lies lifeless, staring up at the sky, a stake through his heart.

"Burn them all," Soren says, pointing to a pile of bodies in the center of the yard. I watch as they put Julien in the back of a van, and try to get in beside them, but a guard stops me.

"In there," he says and points to Soren and Michel. One guard closes his door while another holds the door to the other side open. The guard motions to me, and I'm forced to get inside with Soren. I sit on the seat beside Michel, trying to contain myself. Soren's lieutenant sits beside him, and the two bend down together to discuss their losses.

I half-listen as we drive off, lost in my grief, glancing out the window to try to calm myself. I can't face Michel, knowing he will be upset that I chose Julien, but he asked to be allowed to die. What was I supposed to do?

"It's all right, Eve," Michel says, his voice soft. "You made the right choice. Soren would have let Julien die if you'd chosen me; this way, Julien is still alive." Michel reaches out and takes my hand in his, rubbing my palm with his thumb.

Soren looks at us, a gleam in his eye. "Aww, are the two of you going to kiss and make up? You know I love to see you two together."

I make a face at him and glance away, barely able to tolerate being in his company.

"Oh, stop it, Eve," he says. "You know you can't resist him. Face it. No matter what, you still want him. Julien alone isn't enough, now that you've had them both."

Michel squeezes my hand as if to warn me to let it go. I try, but of course, Soren is very pleased with himself and can't stop.

"You can't hope to keep up with me, Eve, so you're a fool to try." He watches me for a moment, a smile on his face. "I'm so glad you two ran off when you did. I needed to find and eliminate Julien's old friends. He was very helpful in leading us right to them. Nothing happens," he says and leans forward, one elbow on his knee. "Nothing happens without my knowledge and without my leave. Give in, Eve. Your life will be a whole lot easier once you do."

"I'll never give in," I say. "Not in spirit."

"In body will be good enough," he says and sits back, watching out the window as if I'm no longer there.

We drive along in silence, but I'm still a mess, wiping my eyes and biting my lip to stop from crying.

I glance at the vehicle behind us, but can see nothing. I wonder how Julien is…how he'll take being a vampire again.

"He'll be fine," Michel says, his voice soothing.

"Unlike Michel, Julien wants to survive," Soren says after examining a clipboard. "I could have let Michel die, and it would have been fair punishment for his murder of my beautiful Marguerite, but that would be too good for him. He'd be out of his misery. You see how easy it is to manipulate you? Use your hearts against your interests?"

"At least we have hearts," I spit out.

Soren laughs and shakes his head. "Oh, Eve… So callous. Of course I have a heart. If I didn't, none of this would matter. It's precisely because I have a heart that I care."

"You only care about getting power," I say, glaring at him. "So you and the Twelve can reign as some kind of pantheon. Humans got rid of the Greek and Roman pantheons. We won't want yours either."

"They were weak," he answers simply." We aren't. We have modern power. We'll step in and take control. It's what mortals want, deep down inside."

"They won't bow down," I warn. I hope.

He smiles. "We'll see about that. When push comes to shove, most mortals are still scared little hominids hiding in the cave, fearful of the lions and tigers and bears circling around just outside."

I watch out the other window, disgusted with his attitude. Whatever he is, his ego is enormous. When I glance at him again, I find him grinning. He's won. He has my compliance. He has both twins. He used Julien to find a cell working against him.

I refuse to look at him for another second, uncertain how I'm going to survive this, but Julien is alive and will soon be a vampire again. Even if my relationship with Michel is over for good, there's still Julien and there's still hope.

I turn my face to the window and watch the passing scenery during the rest of the trip back to Soren's mansion. Despite his win in this current battle, I'm more determined than ever that I will never let him resurrect the rest of the Twelve. Even if it means all our deaths.

CHAPTER 25

"WE ARE BORN OF LOVE; love is our mother."

Rumi

THE TRIP back to Soren's compound takes barely an hour.

"Will you stop the plague before it circles the globe?" I ask when the vehicle stops at the gate.

"Don't worry your pretty little head, Eve," he says in a patronizing voice. "I won't let too many mortals die. Just enough, no more and no less."

"How can you say just enough? If you were a real god, you'd prevent deaths."

"Michel's real god lets millions of humans die each year. Don't talk to me about real gods."

I bite my lip, knowing my words will have no effect except to upset me even more. I try to blank my mind instead of thinking, letting things happen until I can be away from him, and able to think clearly without his constant snide and gloating comments.

Soren turns to me, his eyes appraising me. "I'm not responsible for the deaths, Eve. Those deaths resulting from the plague aren't on my head."

"You let them die. You could have stopped Blackstone and then none of this would have happened."

"I tried to stop him," Soren says, looking out the window. "I failed. This is Plan B."

"You mean to tell me you were going to stop Blackstone before he let the plague go?"

Soren turns to me, his eyes opening slowly. "I was going to stop things a lot sooner than they did. Let's leave it at that, shall we?"

"It's easy to say that, but where's the proof? You're benefitting from the plague too. You let it happen."

We drive up to the entrance and a guard opens the door for Soren. He steps out and I follow, but I go around to the back of the vehicle where they are removing Julien's body. His body is limp, his arms and legs sprawled in their grip, his head lolled back. He's dead. I touch his face. It's cold.

"Don't worry about Julien," Soren says from the steps, Michel standing beside him. "He'll wake up with a nasty headache in a few hours and a very powerful thirst. Come. We have business to attend to."

They start up the stairs to the door, but Soren stops at the entrance, waiting for me. I refuse to follow, wanting to stay with Julien.

He looks at me directly. "Blackstone wants the plague to wipe out almost all fossil fuels, but I won't let it. The more you delay this, the longer the plague has to spread."

I sigh. He's right and I relent. Julien will be fine. I watch as the two guards haul him inside past Soren and then follow up the steps.

Soren leads us in and I wonder why he's suddenly being so courteous. "The Twelve and I will save the world from catastrophe, Eve, so you can stop feeling so bad about your part in this. We have the off-switch. It's just a matter of deploying it at the most opportune time. I don't have enough power yet, but once I do, I'll make a big show of saving the world, stopping the plague in its tracks. It will be a miracle."

"Hardly a miracle," I say, clenching my fists. "Just biochemical engineering."

Soren clucks his tongue at me. "Oh, Eve. Such a Debbie Downer. Don't you think it's a miracle that I was able to get the antidote? Your brother helped me, and considering his ties to Blackstone, that was a miracle."

"Dylan helped you?"

Soren raises his eyebrows. "I know, right?" he says, laughing. "Like I said, a miracle!"

He chuckles to himself while he walks down the hallway. Michel reaches out and touches me as if to stop me from responding; I do my best to swallow my anger. I follow without speaking, wondering about Dylan's role in all this and what exactly Soren did to force his compliance. I can't believe that Dylan complied willingly.

Does Soren have Dylan's parents now? Was that part of Soren's agreement with Blackstone? Does Soren have mine?

I bite my cheek, doing my best not to run after Soren and throw myself at him in a blind attempt to kill him with my own bare hands. However good it would feel to try, I know it would end with me dead and Soren no worse for wear.

"I hope you saw all this," I mutter to Michel.

He smiles but doesn't answer.

"Well?" I say as we follow Soren into the study. "Did you?"

"Don't worry, Eve," Michel says softly. "Everything will be fine."

He looks calm, as if he's accepted what's happened and what will happen. I wish I could feel his optimism, but I don't. I fear that Soren will screw us over and we'll be faced with watching as the world falls into the steam age, millions of people dying from starvation and the chaos that ensues.

Soren goes to his huge, ornate desk and sorts through some papers. He finds one and brings it to me. "I believe you've already seen a version of this," he says and hands me a map similar to the one Chris showed us at Fort Devens. It marks off the spread of the plague and the world's largest oil fields. I see that the largest ones are not yet affected by the plague. "There's a tiny bit of wiggle room left before the plague hits Ghawar in Saudi Arabia, the natural gas fields in Russia, and the Athabasca Tar Sands in Canada, but not much. We have to get this show on the road, so to speak."

"How much time?"

Soren's busy flipping through a file. "About a month to six weeks, give or take a few days."

I look up in alarm. "So if you don't stop it in six weeks, it could mean the oil fields are affected?"

He nods. "And once any part of a reservoir is affected, it will be almost impossible to stop it. As the biggest conventional oil field in the world, Ghawar is pretty damn important." He points to a sofa on the other side of the room. "Now, take a seat for a few moments. I have to make a few arrangements."

"If you don't need me right now, can I go to Julien?" I ask and glance quickly at Michel, who is already seated, and unfolding a newspaper.

"He'll be out for a few hours so no," he says and points back to the sofa. "Sit. We're expecting company."

I sit beside Michel, who takes my hand and squeezes. "Julien will be fine," he says, then drops my hand before turning back to his paper.

"I wish I had your confidence."

"You did the right thing, Eve," Michel says once more. "I won't be angry with you, or jealous. This was the only way. Because of this, Julien will survive. If you'd chosen me, Soren would have let Julien die. I didn't want that. He's valiant. He deserves to live."

I nod and take in a deep breath, trying to calm myself and trust that Michel has seen this and knows the outcome. It's not easy to do. He's been wrong before—he's missed things. He could be wrong about this as well.

The door to the study opens and in walk two guards with my brother. Dylan looks pale and slightly gaunt, as if he hasn't had enough blood.

Has Soren been starving him? My heart rate increases and I have to try once more to calm down.

"Eve," he says and comes over to where I sit. I stand up and we embrace, and he hugs me so tightly. "I'm so glad you're okay. I was worried that he'd kill you in anger."

I shake my head and step back, looking him up and down. "He let us leave so Julien could lead him to one of the rebel cells in Fort Devens. It was all a setup. I had to turn Julien to save him when he was wounded."

Dylan nods. "The guard told me. He's better off vampire anyway. A great warrior like him? We can't afford to lose him to some stray bullet."

I nod and Soren comes over to us, standing with his hands on his hips, his legs spread like a general inspecting his troops.

"You look like you need a drink," Soren says to Dylan. He turns to one of the guards. "Bring us some blood. Fresh." He makes a face at me. "None of that preserved dreck for us. It's time to celebrate!"

I try to hold back my anger and say nothing, but I don't smile either.

"Oh, come on, Eve," Soren says and frowns. "Don't be a spoilsport. Things are going as planned. Soon the plague will stop, the Twelve will be resurrected, and order will be restored. Those wrongfully prevented from ruling will be returned to the throne. All's right with the world. You should welcome the return to stability."

"I'll believe it when I see it."

"Empiricist to the end," Soren says when a guard returns with a tray holding a carafe of blood and several glasses. "You and Dylan are like two peas in a pod. My little scientists."

Soren pours and hands a glass to Dylan, who takes it and drinks down hungrily. I take one as well, for I'm starving and exhausted from the events of the past two days.

Michel remains sitting on the sofa, looking as if he's glad he no longer is plagued by the bloodlust of being vampire. Seeing him sitting there all alone, I think of Julien in the other room, his body undergoing the change that will make him undead once more. Since I was a child, I've wanted to study exactly what it is that turns a human into a vampire. What does this virus do that infects our blood? How can we eradicate it? How can we harness its unique characteristics for our own benefit?

Immortality… That has been the Holy Grail of all human desire since we developed a sense of our own mortality. It's there, hidden in the genome of the virus that turns a mortal into a vampire.

I bring Dylan over to the seating area and we sit across from each other, me beside Michel and Dylan sitting on a wing chair across from us.

"How are your parents?" I ask. "And my father?"

"As well as can be expected," Dylan replies. "As long as Blackstone believes you're cooperating, they'll be fine."

I turn to look at Soren standing behind his desk, looking at papers.

He glances up. "I never said anything to Lord Blackstone about your little escape attempt, or Michel's attempt to walk out, so don't worry."

He returns his focus to his papers and I wonder why he's being so accommodating. He wants things to go well with Blackstone so he can take power over everything, shut Blackstone down and stop the plague.

Exactly. You're finally getting it. Now, cooperate and you'll get what you want. Every bit of it, Eve. Every inch.

I see him smile to himself and I glance away, hating that he can read my every thought.

That's what a god is, isn't it? Omniscient? And once I bring back the Twelve, we'll truly be omniscient, the way we once were, connected, thirteen minds combined as one beautiful perfect form. That's heaven, Eve. That's heaven.

Finally, Soren looks up and addresses the group, not just me. "You want to see another miracle?" he asks, leaving his desk and papers. "Shall we show her, Dylan? The reason you helped me?"

Dylan looks at me, his face unreadable, as if he doesn't know how to feel. "Yes."

"Good," Soren says and rubs his hands together. "This is so much fun! I love reunions!"

I frown and follow Soren and Dylan as they lead me through the doors and down a hallway. We go downstairs to the basement and to a room in the back. It's small, dark, and cold. Inside is a table and on it, I see one of the cement tanks from the SCU.

Dylan stands over it, his hands on the side. He glances down, a smile on his face.

"Come and see, Eve," Soren says. "See what miracles I have wrought."

I step closer and stare into the gel that fills the tank, catching sight of a mass of orange-red.

Curls. Strawberry blonde and floating in the gel like kelp.

Sarah…

"Oh my God," I say and step closer, leaning over the edge. She's pale, her skin white in death, her lips blue around the edges. Her eyes are closed, her mouth slightly open.

"Dylan agreed to help me get the antidote to the plague. I agreed to help him. Once he delivers and I can see that the antidote is working, I'll revive her."

"Dylan," I whisper and glance at him.

His eyes are wet and he's struggling to keep control. "I had to," he says, his voice barely above a whisper.

I cover my mouth, remembering the last time I saw her on the floor in her parents' cottage, her hair spread out around her head. She was beautiful even in death. His betrayal makes complete sense.

"Now, off to your room to rest for a while," Soren announces, clapping his hands together like he's a happy cruise director. "You can change for dinner. Your things are in the closet." He smiles. "Once we're all done, Julien should be awake and ready for his first meal. Then, tomorrow night, it's off to the cathedral for the show."

He turns and points to the stairs but I'm too stunned to move, my eyes riveted to Sarah lying in the stasis tank. When did this happen? When did Soren take her body?

Dylan turns away with reluctance. I imagine he could sit and stare at Sarah for hours. I know I could. As I turn to go, I wonder if Soren will really resurrect her. How could Dylan not comply with Soren, given the chance to have Sarah back?

I follow Dylan up the stairs and the guard leads us to our rooms. Once there, I throw myself down on the bed, exhausted from the ordeals of the past few days. I can't help but cry because of everything that's happened, overwhelmed at last.

Dylan sits on the side of the bed and rubs my back. "Do you understand now, sister? I had to save her. I'd do anything to save her. Just like I'd do anything to save you."

I turn over and sit up, wrapping my arms around him, understanding completely.

Even so, even as happy as I am to know Sarah may be resurrected, I have to find a way to fight Soren and prevent the resurrection of the rest of his monsters. There's no way I can accept their return. But at the same time, I want Soren to resurrect Sarah for Dylan. I used to have a plan. Now I'm torn.

But at the same time, I remember the deaths of all those who came to watch Kael's resurrection and I know I can't be a part of Soren's plans to resurrect all of the Twelve, no matter what he promises about stopping the plague or bringing Sarah back to life.

There has to be a better way and I intend to find it. Once Julien is alive again, the two of us can meet with Dylan.

I won't give in.

I WAKE when there's a knock at my door. The old wind-up clock on the wall shows that almost two hours have passed since we arrived.

"Come in," I say and in walks Michel. He's changed out of his bloody clothes and has washed up, for his hair is wet and hangs in his eyes. He's wearing a clean set of vestments, a black cassock coat, and a large wooden cross. He looks very priestly.

"Have you checked on Julien?" I ask, my heart squeezing just a bit at the thought I cursed him once more with vampirism.

"He's still out. I expect he'll wake up in another hour or so. Soren wants you to get dressed and ready for a meal. We'll be planning all evening for the event to bring back the rest of the Twelve. You're not needed, so you can spend time with Julien when he awakens."

"I don't like this," I say. "I don't want to preside over another massacre like the one that happened when Kael was resurrected."

"Do you think I do?" he says, exhaling in exasperation. "I despise them, but this is the only way to stop the plague. Don't fight me in this, Eve. If you do, you'll make it even harder."

I glance away from him; I plan on doing precisely that.

I go to the bathroom to splash water over my face, not wanting to argue with him about the merits of his plan. I return and Michel has laid out a dress on the bed, the same long white gown I wore previously. I shake my head and take it back to the bathroom to change, feeling shy in front of Michel now that he's once again a priest. I fix my hair, placing it up as before, although Michel shouldn't be taking any pleasure in seeing my bite mark anymore.

I return to the bedroom to find Michel standing at the window, looking out over the grounds. He turns and takes me in, his eyes moving over my body. I can still see the possessiveness in them, the pleasure in seeing me.

Not totally a priest, I guess.

"I want to check in on Julien before we eat," I say as we prepare to leave the room.

Michel nods. "By all means," he says and holds the door for me.

He leads me down the dim corridors, the walls lined with dark wood paneling and adorned with paintings of European landscapes and ships at sea. Soren has really tried to recreate an old aristocratic environment for himself, no doubt wanting to reinforce his age and power.

Michel stops at one door and waits for me. "He looks worse than he is," he warns. "Once the virus has finished its transformation, he'll revive. The medic was able to suture most of the wounds, but they won't heal completely. He'll bear scars from the battle for the rest of his existence unless he ascends again."

"Do you think he will?"

Michel shrugs and leads me into the room and over to the bed where Julien lies. I gasp when I see him. They've stripped him naked, the long, bloody slashes on his arms where he was struck by a sword clearly visible. He has bullet wounds in his shoulder and belly. Someone has cleaned the blood off his skin but he does look terrible, pale once more from loss of blood. Vampire pale.

I sit beside him on the side of the bed and lean over to stroke his cheek and brow, not caring if Michel sees me. He has to understand that it's hard for me to see Julien this way, despite knowing he will awaken once more. I bite back tears. I'm happy he won't die, or at least, won't be dead. He has died, but will be reborn once the virus finishes its work.

"Come," Michel says, his voice soft. "It's time for dinner. Soren doesn't like to be kept waiting."

I wipe my eyes and take one last look at Julien before rising and following Michel out of the room and down the hallways to the dining room.

Soren and Dylan are already seated at the long burnished wood table, dressed with white linen and pewter bowls filled with flowers and lit with candelabras. There's roast game and grilled fish and vegetables on platters as well as loaves of bread and of course, carafes of blood and wine. It smells marvelous and I'm hungry for both food and blood, the latter craving never really fulfilled except for a brief few moments after gorging.

Soren stands when I approach. "Eve, Michel, please come and join us."

Dylan stands as well and kisses me on the cheek as I take my place between him and Soren. Michel is seated across from us, and I wonder if Soren has arranged the seating on purpose. Is he taunting Michel by having to sit across from me, or was it entirely random?

I wouldn't put it past Soren to do anything he might think would make us uncomfortable.

"Are you?" Soren asks, taking a sip of blood from a crystal glass with delicate etching on the sides. "Feeling better?" he adds, as if to cover up.

"Yes," I reply. "I'm still a bit emotional from seeing Sarah. From everything."

"You'll have to get over it," he says and examines a bowl of soup that a servant places in front of him. "We'll all be together most of the time for the next while. At least, until order has been restored. We have to show a united front, the four of us."

"What about Julien?" I can't help but ask.

"What about him? He's a warrior. He can stand guard, but he's not key to my plans."

We eat our soup in silence. It's delicious, taking the edge off my hunger. A waiter pours some blood into our glasses and wine into Michel's. Soren stands and holds his up.

"To the Twelve," he says. "May their resurrection bring peace to our troubled world."

I put my glass down and watch as the three men drink a toast.

"Not very polite, Eve," Soren says after sitting down and selecting a piece of meat from a tray a servant holds for him.

"I find it hard to be excited about the ceremony, knowing it will mean the death of so many people."

"My brethren have been fighting off the nanovirus all this time. They'll need a big drink, and many souls. So what if a few hundred die to save several billion?"

"They don't have to kill," I say, wondering about his reference to "souls."

He smiles but says nothing.

I eat until I feel satisfied and then push my chair out from the table. "I'd like to go and be with Julien now," I say and wipe my mouth before putting my napkin on the table. "If you'll excuse me."

"By all means," Soren says and waves his hand with a flourish. "Go. Be with Julien. Hold his hand when he wakes. When the time comes, I'll bring him some blood to drink so he can become immortal. He won't say no."

I leave the room and follow a guard down the hallway to the room where Julien lies in transition between death and immortality. The guard unlocks the door and opens it for me, and I go inside to find him on the bed, another guard standing inside as if to watch him.

"He hasn't woken yet, m'lady," the guard says, nodding towards Julien. "He's due any time now."

I sit on the bed beside him and pull up the covers to hide his nakedness. He should have some dignity when he awakens from the dead for the second time. I watch him, waiting for a sign that he is revived.

He's so beautiful in his paleness, with his dark hair cut short, his jaw and chin covered in a few day's worth of dark stubble, his lashes long and black, his lips full. His body is beautiful as well, with a strong neck and shoulders, well-defined pecs and abs. I know his body so intimately, having been his lover now for these past months, but I am still struck by how perfect he is, despite the scars from his wounds.

They're slowly healing, the red gashes closing up, replaced by thin, silvery scars. I've never watched someone become a vampire before and I'm anxious that he'll come through okay and will agree to drink the blood so he can complete the transition. I'm certain he will. Julien said he didn't want to die.

WHEN HE FINALLY DOES AWAKEN, he sits up and cradles his head in his hands.

"Holy fuck, I forgot how much this hurts," he says, groaning and grinding his fists into his temples.

My heart squeezes to see him alive once more but I know he's not quite a vampire yet. He has to drink blood to complete the transition.

"Quick," he says, squinting at me as if the light hurts—which it does. "Get me some blood before my head explodes."

I turn to the guard, who goes to the door. He leans out and says something, and I expect them to bring in a carafe of blood. Instead, Soren arrives hand in hand with a beautiful woman with long pale hair, her body naked beneath a thin chiffon robe.

"What are you doing?" I say, taking the young woman in. "All he needs is blood, not a mortal."

"We're going to do this right," Soren says and pushes the young woman over to the bed. "Crawl up on top of him and offer him your neck, sweetheart."

She looks calm. It's obvious she's been compelled to cooperate, her fear erased. She complies and before I can say anything, she straddles Julien, who stares at her through narrowed eyes. He glances at me as she pulls her hair aside and leans down closer to him. I know what he sees and feels—he sees her as a ripe plum, juicy and delicious, ready to pluck. He smells the blood in her and it feeds his bloodlust. His teeth, just beginning to elongate, ache to bite down hard on her flesh. His body craves the sensation of a living human, beneath him, in his arms, his mouth on her neck, his lips sucking her blood.

"Eve," Julien whispers to me, and he's clearly torn between his desire not to hurt me and his bloodlust.

I stand and go to the door, realizing that nothing I can do will stop this because this is what Soren wants. He wants me to watch and feel jealous as Julien drinks the beautiful woman's blood. I can't deny him this, but I can deny him the kind of response he wants. "Go ahead," I say, my eyes meeting his. "I know you need it. I won't watch."

He nods and before I can leave, I see him take the woman in his arms and bare her throat before clamping his mouth over her carotid.

Soren grabs my arm and stops me from leaving. "If you think you can escape this, you're crazy. If you think you can escape your fate, you're even crazier. But go ahead and try, Eve," he whispers in my ear. "Go ahead and try. I so love a good fight."

I try to wrench my arm from his grip. Of course, I fail. He grabs me and holds me in front of him, facing Julien and the woman on the bed. He holds my face forward and I watch as Julien drinks the woman's blood, his arms squeezing even more tightly. I know what he's feeling—an almost orgasmic high from the effect of the blood on his body as he transitions to vampire.

"Why are you such a sadist?" I whisper, trying my best not to sob.

Soren chuckles behind me. "Years of torture do that to a person."

"So you torture the rest of us?"

Soren laughs out loud. "Eve, you have no idea what torture really is if you say that. "

"Maybe not," I reply, and turn to him, my eyes brimming. "But I know that you enjoy seeing others suffer. Just leave us alone. You got what you wanted."

He lets go of me and goes to the bed, taking hold of the woman's arm. He pulls her away from Julien, who lets go with reluctance. I expect to see him snarl at Soren, but he doesn't. Instead, his face is almost beatific from ecstasy, his mouth, chin, and part of his naked chest stained from the woman's blood.

I take a cloth and sit on the bed next to him, wiping off his face, wiping my tears with the back of my other hand.

"Just remember, Eve," Soren says from behind me. "When you fight me, I get even more enjoyment."

I say nothing, and keep cleaning Julien's face. I hear the door close behind us, and when I finally glance back, I see that we're alone.

Julien takes the cloth from me and wipes the blood from his body. He can barely stand to look in my eyes, embarrassed at how weak he was when faced with the woman. How bloodlust dominates every other sense.

"Look at me," I say, my voice soft. I touch his face. "I'm not judging you. I know what it's like."

He finally turns back and looks me squarely in the eyes. I lean closer and kiss him, my love for him flowing between us so strongly it makes both of us gasp.

"Julien, I'm not helping him resurrect the rest of those monsters," I say when I pull back.

"What choice do you have?" he says doubtfully.

"We all have a choice," I say. "We can choose how every moment goes, even when there's a gun at our heads. I choose not to help him bring back the rest of the Twelve."

"Even if it means the plague stops?"

I nod. "Even if it means that. If he has the antidote, we can get it as well."

"What do you propose we do?"

"You're the security expert. You're the one with all the military skills. There has to be some way."

"What about Michel?"

"He's a priest again, determined to help Soren and preserve the Church," I say and even now, there's a stab of regret in my chest. "He's made his choice. Now I'm making mine."

I have no idea what we can do to fight Soren, but I can't face the prospect of reviving those monsters only to watch them kill hundreds of innocent mortals.

If it means that I have to die, so be it. I'd rather take the chance and fight back than comply and share the guilt for all those deaths.

Julien and I embrace, lost momentarily in each other, all thoughts of the future we face blotted out for at least a few blissful hours.

END OF BOOK FOUR

ALSO BY S. E. LUND

PARANORMAL ROMANCE / URBAN FANTASY ROMANCE

THE DOMINION SERIES

Dominion: Book 1 in the Dominion Series

Ascension: Book 2 in the Dominion Series

Retribution: Book 3 in the Dominion Series

Resurrection: Book 4 in the Dominion Series

Redemption: Book 5 in the Dominion Series

Eternity: Book 6 in the Dominion Series

❧

Contemporary Erotic Romance

THE UNRESTRAINED SERIES

The Agreement: Book 1

The Commitment: Book 2

Unrestrained: Book 3

Unbreakable: Book 4

Forever After: Book 5

Everlasting: Book 6

Drake Forever: Book 7

Endless: Book 8

Limitless: Book 9

THE DRAKE SERIES (The Unrestrained Series from Drake's Point of View)

Drake Restrained

Drake Unwound

Drake Unbound

THE MR. BIG SERIES

Mr. Big Shot: Book 1

Mr. Big Love: Book 2

Mr. Big Daddy: Book 3

Mr. Big Deal: Book 4

THE MCINTYRE BROTHERS SERIES

Tempt Me: Book 1

Tease Me: Book 2

Tame Me: Book 3

Military Romance / Romantic Suspense

THE BAD BOY SERIES

Bad Boy Saint: Book 1

Bad Boy Sinner: Book 2

Bad Boy Soldier: Book 3

Bad Boy Savior: Book 4

THE BOYFRIEND SERIES

Boy Toy: Book 1

Man Bun: Book 2

STANDALONE BOOKS:

Matched

If You Fall

ABOUT THE AUTHOR

S. E. Lund lives on the side of a mountain in the shadow of an active volcano with her family of humans and pets. Besides writing paranormal romance, urban fantasy and contemporary romance, she dreams of living in a warm climate where snow is just a word in a dictionary.

Sign up for her newsletter and get information on new releases, sales and news. She hates spam and will never share your email!

https://www.subscribepage.com/x8t1t7

www.selundauthor.com
selund2012@gmail.com